Andy Creighton is Dead

A Thriller

Richard Panchyk

For Amanda
Look what you made me do.

CHAPTER 1

SLOANE

Andy Creighton is dead.

I feel like everyone hates me for it, and I mean literally everyone.

If I knew it was going to be this bad, I might have reconsidered killing Andy. But it's done and I can't take it back. I've just got to take a deep breath and try to get through each day until the furor eventually calms down and my life returns to normal.

For right now, getting through today means being able to successfully back my Nissan down the thirty feet of my freshly paved asphalt driveway without killing anyone so I can go to the store and get some groceries before I starve to death. I've been holed up at home by choice for the last few days, and I finally decided it's time to prove to myself that I am not going to be afraid to leave my house, that I am not going to be afraid to confront the protestors. Unfortunately, one of them is standing at the end of my driveway with a big handwritten sign proclaiming me as a murderer. Not even figuratively, literally.

I honk my horn in a polite, *Hi there, can you please move* fashion. The young blonde woman standing in my driveway apron does not budge. Instead, she raises her sign and unleashes a torrent of expletives at me.

This is getting ridiculous. I honk again and continue backing up. Lord knows the last thing I want to do is run the girl over, but I am not going to be trapped in my own driveway on account of someone who is trespassing on my property.

"Andy was perfect!" her sign says in part. To which my reply would be, perfect people die too, and then I'd add, get over it already. I lay on the horn and keep reversing. Thankfully, when I am ten feet away, the girl finally steps aside, hurling epithets at me through my closed window. Her tear-streaked face is red and puffy and as I switch gears to drive, she yells repeatedly "Why? Why? Why?!"

It's been five long days since the world found out about Andy's death, and it has not been at all how I imagined. I tell my car to call Mandy and the phone rings. She picks up right away.

"Hey girl, how are you holding up?" she asks, a little too chipper by my estimation.

"Not great. Nearly ran over a protestor in my driveway." I wanted to but didn't.

"I can get a police detail assigned to your house," she offers.

"I'll think about it, Mandy," I say. After what happened in Boston two nights ago, vandalization and a small fire, that might be a smart move. In Denver, someone threw rocks into a bookstore window because of me and the broken glass cut a clerk's hand; she needed ten stitches. The thought that I am causing destruction of property and endangering people's lives is disheartening to say the least.

"We've been talking about damage control," Mandy says. "I've made calls."

"Damage control." I pause and then say what is floating through my head. "This was supposed to be an exciting week for us, not the worst week ever."

"There are ways to fix this, ways to be smart and come out ahead of the curve."

"Yeah how? Revive Andy? Impossible." This is not some fantasy or sci-fi book, I can't simply bring back the dead. I can apologize. I can be penitent. I can try to make it up to everyone who loved him. But I can't bring him back because he's gone. I killed him, as everyone loves to remind me the last few days.

"We are in discussions. I talked to Micah and Jonah and the others. We are tossing around some plans." Mandy sounds a little too confident and I don't like it. Or maybe smug is the right word.

"Care to clue me in? Since I am the one…"

"Babe, it's too early. But trust me, I've got you on this. We may be able to get you off the hook."

"Maybe I should plead insanity." It might work. Anyone who would kill Andy Creighton would have to be insane, right? High school football quarterback, valedictorian of his graduating class, full college scholarship, and then a dream job and the perfect girlfriend. He had the perfect life, and now he's gone. Insanity. I was crazy thinking I could get away with this and not thinking of the consequences.

"Can I ask you something? And you don't have to answer me." Mandy knows I will answer her. We share everything. Or at least we used to until the whole Ellis thing happened.

"Sure." I signal left to merge onto the highway. I decide to go to the supermarket the next town over to lower my chance of being recognized. I'm wearing a baseball cap and my hair is braided so I look less like me.

"Why did you do it? Why did you kill Andy Creighton? I never really asked you that."

"For the money," I say without hesitation, and I don't feel guilty about that. It was for the money. Well, okay, to be honest, and I want to be honest with her and with myself, it wasn't just that. "And because I was tired of him. Andy this, Andy that. I had enough." Which sounds awful, I'll admit. Killing someone for that reason. Money is a better motivator; at least more people can understand that whether they like it or hate it, they can comprehend that as a reason. But it backfired, because now people are talking about Andy even more than before.

"But did you have to…kill him? Did you have to go that far? Couldn't you have just stopped writing the series? Left it on a happy note, Andy and Ciara walking off into the sunset holding hands, drop the mic and go?" I can picture Mandy shaking her head and pursing her lips like she does. I can picture most of her expressions because we know each other so well. Like I said, we are very close. I trust her with my life. Though the last couple of days I am getting a strange vibe from her.

"If you had such strong feelings you could have tried harder to talk me out of it." I know I'm laying an unwarranted guilt trip on her. Maybe she didn't like what I was going to do but she couldn't have predicted this backlash. I sure as hell didn't. I step on the gas and pass a few cars. Maybe if I floor it and hit eighty-eight, I'll go back in time. I'm really tempted to go to my cabin in the woods where I can be alone, and lay in the hammock until the storm passes.

"Would you have listened to me anyway? Let's be honest here," Mandy says in a rather milquetoast voice.

"I suppose if people were celebrating instead of lamenting his death, then you'd be happy with me right now?" Gotta love how fast she turns on me. When you think you have a pal and confidante and she is just like everyone else, it hurts.

"Probably. But that doesn't matter does it?" She pauses. "Hey. Listen. It's going to be okay."

"Not if I run a protestor over with my car. Repeatedly. Until she's dead." Seriously considering it at this point.

"Which you won't do. Right?" She doesn't wait for my reply. "Where are you now?"

"On my way to the store. I ran out of food."

"That's because you locked yourself in your house."

"Sure did." The backlash from Andy's death was swift and kind of frightening, that's why.

"Listen, to quote a book I read recently…All things must…pass," Mandy says with a chuckle.

I know she's only trying to help, but sometimes she thinks she's being funny when she's actually being cringey. I have to remind myself why I hired her to begin with. Because she was kind to you when you were nothing. Because she believed in you, that's why. *One day, you'll be huge, just wait*, she'd tell me. And now here we are seven plus years later and she is telling me to get food delivered to my house instead of going out into the world. Instead of facing up to reality. I take the next exit off the highway and swing a tight right and another right to get into the shopping plaza that has a colossal Stop and Shop. The parking lot is only half full, which is better than my local store would have been anyway.

"I'm aware. But I'm at the store now, so I'd better hang up." Not that I can't talk in the supermarket, there's just nothing else to say right now. I pull into a parking spot and grab my bag. I feel suddenly relaxed. It's a sunny day, fifty-some degrees and the sky is bright blue. The air feels delicious when I step out of my car and inhale deeply.

"You do realize there's this thing called delivery," Mandy says with exaggerated snark.

"I hate getting food delivered and you know that." It's always been the case even when I lived in the dorms at college. I could be in my jammies at midnight but I'd still make a run to Domino's rather than having them come to me.

"I worry about you, babe," Mandy says softly. She's sitting in her home office right now, I can tell, because I hear her Cartier pen tapping against her mahogany desk. Tap. Tap tap. Tap tap. Like she's trying to send a secret SOS message. But it's just a nervous habit. "Anything else you need?"

"I don't even remember why I called you to begin with," I admit. Just to hear a friendly voice, that's why. But right now, today, she's not very reassuring. Having secret meetings with the others to decide how I can fix this, that's not reassuring. It's mysterious and non-inclusive. It's like I'm a child they can't trust to solve her own problems. For the money. Isn't this what Micah and Jonah wanted? To make more money?

"Well, I'm here if you need me, don't hesitate to call. As long as it's before five-thirty, after that, I'm off the clock." She laughs but I don't think she's joking.

"Thanks, Mand, I appreciate it. And yeah, this will all blow over soon. And we can sit down next week and talk about next steps." The fresh air gets to my lungs and fills me with hope and renewal.

"One day at a time, girl. And don't do anything stupid!" When I don't say anything she adds: "Just stay safe please." And she hangs up before I can tell her I love her (even despite what happened with her sleeping with Ellis). She's been reliable...professionally at least. When things went bad, the day the reaction to Andy's death blew up the internet, Mandy was my rock. She gave a statement to the press right away, crafted that thing in thirty minutes, sent it to me for approval, got it out to all the major news outlets, and then spent an hour on the phone with me, talking me down from my near suicidal thoughts. That was a few days ago. I thought that would do the trick, but it only got worse from there. I honestly don't know what anyone can do to fix this. There is nobody who can make it better now, no matter what they think. Micah did have the power a few months back – he could have overruled me and stopped me from killing Andy, but he didn't. Because he knew how mad I'd have been if he did that. And now it's done and I've got to move on. All they can do is support me and help me get through this. Andy Creighton is dead and nothing can bring him back now.

CHAPTER 2

MANDY

The sound of my pen rapping against the desk is inexplicably comforting to me. It's been a nervous habit since I was a kid studying for a test one spring afternoon in the fifth grade, freaking the hell out because I didn't know where to begin. The massive social studies textbook was sitting in front of me, a dense chapter on the Civil War waiting to be read, and I was frozen in place, unable to focus on the task at hand. I grabbed my blue Bic pen and started tapping and suddenly I could read. I breezed (and tapped) through the entire chapter in twenty minutes and aced the test the next day. I've been through a lot of pens (and a few desks, too) since then, but they've all been called to duty in times of stress. Times like now, five days after the death of Andy Creighton.

It's great to hear Sloane's voice, but the whole Andy Creighton mess is causing me severe mental indigestion. In the past, I've carefully curated and controlled the whole reader experience from months before release and through to a full schedule of events and appearances afterwards. This time the entire plan was upended based on the outsized reaction to Andy's death. Tour dates, cancelled. Special events, postponed. All my carefully coordinated plans, trashed.

Micah and Jonah blame me. They have not said as much, but I know they do. I'm the head of publicity, so I'm fairly certain they are sitting over there cursing me out, thinking if I'd done my job right none of this would have happened. That I could have anticipated the mass hysteria and counteracted it somehow through some kind of proactive marketing campaign.

But I know nothing is my fault. Sloane killed Andy Creighton, not me. Not Jonah, Micah, Ireland, Phil, or Katrina either, though I'm sure they'd all argue that it's on me to get in front of the backlash, to be clever and come up with some good talking points to quell the outrage. I'm sorry, but I'm all about hype and publicity; not suppressing and calming. I'm supposed to stoke the public, not tranquilize them.

I'd better think fast though, because my job is on the line, despite my close relationship with Sloane Rylie and my years of service to the company. I lied a little to Sloane just now, telling her we have some ideas to get her out of this. We actually have nothing just yet. We're working on it though.

"Nothing excuses accountability," Micah once said at an annual board meeting before firing three people on the spot. "Not longevity, not likeability, and not even importance."

It's been hard to watch my old friend suffer the last few days, knowing she's being skewered and trashed over something that is at worst a bad decision, not a malicious act designed to rile up the public. She didn't kill Andy to spite everyone (at least from what I can gather). She's a writer. She's human. And at the moment, she's crying to me on the phone, spilling her fears in a torrent of insecurity. She blows her nose, probably into the pink hankie I gave her for Christmas five years ago. She's carried it around in her purse ever since, for rare nasal emergencies like this.

"I worry about you, honey," I say. "You need to calm down." Normally, I'd break into some lyrics from the Taylor song, but this is not the time.

She is silent for a moment, except for an audible sigh. "I forgot why I even called you to begin with," Sloane says. She'd never admit it, but I'm pretty sure she called me to guilt and pressure me into making her troubles go away. Problem is, she doesn't truly grasp just what a tall order that is, which is why the entire team is working on it trying to fix the mess she created when she killed Andy Creighton.

"I'm here if you need me. And hey, you can call me after hours too. Anytime, day or night. We're friends for real, not just when the business clock is ticking."

"Aww, thanks, Mand, I appreciate you. This whole shitstorm had better blow over soon, cause I'm sick of it. This is not what I signed up for. To be honest, I'm considering a career change at this point." I tap my pen even more rapidly, in what I actually think is the Morse code sign for SOS. Sloane changing careers would not be very good for my career. I'd definitely get fired if she decided to open a flower shop or become a librarian.

"Okay, go do your shopping in peace. Talk soon. I've got your back, babe." When she doesn't speak I add: "No matter what."

"You'd better fix this," she says through a sniff as if we're kids and I just broke her favorite toy.

"We will do our best!" I say we because I want her to realize it's not all on me. The entire team has to figure out how to minimize the damage.

"Okay, thanks."

"Love you, bye," I say.

"You won't love me by the time this thing is over, everyone else is turning against me so why not you too," she says on a sigh. I want to reassure her that I'll always be on her side but she hangs up before I can say anything else. I wish Andy Creighton was still alive, and I need to make sure we figure a way out of this mess.

CHAPTER 3

SLOANE

I start in the produce aisle, checking out the fruit. Oranges and apples mainly, because they have a long shelf life. I love bananas but they're too fickle. They all ripen at the same time and then you have exactly one hour to eat them before they turn to mush. I adjust my Sabrina Carpenter cap and make sure my braids remain tucked underneath. I purposely didn't put on any makeup before I left the house; in all my public pics my hair is down and I'm wearing violet lipstick and matching eye shadow, so I should be incognito here. I'm thirty-four and this is probably only the third time I've left home without makeup since I was a teenager – and the other two times I had a rash.

I turn the corner at the end of Aisle 1 and enter Aisle 2 – breakfast cereal and coffee, neither of which I particularly need right now, so I push the cart relatively quickly. Just as I reach the end of that aisle, I hear a female voice call from behind me: "Hey!"

I ignore it of course. They could be talking to anyone. But then I freeze when they say, "You're Sloane Rylie."

My heart pounds and I feel dizzy. I thought I was amply disguised and would avoid any confrontations here, which was apparently a foolish assumption on my part. It's not like I'm known only in my town. The death of Andy Creighton made headlines across the country along with my picture. Even though I look different now, maybe I don't look different enough. My face is still my face, makeup or not. Maybe that annoying driveway woman followed me here or told the media I was heading north on the highway. They know my car, probably saw me pull into the parking lot. I'm screwed, royally. Where's Ellis when I need him? Working, that's where. And we broke up weeks ago so that's not even an option. Anyway, Ellis wouldn't be enough. I need an actual bodyguard. That's what I should have asked Mandy to get me twenty-four hour protection. I make my decision and swing my cart around the corner to the next aisle, cookies and snacks and my eyes light up because sweets always make me happy (especially in large numbers like a supermarket display). I tend to binge eat when I'm depressed or anxious. And for the last two days I've had nothing to munch on except my fingernails, and those don't taste very good at all.

Hopefully, the woman went away when I didn't respond. Who says I am Sloane Rylie? I am a nobody. Sloane Rylie does not come to this store. I select some Keeblers and a few bags of Milanos, double dark chocolate, of course. But when I look up, I see her at the end of the aisle. She's not the driveway woman; she's older, maybe mid-forties and built like a barrel. Square face, thick dark eyebrows, short brown hair in a kind of ugly bowl cut, and wearing a tan jacket with…what looks like a few Andy Creighton buttons pinned on her chest. Her eyes narrow when she sees me.

"Sloane Rylie!" she says, and my name sounds vile on her lips. Like both a curse and a promise of revenge. I half expect her to chuck a can of Folgers at my head. Instead, she just rolls her cart slowly up the aisle, right toward me. Instead of sticking around to discuss Andy Creighton, I hightail it back where I came from, and sprint along the front of the store, then duck into the cleaning and seasonal products aisle. I bend over, trying to catch my breath. I am definitely not used to running anymore. My track and field days are long gone. I can hear my heart thump away in my chest, almost to the beat of the Huey Lewis song playing on the store radio. Yeah, I want a new drug too, Huey. One that won't make me nervous. I stand next to the mops and try to assess my next move. I can't just leave here without getting what I need. I can't leave in defeat. I still want bread and milk and eggs. And some cheese. And a few packages of ground meat. Maybe the woman just wanted to tell me off and then move on. Maybe in denying her that pleasure I have only made her angrier. I should just face her, take the heat and then go on about my shopping hoping nobody else here recognizes me. Or cares. Not everyone cares about Andy Creighton. Not everyone knows who he is.

Do I need a mop? Maybe I do. If nothing else, a mop in my cart looks like protection. I can wield it if necessary, pull some imitation ninja moves on my would-be attacker. I grab the twenty-dollar mop, lay it diagonally in my cart, and keep going. When I'm alone with you, Huey sings. It's been so long since I was alone with Ellis. I could use a little Ellis time, but we are broken up.

I get to the end of the cleaning aisle and turn into the next aisle – paper products. Ah yes, one can never have enough toilet paper. I grab a few four packs and some tissues (I have been crying a lot recently) and am about to make my way down the rest of the aisle when the barrel woman appears at the end.

She holds up a hand. "Stop," she says.

I obey, glancing at the mop, my fingers flexing and ready to grab the handle if needed. "Hello," I say with an attempted smile. Being friendly can't hurt.

"Why did you kill him?" she asks, tilting her head. It's not like this question hasn't been floating around various articles and a topic of discussion on the daytime shows and nightly news as well. But I can't give the answer I gave Mandy: for the money. That would not go over well at all. And it would leak to the press and they'd have a field day with it.

"I regret it now. I should not have," I say with gravity, lowering my head. "It was a mistake."

"It was premeditated," she says matter-of-factly. "You planned it all along. I can see that now." She's wrong about that. I did no such thing; I only decided to kill him recently.

She rolls her cart closer. I don't move mine, but I do grab the mop with my right hand, just in case.

"I mean, inasmuch as these things require some degree of planning, yes. But I regret it, that much is true. I had no idea of the ramifications of what I did." This is also true. Goddammit if I knew this would have happened I'd never have killed poor Andy, not in a million years. Not for the money and not for anything. It wouldn't have been worth it to lose my privacy and sanity over that, no matter how much money it brought me.

"I loved him," the woman says, and I can see she is on the verge of tears. Here we go. Well at least it is going this direction, sobbing and distraught rather than screaming and angry.

"He was popular. A lot of people did." A whole lot. More than I realized, I guess. Because he was perfect. Nobody in real life is perfect but he was, because I made him perfect. In doing so, I set him up for a big fall. They don't understand that. I was supposed to be traveling now, across the country on a book tour. Not shopping for butter in a supermarket. The trip was canceled pretty much right away. Thanks to people like this loser.

"Now what am I supposed to do?" She is asking this honestly, and I have no idea how to comfort her over the loss of Andy Creighton, someone she's never even met. She will live and get through this. But I may not live if people like her keep accosting me.

"There are groups you can join," I offer. Already. Support groups. As ridiculous as that seems. They popped up immediately on Facebook, at least ten of them. A couple have tens of thousands of members. "I'm in mourning too." It's true, I am. I liked Andy a lot. I've known him for seven years. He made me who I am and that's part of why I killed him – to escape from his grasp on me, to separate myself from him.

The woman looks into her cart, at her large black purse, and then she plunges a hand in. I grasp the mop with two hands now, perhaps more to steady myself than to use it in self-defense. But she does not remove a weapon. She removes a liter bottle of what looks like gin. Yes, it is gin. I can see that when she holds it up.

"I brought liquor into the supermarket so I can swig while I shop," she whispers as the tears start to flow. And to demonstrate, she unscrews the top then pours more than a gulp down her throat. She coughs and exhales hard as she recaps the bottle and replaces it in her bag. She is not a drinker, or at least she wasn't one before a few days ago. Bile rises within me and I reach my breaking point. Mandy told me that first day not to be rude or blunt with people, not to insult them if they seem highly agitated over Andy's death. But I have reached my breaking point. And though I could easily disengage and call Mandy right now, I don't want to do that.

Instead of backing away, I let go of the mop and roll my cart closer to the woman. Instead of offering more penitent words or soothing thoughts, I get within ten feet of her. I can tell her chest is burning and she is in discomfort. I glance at her left hand and see a ring.

"You're married," I say.

"Do you want to kill him too?" she replies.

Ouch. That one hurt. But also it just makes me angrier.

"What does he say about all this?"

"What does he say?" She blinks at me as if I have four heads.

"Yes. What does he say? Does he care? Is he sympathetic?" I somehow doubt he understands.

She shakes her head, then reaches for a package of scouring pads and tosses it into her cart. "He's an ass."

"He doesn't care what happened to Andy, does he?" I say it and know it's true. The outrage has been almost all women. Which makes sense. I remember that I need some laundry detergent so I grab a box from the shelf and drop it into my cart. The clunk startles the woman. She looks up at me and blinks.

"Never mind him. You killed my true love, Andy Creighton. It's an outrage."

"You can mourn him without feeling angry." Sounds like he really was her true love, so I soften my tone.

"You broke my heart," she pokes the air with her finger.

I take another step closer to the woman, close enough that I can smell the alcohol on her breath. Be sympathetic, Mandy warned me. These are your fans. You owe it to them. You gave them something amazing and then you took it away from them.

Fuck that and fuck Mandy.

I lean in close to the woman and say, slowly and with emphasis. "Andy Creighton is a fictional character in a series of books. He's not real. He may have been nice, smart, funny, kind – pick your adjective…but he's not real. He had a good run and now he's making his exit. Do us all a favor and grow up and get over it already. The book series will continue. Life goes on." And I turn away and roll my cart past her so I can finish my shopping trip.

CHAPTER 4

SLOANE

As the checkout girl scans my items, she throws me a strange look, but I think it's because of my multiple bags of decadent cookies, rather than any sort of recognition. Besides, she's only about sixteen and the average age of my readers tends to be twenty-three to forty-nine.

Because I'm feeling self-conscious, I say, "I've been looking for these cookies everywhere," which sounds really ridiculous, I suppose, because they are not uncommon. They can even be found at my local chain drugstore.

But the girl nods and flashes a smile as if she believes me, and says "Nice," and then "Eighty-one fifty-seven." Dark-chocolate robed decadence isn't cheap.

I wonder if that angry woman is still standing by the Tide, in shock at being scolded by a famous author. I almost want to go back and tell her not to fear, that my intrepid team is right at this moment working on solutions to fix this. Her eyes would light up and she'd ask if that means Andy is not dead. And I'd say, that's not possible, he's very dead. After how I wrote that scene, he's incontrovertibly deceased. Now if this were a fantasy book, I could have Ciara cast a spell and bring him back to life. Or if it were sci fi, he could be whisked into a time machine and transported back an hour to avoid his tragic fate. Nope, no such luck here. I can't undo what I did in a romance novel.

I get back to my car, arms full with three badly packed paper bags overflowing with groceries. I forgot my reusable bags at home again and had to pay five cents apiece for these. I'm terrible about being environmentally friendly. Don't hate me, but as much as I want to save the earth, my brain is not programmed for it. I mean well! I really do. But I am constantly forgetting the little things, like recycling for example. How many cans and bottles have wound up in my trash? A lot. I used to be more in touch with nature, in the days when I spent time at my dad's cabin in the woods. I should really go there soon, to clear my mind and get away from everything.

My mind is lost in those thoughts as I try to snake my hand into my pocket to unlock my car, when a familiar voice startles me from behind.

"Thought you could just insult me and then walk away?" I fumble the three bags and would have dropped them if I hadn't leaned up against my car door to brace myself. I turn my head slightly and confirm it's the distraught woman from aisle ten.

"Can we not do this here in the parking lot?" I say, finally managing to press the button on my key fob and hearing the lock disengage. What I mean is more like, can we not do this period. I make my way to the trunk, well aware that the woman is standing a few feet away, arms folded, shaking her head. She must have already loaded her car and decided to skulk around the lot until I came out of the store. If that doesn't make me feel special I am not sure what will. If she wants to continue our little discussion, then she is going to need to be helpful. "Could you get the trunk for me at least so I can give you my full attention?" I say. She grunts in assent and the trunk pops open. "Thanks," I say.

I quickly load the groceries and then slam the trunk shut and turn to face the woman. I used to admire persistence, but lately I am seeing the negative aspects of that trait. People need to forget about me and Andy and my book and just move on with their lives.

"How about telling me your name? If we're going to continue this," I say.

"Glenda," she says, looking at my car. "You drive this?"

"Yeah. What did you expect? A Mercedes? I'm just an ordinary person like you." Have I insulted her just now? Does she think she's more than ordinary? Who knows. I am not built for this. I became a writer for two reasons – one, I love writing, and two, I generally hate people and prefer to be by myself. Sure, I can afford a better car now, but I don't really want one. The truth is, I have not changed that much since the money started flowing in, since my books started selling over a million copies. But the truth also is, the book world is fickle. My sales have been declining. Authors can't take anything for granted, even if they are Sloane Rylie.

"I wish you hadn't killed Andy," she says, eyes watery. I should have taken Mandy's advice and been kind to anyone who approached me. But no, I had to be a complete bitch. Honestly, do you blame me? There are thousands of people dying every day from violence, starvation, preventable diseases; who is protesting that? Meanwhile, a fictional death is causing an uproar and resulting in supermarket confrontations? As my college film professor told us on the last day of class: Life sucks, people expect more from movies, television, and books. I never really bought that concept. I think it goes both ways. One could argue that bad endings can actually be enjoyable because they are reminders that your life is better than that. On-screen disasters and on-page deaths make reality seem better. I used to believe that at any rate. Until the real world started to become scarier than anything a writer could conjure up. But instead of getting lost in an internal debate over the merits of bad endings, I have to think of what to say to Glenda before she decides to shove me in front of an oncoming car.

"The next book will…" I stop myself from spilling my planned plot to a random person. She would probably take it to the press and tomorrow my plot would be all over the news. No thank you. "It will be very good. And you will feel better."

"When will it be out?" she asks. Fair question, but I have no idea. I've only just started writing it.

"Oh, shouldn't be long at all. Maybe six months?" I lie because it's the most convenient way to get her off my back. It will be at least eighteen months.

She stands there staring at me. She looks younger than I originally thought. She is probably close to my age. She swallows hard and then says, "Can I take you somewhere? I want to show you something."

As an author, that is not a question you want to hear from a "fan." I start to decline the offer. "I don't think that's a good…"

"In separate cars. It's only five minutes away." There is a softness and supple sadness in her eyes now, like she's suddenly reconciled the anger she'd been feeling toward me.

"Fine. I'll follow you," I say. Any sign of trouble, and I'm going to turn the hell around and leave. But curiosity takes over and now I need to know what she has in mind. We get in our cars, and I watch her drive away. I consider just ditching her, but I wind up going left and staying on her tail.

We wind through a few narrow local streets, the last of which dead ends onto a broad boulevard. She turns right and drives painfully slowly. After a minute we come upon a large old cemetery on our right. She signals and turns into the main gate. I follow. She pulls her car off to the side about a hundred feet in. For a couple of minutes, she remains in the car and I start to panic. What if she's got a weapon and is going to spring out and run toward my car and shoot me through the windshield? Her door opens and I brace myself but there is no gun visible as she strolls toward my car. I quickly get out and stand waiting, hands on hips.

"Follow me," she yells, gesturing. She walks along a row of low and broad granite gravestones that must be the newest in the entire cemetery, the rest of which look like they are from the late 1800s. I stay about twenty feet behind, leaves crunching under my sneakers as I study the names we pass. Berman, Cydester, Albertson, Sommers, Ardinkle. She stops a few feet past Ardinkle and lowers her head. I stand next to her and look at the stone. Frank Milman is chiseled onto the rock in large block letters. The date of death is last year; he would have been fifty-seven then according to my math.

The woman sniffs twice and then starts bawling uncontrollably. She's no monster, she just lost someone close to her. I put an arm around her and let her sob for a minute.

"Your dad?" I guess, feeling her loss.

"Dad? No! That was my husband." And she sobs some more and wipes her eyes and nose on her jacket sleeve. Gross.

"Oh no, I'm sorry. But wait, you'd said your husband is a pain in the ass."

"Well, he is, for going ahead and dying on me." She stifles a smile and flips a finger at the gravestone. "He passed away last year and all I had left was my number one book boyfriend."

I brace myself for what is about to come next.

"But you took him away from me." And there it is. She shakes her head slowly and leans forward to run her fingers over the name on the smooth gray stone. "It's okay," she says, patting my shoulder gently. "You're right. It's just a book. I should be mourning the actual loss, not words on a page." I resist the urge to recoil at her touch; though I don't want her hands on me I'd rather not alter the momentum of this encounter that seems to be improving by the second.

"The next book will make up for it," I promise her baselessly, following her lead and placing a pebble on her late husband's gravestone. The next book will do nothing of the sort. In fact, I may quit writing altogether, change my name, and move to an island off the coast of South Carolina like I'd fantasized as a kid. Yeah, I was a strange kid. But I think strange kids are the ones most likely to turn into successful writers.

"I'll read it, even though I'm sad and mad and upset over All Things Must." She looks up at the cloudless sky and shakes her head, tears streaming down her cheeks. "Aw crap. What is wrong with me? I'm sorry I dragged you here. I never met anyone famous in my life, well besides a third-place finalist from American Idol. But besides that, nobody. And what do I do when I finally meet a celebrity? I take her to a cemetery. I suck," she says, her voice breaking, as she wipes her face on her sleeve. A celebrity. Never really thought of myself that way. Ellis rarely treated me like a famous writer, even though my books have sold a ton of copies. I guess we tend to frame ourselves through the eyes and hearts of our significant others. By we, I mean me.

"You're good," I reassure her as we walk back to our respective cars. "This was actually important. For me to see how my writing has a real impact on readers. I think it will make me a more thoughtful author." Or maybe it will lead me to give up writing altogether. One or the other.

"I just wish you hadn't been so violent," she says softly, head lowered." I think that's really what did it for most of us fans. Not just that it happened, but how it happened."

I stop in my tracks. "Violent? I made it as peaceful as I could." Hands on hips, I face her. See, this is the level of crazy I deal with as an author. Everything is exaggerated. Not that I've ever died before, but on a scale of 1 to horrible, I'd think fast acting poison is not atop the list of most violent ways to be killed.

Glenda kicks at the dirt with her sneaker. That look she gave me back in the supermarket has returned. "Seriously?

I thought we were good, and now you say this? Peaceful? It was heartbreaking!" She shakes her head slowly, stomps past me, unlocks her car door and plops into the driver's seat, mouth twisted into quite a scowl. She really is insane. If I had remained a mid-list author I'd have never had to deal with this level of crazy. Nobody has delusional tantrums over what happens to characters in mid-list books.

CHAPTER 5

SLOANE

What the general public doesn't get is that the Andy Creighton series was tanking. Sales were down the last couple of books. Another ordinary Andy book and the trend would continue. The series had run its course. America's favorite book boyfriend was on the decline; soon enough my books would wind up on the dreaded remainders table. I needed a huge twist, a big deal that would send everyone running to the bookstore to buy it. Micah thought sales would tank even further with All Things Must, and I thought (correctly) the opposite. The pre-orders for this book were double that of the previous one thanks to Mandy's efforts in pre-publicizing it and placing carefully worded teasers that described a huge shocking ending without giving anything away (Everyone loves Andy Creighton…right?).

I did in fact have a plan for the next book: change the focus to Ciara Derryfell, who while still mourning Andy falls for the detective who is brought on to help solve Andy's murder. That was my plan for how this plays out.

And the readers don't know this yet, but Crenshaw is quite a catch himself. Maybe even better overall than Andy was, if only the readers would give me a chance to show them that.

I decide to take local roads home instead of the highway to help calm my nerves. I pass through sunny little streets with cheery 1920s cottages painted in bright reds, yellows, and greens and wonder how many of their residents have read my book. While each book in the series has been a bestseller, overall, that still amounts to a tiny fraction of the American populace that cares about Andy Creighton. The vast majority don't. That old man walking his dog, definitely not. Those kids playing ball in their front yard, nope. The book has already sold 700,000 copies. Add to that library borrows and kindle reads, maybe we're talking four million people who've read it so far? Out of how many people in this country? And yet, that's plenty enough to cause an uproar and make my life hell. The older girl misses the ball, and it bounces out into the street in front of my car. I screech to a stop and allow the girl, maybe eight, to run out and retrieve the ball. She smiles at me and yells a happy thanks before scampering back to her lawn. The second girl, a year or two older, waves and gives me a thumbs up. Probably the first time in five days I've registered a positive reaction from anyone, and it feels damn good.

Maybe it's true I am known across the country, but I feel like getting away could be useful. If I was incognito in Bar Harbor, Maine I think I'd be fine. That Stop and Shop was just too close to my home to get away with escaping unnoticed.

When I reach my house, that protestor is still at the end of my driveway. Feeling emboldened, I roll down the window as she steps aside, and say, "Hey, why don't you go home? Surely you have better things to do?" I glance at my watch for effect and then pull into my spot. Apparently, she takes my advice because she is gone by the time I open my trunk to start unloading groceries.

I get inside and my phone buzzes. It's Mandy. She probably already knows that I berated the woman in the store. Word travels fast. I prepare myself to be scolded and answer the phone, which I set down on the marble center island as I shove food into the fridge, stuffing a Milano into my mouth as I do so.

"Hey!" she says as if we haven't talked in days.

"Hey to you, too," I answer.

"Successful shopping trip?" She doesn't know what happened, good. Maybe I tell her a sanitized version of it. Let's see first what she wants.

"Yeah, it was okay I guess." Did I really buy this many bags of cookies? I take another bite, and crumbs fly out of my mouth and onto the floor. I should have kept the mop in my cart; this floor is filthy.

"Great. Hey, listen! Just got off with Jonah. They've had a couple of interns scouring all the groups about our Andy Creighton quandary, to monitor the chatter and try to deescalate discussions when they get too heated." I roll my eyes. Andy Creighton has been described in many ways, but never as a quandary.

"Deescalate things? You mean like defend me?"

"Yeah, kind of. Not overtly, just subtly. Like if someone says they hate you, one of them, through one of their several accounts, will say, aww, but I feel bad for her. Anyway, not my point. So they were monitoring this one group – We Love Andy Creighton, mind you that has existed for four years now. Anyway, Trish, the one intern came across a comment, a theory from this thirty-year old in Des Plaines that the whole last chapter was nothing but a dream sequence."

I nearly drop the eggs I am cradling on my way to the fridge. "A dream sequence? What the fuck?" I badly needed that laugh.

"No, hey. Focus here. The girl laid out the theory in some detail, and it has merit. The fact that Andy was always tired, the references to clouds in several places in that chapter, there's a list of things."

I don't know where Mandy is heading with this, but I just want to finish unpacking and eat a few more cookies while I watch reruns of One Tree Hill. I clear my throat and place the eggs on the shelf realizing I apparently already have enough eggs to last me three months. Oops.

"Okay that's cool. And?"

"And? Babe, don't you see? This is our opening. We are going to run with this."

I cannot even pretend to be following, because it makes no sense. What is she saying? Run with what? Is she proposing some kind of revisionist history here? Before I can speak again, she continues. "Listen, can you get down to Cabinet in like ninety minutes? We are all going to meet in the boardroom and it would be best if you were there in person."

Going into the city would mean either driving, taking an Uber, or riding the Metro-North train. Parking is a pain in the ass; I do not want to be caught by angry "fans" on a train where there is no escape. So Uber it is, because I'm pretty sure the driver will not be a thirty-something single white girl, my typical demographic. I set it up and grab a bottle of spring water, my purse, my phone, and a couple more cookies which I toss into a Ziploc.

Thankfully, the protestor is still gone when the Uber pulls up. I have not been to the city in over a week and I kind of miss the chaos (unrelated to me chaos, that is) of it all. And also the anonymity. I feel like walking down Fifth Avenue nobody will recognize me in the crowd and I'll feel a little better. I stare out the window of Mo's vehicle as the houses and stores flit by. My eyes glaze over and all the passing things morph into one streaking blur.

I guess it's been more like two hours, because they're all waiting for me when I walk into the 33rd floor conference room. There's Mandy, flashing a warm and genuine smile. And then Micah, the chief editor; Jonah, who's my personal editor; Terrance, the CEO; Ireland, the bookstore sales rep; Jessica from Accounting, and a few others I have never met. At least one of them must be the intern who found that woman's comment in the Facebook group thread. They saved me the spot at the near end of the long, smooth teak table.

Everyone's eerily silent as I take my seat and roll the chair tight to the table. Each of us has a copy of All Things Must sitting in front of us, along with a dark purple Cabinet Publishing folder to its right. All eyes are uncomfortably on me until Micah clears his throat. Good old Micah, forty-five, with a bushy head of dark black hair and a carefully trimmed salt and pepper goatee. He peers at me from across the room, through his wire-frame glasses.

"Our head of publicity is going to fill you in on where we're at," he says and then folds his hands, shifting his gaze to Mandy, who flashes me a nervous smile and then addresses the room in a cheerful voice as she glances at a paper in front of her. "As some of you already know, we've had our interns tracking all the chatter in the various groups dedicated to the author, the book, or to Andy Creighton himself. On Facebook alone that's fifteen different groups, ranging in size from thirty-eight members to 650,000 members. The comments went from overwhelmingly upbeat and anticipatory before the book was released, to overwhelmingly negative starting about six hours after when the first people began to finish the book." She pauses and peers at Micah from above her glasses, then brings her attention back to the paper. "We set out to do this to monitor the reaction to the book, expecting to have many positive reviews and comments to report. But the reaction to Andy Creighton's demise was far more severe than we could have predicted. That overshadowed any positive thoughts on the rest of the book. It overshadowed everything. Andy Creighton's death became the only important moment in the book. The comments in these groups took on a life of their own and there was much complaining, anger, sadness, and disappointment. While one might expect discourse or debate with a negative comment, in this case, the only discourse was in what way it affected the reader and what emotions they were feeling."

"What is the point of this little monologue?" Ireland asks, drumming her fingers on the table. She should be thrilled; bookstore sales are through the roof. Everyone wants a copy of the book so they can read it and weep, literally.

"Patience, I'm getting there," Mandy says without missing a beat. "Well, a couple of hours ago, our intrepid interns (sure enough, she gives a subtle nod to the one girl at the table) stumbled across a lengthy comment from Dez Maxwell of Des Plaines, Iowa. While she, too, is devastated by the death of her beloved Andy, she puts forth a theory that the entire thing was a dream sequence." There are a few snide chuckles from the room and some head shakes to go with them. Mandy waits until the room is silent again and continues. "This may seem ridiculous, but Dez, short for Desiree by the way, lays out several proofs for her theory. And they are good ones. For one, Andy has been very tired in the days leading up to his death. Second, in the scene where he dies, he describes a recurring nightmare he has of being killed. Third, just before he dies, he says he wishes he felt more awake. And it goes on." She turns the paper over. "In your folders you will find all the relevant points that Ms. Maxwell raised."

Now it's my turn to chime in. "Okay, that's cool. So, what are you suggesting?"

"That death of Andy Creighton was nothing more than a dream sequence," Micah says flatly, glaring at Mandy, and then at me. "We will be engaging in a full-on social media and PR campaign to promote this fact."

"Whoa there, Micah. Slow down. I haven't approved anything yet." While I normally appreciate his decisiveness, this seems preemptive. I usually get final say in what happens with my books.

"I'm afraid it's already been decided," Terrance growls in his smoke-addled voice from the seat to my left. He's one of their senior editors. I've never liked him.

"What if I don't go along with it?" I say with a shrug. My opinion here has to count for something. I have lined the pockets of pretty much everyone in the room. Except maybe the interns, I think they're unpaid.

Micah shakes his head slowly and opens his Cabinet folder. He extracts a stapled sheaf of papers and flips through a few pages to get to a neon green sticky note. He plucks the colorful square off and slaps it onto the conference table, clears his throat, and proceeds to read from the paragraph he's marked with yellow highlighter.

"Page nine of your contract and I quote – 'Author hereby relinquishes final control over all decisions regarding the promotion of the work and gives publisher complete authority without limit to handle any crisis situation emerging from content of the work such that it is in the best interest of the publisher.'"

"Are we really citing my contract? Is that necessary?" Apparently, it is necessary, which annoys me to no end. Times like these I wish I was still an indie author making waves on her own without a corporate juggernaut calling the shots.

Jonah's been quiet so far, but I can see he's been wanting to speak. Jonah always takes my side, he has from the very beginning when I handed in the first book in the series and insisted on Andy's name not being changed to Clay. And not only does he speak, he stands up to do so, so abruptly he almost sends his chair toppling over before Ireland reaches out to steady it.

"It's not necessary, Micah. She's right. We do have a good plan, and it's on us to convince her not force her. We're a team. We're in this together. We published the book, but she wrote it. This won't work without her buy-in, no matter how much we twist her arms." He strokes his angular chin and his brown eyes scan the room for signs of dissent. There aren't any. He nods, satisfied. "Good then."

One of the women I don't know speaks. She's wearing a tank top that reveals green and orange dragon tattoos on both muscular upper arms. "And now for the best part. Dez Maxwell is going to be our winner!"

"Our winner?" I repeat, blinking at the woman.

"Yes! She is the first one to correctly guess what really happened in the book…"

"But it didn't really happen. Andy Creighton is dead," I say flatly, trying to remind everyone of reality.

"Ah but it did happen, and Dez figured it out," Micah offers. "Cabinet Publishing has been scanning the socials to find the first reader, the first fan, to guess the truth as part of a secret contest we were holding. This will be the biggest surprise promo in the publishing industry since 2015 and the golden bookmark that was slipped into five copies of Desert Plume. So, as she is the winner, we are flying Dez and a guest here to New York immediately for a one-week all expenses paid trip. She will get to tour our offices, meet you, be part of a major press conference and social media campaign, and receive a thousand-dollar swag bag filled with books and merch before we send her off on her merry way back to the sticks, with our problem solved and everyone happy" Yeah, everyone except me. But nobody seems to care what I want.

"So, what Micah was saying, the social media campaign, it's going to be all about the dream sequence theory, and we will elaborate on it. We're thinking up a catchy title but something along the lines of Andy's Alive! We'll take out print ads, radio ads, maybe a billboard in Times Square, maybe even a TV spot. And not only will this free us from the stigma of Andy being dead, it will also get the book even more buzz and sell more copies." Mandy smiles but I can't be convinced she's okay with this.

"But Andy is dead," I say. I am reacting to news of his unlikely survival the way most people react to the news of a loved one's death. I killed him and now he's alive again? This is unreal.

Micah laughs. "Damn, Sloane, you've got to stop saying that. A few hours ago, he was. But as of now he's alive because Dez figured out our surprise." I wish I didn't care so much. I wish this didn't matter to me. But into every good book goes the author's entire life for months and sometimes years. It's hard to just sit back and suddenly not care.

Now Jonah chimes in: "And in a week's time, we are going to release a teaser from the first page of the next book in the series, proving that Andy is alive and well."

The room falls silent, and all eyes turn to me. As if I know what to say. I'd already started plotting the next book, without Andy Creighton. To suddenly come up with an entirely new plot and opening page of the book within a week will be nearly impossible. Dream sequence clues or not, everything in the book was leading toward the death of Andy Creighton. What do I do, just start off with Andy sitting at the breakfast table digging into a plateful of lightly scrambled eggs with home fries, as per usual? And then all the fans can relax and stop stalking me wherever I go? Maybe they won't even care if his resurrection is not believable. Maybe they just want him back, pretending nothing happened. Because in real life, if you thought grandma was dead and it turned out she wasn't, would you be obsessed with the why and how, so long as you could see and touch her? Would you care if the doctors pronounced gran dead and she popped up and started walking out of the ICU? Nope.

Everyone is still staring at me because I have not spoken yet. "This is happening too fast," I say gently. "We need to be careful and go slowly."

"No," Micah says. "The opposite. Speed is of the essence or it won't seem organic. It has to feel like this was planned. We can't stumble out of the gate if this is supposed to be a contest."

Organic. A word I've come to greet with skepticism ever since my primary care physician launched into a dissertation about how the whole organic movement is misleading and organic food is not in fact better for you. And that is my fear, that this whole contest and reversal will seem fake, contrived. That it will make a joke out of me and my books, my career will be sunk on account of this stunt. Better to let Andy rest in goddamn peace.

I glance around the conference table, at all the expectant faces, and can't decide why exactly they are doing this. Surely it's not to save and protect me personally. I doubt that they care about me in that way. No, they are more concerned with my brand, with their reputation, with the sales outlook for my past and future books, with the very existence of Cabinet Publishing. And swirled into that is their desire to be clever and turn an unexpectedly bad situation into a goldmine.

All I want to do is go home, open a bottle of white wine, and soak in the tub under a frothy lather of rose scented suds while my Gracie Abrams playlist cycles through my eight favorite songs a couple of times. I am badly outnumbered and all this attention on me is making me squirm in my chair. I seem to have no choice here, so in the interest of more bubbles and less troubles, I agree to their stupid plan.

CHAPTER 6

SLOANE

According to her Facebook profile pic, Dez Maxwell of Des Plaines, Iowa is in her mid-thirties, has short, pink hair, a dragon tattoo on her left shoulder, and owns a scrawny looking calico cat. Looks like your typical reader, is what Micah told me when he sent me the link to her page. This whole contest was their idea, but Micah insisted that I be the one to make the call. The call! Like this is 2007. Why can't we just email the woman? I was feeling uncomfortable about the degree of sketchy activities that must have yielded her phone number so I said as much. Micah cracked a wry smile and told me she's a member of the Ciara's Besties Fan Club; Cabinet has all her info along with that of about 200,000 other rabid fans who've paid ten bucks to join the club in the last few years. In return, Ciara's Besties get an annual goodie bag of stickers, a keychain, a pair of socks, and exclusive sneak peaks and chances to win signed copies of my books. So Dez Maxwell gave up her personal info willingly. Okay then, I can make this call without feeling too bad. No worse than I already feel for pulling the whole contest ruse on the poor woman, at any rate.

Thankfully, Micah didn't insist on me doing the call while he watched. He handed me a half-page script with some extra talking points and answers to possible questions, and sent me on my way. I turned to look at him on my way out. The man is handsome, I'll give him that. A year ago I developed a small crush on him, but it passed when he decided to grow that goatee. I normally don't have anything against goatees or beards in general, but I have a weird thing where if I know and like a cleanshaven guy and he suddenly grows facial hair, I can't deal with it. My second boyfriend was one of those. Not only was it disconcerting when he stopped shaving, it kind of hurt when he kissed me for the six weeks that it took to grow out. I broke up with him when I looked at him across the table in the Applebee's and didn't recognize him as the same guy I'd started dating six months before.

"Do it today, and let me know right away once you reach her." Micah seemed very pleased with himself, but as the call rang through to Des Plaines, I was less than enthused. The whole idea was a ridiculous attempt to save face, to pretend the bad thing I'd written never happened. It happened. I wrote it into existence and not one of those editors over at Cabinet thought it was a problem at the time. When I said this to Micah as I snatched the paper out of his hand, he replied with two words. Damage control. I blinked at him.

A woman picks up on the fifth ring and says a bland hello. She sounds small and distant.

"Hey! Is this Dez Maxwell?" I ask, wanting nothing more than to get this over with.

"Who the hell is asking?" the voice says. And this is why cold calling was a terrible idea. People generally do not like talking on their phones, they prefer texting. And that's for people they know and like; this is an unsolicited call from an unknown number.

"Sloane Rylie," I reply. "The author."

Her tone lightens a little. "Haha, Dana? Is that you? Are you pranking me again?"

"It's not Dana." Though I am tempted to just say yes and hang up. "It's really me, Sloane. You are a member of Ciara's Besties Fan Club, aren't you?"

There is silence as Dez considers my words. "Yeah, okay Dana, nice try." She pauses and I hear a gasp. "Wait, what? I just texted Dana and she swears it's not her and now she's calling me on the other line. So, who the hell is this?"

"Like I said…it's really me, Sloane Rylie. I am reaching out because you are the winner of Cabinet Publishing's secret contest." Secret indeed, so secret I just found out about it myself. I'm lousy at faking emotions. I had wanted to be an actor when I was in middle school, and I won the lead female role in The Music Man but gave up after a few rehearsals. I couldn't come across as convincing. I couldn't be anyone but myself.

"Secret contest? What?" I have her attention now. "And by the way if you really are Sloane Rylie, then you can tell me I'm right."

I know what she meant without even asking. "You are right and that's why I said you won our contest." I try to fake some enthusiasm and excitement. "You figured it out that the whole thing was a dream sequence, so congratulations for that. You win a grand prize package that includes an all expenses paid trip to New York City and a tour of Cabinet Publishing headquarters, a meet and greet with me and one other Cabinet author of your choosing, and a copy of every single book Cabinet has published in the last ten years." I take a breath after finishing my prize monologue. As I spoke the words, I had a really bad, sinking feeling about this lie, that it would come back to bite me hard, and my body reacted immediately – my stomach tensed and my intestines twitched. I felt like I was about to shit my pants.

There is a deep exhale at the other end of the line, followed by a muffled few words like she is talking to someone else in the room, then she comes back to our call. "This is crazy. This is great. It's an honor to talk to you, Sloane. I almost got to meet you at one of your book signings in Davenport a few years ago but the line was too long, and they turned me away. And now I get to fly to New York and get you all to myself? Crazy!" She seems genuinely excited, making her the first fan I'd encountered who had not greeted me with anger and disappointment. My anxiety eases its grip on my digestive system a little.

"We're looking at the next few days. Someone will be in touch shortly to make all the arrangements with you, and congratulations again," I say per the script Micah has provided me.

"Thank you!" Dez replies; I can almost see her smiling through the phone. I am about to hang up when she says, softly, "Between you and me, I pulled that dream sequence thing out of my damn ass, it was wishful thinking. I was just trying to stop all the negative comments on the fan club page because it was getting out of hand and I felt bad for you. So, I was really right about it? That's a relief, I have to admit."

I glance down at Micah's script again. "Yes, you are right. But we at Cabinet Publishing ask you to refrain from mentioning it to anyone at all, until we officially announce you as the winner. It's a whole thing we have planned to reveal it." I pause for effect. "If we find out you've told anyone then you forfeit your prize package. It's all in the documents we will be emailing you for your review and electronic signature later today." I shake my head, annoyed at this whole thing. If we find out you told someone about the thing we just made up on the fly, you lose the prize we were going to give you for inventing a way out of this. Unreal.

She goes quiet and then I hear a light sobbing and sniffing on the other end.

"Hey, what's the matter, Dez?" I ask tenderly.

"When you told me a few minutes ago, I told my boyfriend. He's right next to me in the kitchen here. That's what you heard probably, I covered the phone and told him. And now I've lost the prize before I even really won it." And she sobs more.

"It's okay," I say, making an executive decision. "I had not told you the ground rules yet. Starting now. Okay? Just tell the boyfriend to keep it quiet and it's fine."

"Alright. Thank you, Sloane. I guess I will see you in New York soon! And by the way, I am thrilled Andy is actually okay!" The excitement is back in her voice and I feel like crap. There go my intestines again. I say goodbye and run to the bathroom, almost not making it there.

CHAPTER 7

MANDY

That was the most uncomfortable Cabinet Publishing meeting I've ever attended, and I've been to a few doozies. Like the time the standup comic Curtis Curtin was negotiating his autobiography and he fired his agent while we were sitting there in the boardroom, then proceeded to demand double the original advance we'd offered. I feel bad for Sloane, having to endure all the attention, having to listen to everyone tell her what was going to happen. And I feel bad for being part of that insurrection, but it's my role as the head of public relations for Cabinet to promote and protect.

We also happen to be friends for years, ever since Sloane walked into that writers conference, just a fresh-faced girl of twenty-four completely new to the publishing world. I was new too, back then. We hit it off immediately and became besties, and then she hired me. When her first book hit the hundred thousand mark in sales, we went out to dinner to celebrate, just me and her. A steak dinner, and not just at the chain restaurant that always runs those commercials – at the place where the eight-ounce filet mignon is well into the three digits and doesn't even come with any side dish. Then Cabinet hired me to work on all their titles, not just Sloane's, and the rest as they say, is history. I've been Sloane's confidante and best friend for the last ten years and I'll admit that it's not all to my credit. I'm not that great of a person or a friend, to be honest. It's more that she doesn't really have anyone else better. One of the first things she told me after we met was that her closest friends were fictional characters either in books she read or books she wrote. I used to think that was kind of pathetic, until I read her series and became hooked. I guess in writing she makes up for the people her real life is missing, and the characters come across stunningly three-dimensional. Confession: Andy Creighton was my book boyfriend, too. Sloane has this way with dialogue that really makes her characters come to life. Andy is so real to me. I think her ability is also her liability in this case. Which is why we find ourselves with this uproar over Andy's demise. Confession number two: I was devastated when I finished All Things Must.

There's unpleasant stuff happening out in the world that I didn't even want to tell Sloane. Like in Seattle, about thirty people met up at Discovery Park and threw a bunch of her books into a campfire (in the TikTok video I saw it was more like a bonfire). Well, they attempted to at any rate, before the local police stopped them but confiscated the books in the process. And in Dallas, Atlanta, and Tulsa some angry readers bought up the entire display of books and promptly made a show of tossing them into a trash can outside the bookstore. People have short attention spans, and I suspect the whole thing will blow over in a week or two. But maybe not. I want to shield her from the full scope of readers' wrath because we're besties, despite the chill I've felt in our relationship since this last book was finished, since the thing with Ellis, the thing where I slept with her boyfriend before I started dating my current guy, Patrick. It's a long story and one that I prefer not to repeat but suffice it to say they were on a break, and we were tipsy and the rest is history, albeit badly written history.

She acted as though she didn't care, but deep down, I knew she cared a lot, and I felt the immediate and maybe irreversible strain in our relationship from that moment on. But also, she's been very stressed lately. I think writing so much so quickly has taken a toll on her, and our friendship isn't the only thing that's suffered. Finishing this book near burned her out. She was rushing to get it done and meet her contractual deadline. I think that's why she killed Andy, to be honest. I think she was down to the wire and didn't have time to execute her original plan for the book's ending so instead she executed Andy. She'll never admit it, of course, but I believe it to be true. It's what I would have done in her place.

I stare out the window at Fifth Avenue, at all the tourists walking and gawking on their way to see St. Patrick's Cathedral or Rockefeller Center, wishing I was also a tourist right about now. I really didn't enjoy having to make that little speech in front of everyone, spouting ideas that weren't mine and citing information I'd only just been made aware of an hour before. Jonah and Micah thought Sloane would listen to me more than anyone else, so I had to be the one to explain what was basically Micah's decision and frame it as a group effort.

"I don't want to be the messenger for your lame idea," I told Micah point blank.

"You're our head of publicity. Your job is literally to be the messenger," he replied, eyes narrowed.

Suddenly I feel nauseous. I want to crack open the conference room window but before I can do it, a tap on my shoulder startles me and I jump. It's Micah. He apologizes with a nervous laugh and then tells me he wants to see me right away in his office. Great. I was hoping to go home and finally do the mound of laundry that's been sitting on the floor at the foot of my bed. The last couple of weeks have been nonstop for me and I'd love to just catch up on stuff. And frankly I used to get more stuff done when Sloane and I hung out a few times a week. I miss that. But anyway, it looks like I'll be here in the Cabinet building for at least a little longer.

Micah has the corner office, and the view is amazing. He deserves it, I guess, though Sloane's name should really be on a plaque next to his door, since he built his cache here by shepherding her manuscripts through to the bookstore shelves. I saw an accounting report for last year and Sloane's book sales represented fifteen percent of the company's revenue. Now that may not sound like a lot, but considering Cabinet publishes 35 books a year and has an established backlist, it's huge. Sloane is everything. I guess that's why the fire drill over Andy Creighton. Nobody is willing to let their top author and her entire body of work just go up in flames. Literally.

Micah gestures for me to sit in the old burgundy colored leather armchair that has been graced by the butts of countless authors, agents, and random celebrity visitors. I flash a perfunctory smile and plop myself into the chair. It's seen better days, but Micah will never get rid of it. I sit with my hands folded in my lap and wait for him to speak. He does that thing where he looks up at the ceiling before speaking; that's how I know he's about to say something important.

"What's up, boss?" I ask to get the process going.

"Mandy rhymes with Andy," he says. Dude says the weirdest shit sometimes, I swear.

"I'm aware," I say.

"Sorry. That just popped into my head."

"And as we learned in second grade, we don't need to say everything that crosses our minds." I say in a singsong voice. I'm glad Micah and I are on this level, where I can tease him mercilessly and not make an enemy out of him. Yet.

"Haha, true," he says, adjusting the snow globe on his desk and picking up a pencil. He doesn't actually use pencils for anything other than fidget toys. Sometimes he fucks with the eraser, jamming his fingernail into it nervously. This time the business end of the pencil goes into his mouth and he gnaws on it. I try not to cringe but fail. That yellow paint can't be good for you. He notices my expression and places the pencil back on the desk, then adjusts the snow globe again. "Mandy Jacobsen, I have a proposition for you."

"Micah! After all these years you're finally going to proposition me," I smile and he rolls his eyes. I think he's had a crush on me all along and just refuses to acknowledge it. Perish the thought though, because that might actually have been worse for me and Sloane than me fucking her boyfriend.

"Seriously though. All this commotion over Andy's death has got me thinking. We need to take advantage of it. A complete turning of the tables." He turns the snow globe around 180 degrees to emphasize his point.

"I thought that's what we're doing with the whole dream sequence idea," I say. Though it wasn't my idea, I think it was a good one. Creative thinking goes a long way in the publishing world, especially these days.

"It's more than that," he says. He picks up the snow globe and shakes it. Glittery snowflakes fall on a quaint village of half-timbered houses. "I want to make everyone pay for this. Literally."

"More," I repeat. "Okay mister Cryptic, care to elaborate? And why isn't Sloane here with us?"

He nods and puts the snow globe back on his desk. Then he picks up the pencil and taps it on the desk like he's trying to do Morse code. "This doesn't concern Sloane," he says. "I mean, it does, but not directly.' He pauses and raises his eyebrows at me. "You published a novel way back when, didn't you?"

Ah, my novel. Take Me Back to Tennessee. My attempt at a grumpy vs. sunshine and enemies to lovers trope book. My failed attempt. Whenever anyone brings it up in conversation, my cheeks immediately turn a blotchy shade of crimson. It was indeed published, and it was not very good. The reviews were not kind. Even my own mom, who put all my shitty artwork on her fridge when I was growing up, only gave it three stars. "You know I did, so why are you asking? It's right there on Amazon." Ranked somewhere between four and five million in popularity.

"Yeah, so it is. Okay. Well, how would you like to publish a book with Cabinet Publishing?" He holds the pencil up in front of his face and looks slightly cross-eyed as he studies the eraser.

"Is this a trick question?" My novel was published by Flying Pony Press, a small outfit that has since gone out of business. Ponies Can't Fly But Our Books Do was their motto. Cute but ultimately inaccurate, unless they were talking about flying straight onto the clearance tables and bargain bins. Cabinet is one of the best-known mid-sized publishers in the country. I would give my left arm to publish with them, though the thought never crossed my mind that they'd ever consider anything I wrote for their list.

"Not at all. I'll get to the point here. This Andy Creighton mess is an opening. We want to seize it. Like what we were saying in the boardroom, turn the tables and take a bad situation and turn it the fuck good."

"I understand all that. Where do I fit in?" Where indeed? The best use of me would be to just do my job and make sure we spin things correctly and put Sloane and her book in a positive light. But he's talking about publishing one of my books! Does he want to read the last manuscript I completed, the one about the sickly British girl who enters a mystical realm where she is recognized as their long-lost Queen and unicorns and mermaids are her army? I actually thought of showing it around at Cabinet, but chickened out when I realized it was kind of ridiculous, both my manuscript and the idea of showing it here.

"We want you to write a book about the fake death and resurrection of Andy Creighton. A Making Of book." He stops and waits for me to react, except I am speechless...and clueless. What is he saying? A book about what? He frowns and leans forward. "Mandy, this is a huge opportunity that we are tossing your way. We are prepared to offer you in the mid five figures by way of an advance."

In the space of five minutes I've gone from helping putting out the biggest fire Cabinet Publishing has ever seen, to being propositioned to document and discuss it in a book, to shine even more attention on it and turn it into a sideshow. I stare into Micah's brown eyes, trying to determine if he was high on crack or something. At least that would explain this.

"A pretend Making Of the pretend killing of Andy Creighton? How would I even write an entire book about that? At best it's maybe ten pages." I pick this to say because it is a legitimate concern. Though I have many others, this one seems to be the most likely to put a halt to Micah's delusions. I've known Micah for years now and though he's shepherded several mediocre books to bestseller status, he sometimes gets these bizarre ideas that result in genuine duds. Like How to Make Your Ferret Dance and Other Life Lessons, which barely sold a thousand copies.

"Oh, there's a book in this, trust me. It's not just about the furor surrounding death, it's about the joy surrounding the resurrection. This will document everything. Not just starting from today, going all the way back in time. You've been with her through the whole writing process, through the development of the series. So you can tell the long story of the clever idea that went wrong. It'll sell a ton and will also help readers feel better about the whole thing."

"This book sounds like an idea that went wrong," I mutter.

"I'll be blunt here. If you won't do it, we can just find someone else…" Micah sighs, shaking his head and avoiding my wide eyes. "But it's happening either way, so factor that in. It's going to make a ton of money, and you could be in on that action."

"Well, okay then, find another author," I say, wholly unprepared and uninterested in accepting his offer. I don't love how greedy Micah sounds right now. It's giving me a weird vibe and I want no part of that. Micah is a decent guy but every now and then he says or does something that just repulses me. Like the time Britt Bonnerson's dad passed away and he made me turn it into a social media post designed to take advantage of her loss and sell more copies of her memoir.

"I meant someone else to take your position here." Micah clenches his fists and stares at me, eyes narrowed. "So what's it going to be?"

"Are you threatening my job?" I would quit on the spot except I have too many bills to pay. And if I left here, my already tenuous relationship with Sloane would completely evaporate, without having an excuse to talk to her. I mean, she could go back to paying me like she did in the beginning before Cabinet hired me so I'd have benefits and a more stable income.

"Not at all," he says with a shrug. "But you are." A smile spreads across his lips. "I'm only joking of course. Well, half joking. But say yes, so we don't have to go down that road."

I don't know what to say except tell the dick I'll do it. "Fine. I'll talk to Sloane about it later."

"You'll do nothing of the sort. This stays a secret until the book is written. She is not to know anything about it, that would defeat the purpose!" He slams a hand on his desk and then winces at his own stupid temper. "Sorry," he says softly.

"That makes no sense. How am I supposed to do this without her?" I can start sending out resumes tonight, but if I leave then I'll be abandoning the best job I've had, and the best friend I've had.

"You start now, today, and you document everything that happens, everything you see. There will be some surprises too. Record history in progress."

"Surprises? I should be in on everything that happens." Me and Sloane both need to know what's up. No ambushes. Never mind I can't be recording what happens if I'm hiding the truth about Andy's resurrection. He wants me to blur the lines between fact and fiction and double down on a lie to millions of readers.

"I understand what you mean but this situation is fluid. We came up with a solution but that doesn't mean we won't be improving and improvising in the coming weeks. Who knows where this could go."

"Write me a contract," I say. "I'll have my lawyer check it out." I have no lawyer, but Micah doesn't need to know that. If it wasn't for the stipulation that I don't mention this to Sloane, I'd ask her. She's been through enough contracts to know what's what.

Micah leans forward, flashing a sly smile. He reaches into his desk drawer and extracts a Cabinet folder, opens it and then nods at me before shutting it. "Here you go," he says with a wink. "I think you'll find the terms for Killing Andy Creighton quite agreeable. This book will make you a lot of money, Mandy."

"Money isn't everything." It is, though. I just don't want to seem greedy. "Isn't this taking advantage of a bad situation though?"

He flashes a crooked smile at me, studying my face as if I'm a naïve child who's just asked how Santa fits down the chimney. "You know what my mom used to say? Before the dementia?"

"How would I know that?" I have never met Micah's mom, either before or after the dementia, though I had heard the story of how she raised him as a single mother in a one bedroom railroad apartment on food stamps.

"She used to say, when life gives you lemons…squeeze 'em into someone's eyes and then take their wallet." He laughs so hard tears begin to stream down his face.

"Your mom was something else," I say. Lemonade is overrated, I guess.

"Made me what I am today," he beams.

I'm about to speak when the door swings open and Sloane marches in.

CHAPTER 8

SLOANE

I storm down the hallway and throw open the door to Micah's office, interrupting him and Mandy having what appears to be a very intense discussion. Micah stops mid-sentence, and Mandy turns to face me, and reading the anger in my eyes, lowers her head and folds her hands in her lap.

"This is not the ending I wrote!" I shout, tossing a copy of my book on his desk. It slides a couple of feet until it's stopped by his snow globe. After the meeting let out thirty minutes ago, I sat in the boardroom for a while, staring at the empty chairs that had just been occupied by the bigshots of Cabinet Publishing. On the table at the far end of the room were stacks of the latest releases. My book and two others. Everyone who worked at Cabinet – even the janitor – was encouraged to read all the new books and spread the word on their socials, post reviews and such. The employee who shared the most book-related posts every month won an Amazon gift card. I stood up and hauled my weary self to the table, studying the dustjacket of my book. It was an attractive cover, one that was bold and colorful. In that moment, I realized that in all the chaos and excitement of the book being released, I'd never actually opened a copy. I had my twenty-six author's copies still sitting in the box under my desk at home, but I'd not cracked one open. I grabbed one from the stack and took it back to my chair, sat down and opened it up, inhaling the scent of the recently printed volume, and then flipping pages toward the end. So many pages when Andy was still alive. I stopped at the last page, to finally confront in print, what I'd done, what I'd written that had started the avalanche of negative reactions across the English-speaking world. And that's when I saw it. At first, I just blinked at the last paragraph, then I closed the book and reopened it, thinking I was hallucinating. But I wasn't. The book had the wrong ending. Impossibly, yet there it was. And not just in that one copy, in every book in the stack. I checked. And then I marched myself down to Micah's office, my head swimming in an unpleasant mixture of rage and confusion.

"What are you talking about?" Micah says, apparently dumbfounded. How can he not know?

"Go on, open it up to the last page!" I say, fists clenched. "Four-thirty-two, open it up right now!"

"Okay, okay, relax," he says, sighing mightily like I just asked him to run down the thirty-three flights of stairs to the lobby and then back up again.

"I'm not going to relax until you look at the page," I say. I can feel a tingling dancing across my fingertips, just like my mom used to tell me happened to her when she got angry. We're so unalike in most ways; this is the thing I've inherited from her?

"Sorry for the interruption, Mandy," Micah mutters. Mandy says nothing, playing with the strap of her smartwatch instead of looking at either of us.

Micah quickly flips pages until he gets close to the end and then slows down until he reaches the referenced page. He squints a little, studies the page, and then looks up at me with a half-smile. "Okay, I see the ending, what's wrong with it exactly?"

As I walk up to his desk, Mandy scutches her chair aside to give me a wide berth. I lean forward and stare down Micah. "What's wrong is that's not my ending. That's not the ending I wrote!" I shout.

"First of all, calm down," he says. "And second, of course it's the damn ending you wrote, it's your book. Who else would have written it?"

I shake my head violently. "Dude, don't be gaslighting me," I scold while Mandy studies her sneakers. "Didn't you read my final draft?" I demand.

"Of course I did," he says, eyes darting around the room until they finally land on me.

"I don't really think that's possible," I answer. "If you had, you'd have seen that ending and known that wasn't my ending."

"That is the ending I saw in the final draft that was approved for print," Micah says, stabbing his finger at the page. "This right here."

"So wait a minute, you didn't read the other drafts?" I ask, incredulous.

Micah must be sweating because I can suddenly smell his musky deodorant wafting my way. "I read the first draft but it was very different, wasn't it?"

He does have a point. It was very different; in that version of the story Andy Creighton did not die. But that was a very rough draft. My first drafts generally suck and are a far cry from the finished product. "So you're telling me between the first draft eight months ago and the final passed for press proof three months ago, you didn't read any of the other drafts?"

"Look, I'm the executive editor here and I have a lot of authors to attend to and drafts to read. If I read every draft of every book coming through our system, I'd be reading twenty-four-seven. Andy Creighton is dead, and you know I didn't exactly like that outcome."

I turn to Mandy, who's finally looking at me now. "And what about you?" I say sharply, instantly regretting my tone.

"I...," she started. "You know my job, Sloane," she continued softly. "I'm supposed to create a buzz, I'm supposed to be your promoter here."

"What are you implying?" I ask. Micah looks at the ending of the book once more and then puts a neon yellow Post-It note on that page.

"I'm not implying anything," Mandy says. "Other than I kind of have the same issue as Micah, if I read all of your drafts then I wouldn't have time to do my job. I read the almost final version that you submitted a few weeks before it went to print," She pauses, trying to find the right words. "And then I ran with my PR campaign. I didn't really have time to read it again. Besides, nobody said there were going to be any major changes after that point. The last draft was just to correct any fatal flaws, errors, and that stuff. Not additions or changes; that would defeat the purpose of a final grammar and typo check if you were adding new material at that point. And yes, I had read the passed for press proof."

Even though she had a point, I still roll my eyes and look up at the ceiling. There are a couple of dings there from champagne corks that have been popped in the last few years celebrating book releases. I see what the problem was here. Unlike my other books, Cabinet did not issue Advance Readers Copies, known in the industry as ARCs, for this title. ARCs are a great way to get reviews ahead of the publication date and build up buzz for a book. In the old days the ARCs were called galleys, and they were physical copies of the book, but that's moved to mostly digital now. Almost every novel on the planet goes through the ARC phase. In some cases ARC readers can even help identify any mistakes or potential issues before the book goes to print. But on this book, Micah decided to skip that step because with the ARC for my previous title, an ARC reader broke a couple of rules; she released her review a month too early, and also included a major spoiler. I tried to insist no harm was done but Micah was furious and put a stop to ARCs for this book, against Mandy's advice. Besides, he was terrified that Andy dies in the book and didn't want that leaking out early.

"So what you're both saying, regardless of whether your excuses are valid or not, is that neither of you read the final draft of my book before it went to print. Or at least neither of you will admit reading it, because then you will admit that you missed the change to the ending." Was I being too hard on them? Maybe, but I was annoyed.

"Sloane, was this something you had written previously and it just wound up back in the final draft by mistake?" Mandy asks.

"I have never written those words," I say, gesturing at the book on Micah's desk. "That is not my ending and it never was."

Micah shakes his head, throws Mandy a quick glance, and then dials Jonah's extension. "We have a situation," he says. "Get in here."

I hear Jonah say, "Another one? What now?"

"Just get in here!" Micah yells into the phone and hangs up.

"We'll get to the bottom of this Sloane, I promise," Micah says. "But is it that bad actually? Andy Creighton is dead either way. Right?" He tilts his head as dramatically as my childhood chihuahua Quentin used to.

"Did you not read that last paragraph after all?" I ask. "Where Andy spasms, coughs, cries, turns purple, and convulsing he gasps and clutches his throat and collapses?"

"I mean yeah," Micah turns a shade of red. Mandy stands up, but I tell her to sit down. She swallows hard and obeys me. "Nobody leaves this room until we figure this out," I say, instantly regretting it and picturing an all-nighter. While there is a great view of Central Park, I didn't fancy the idea of spending a night at Cabinet Publishing. I'm tired enough already having barely slept the last few days. "Who exactly are the people who read my final draft?"

"That is a question for Jonah," Micah says, drumming his fingers on the desk. On cue Jonah saunters in, enveloped as usual within a swirl of his musky cologne.

"Hey guys," he says casually, "I get to hang with the cool kids, eh?" He stands a few feet to my left. If he senses the tension in the room, he ignores it, flashing a broad smile at Mandy. We all know he's had a crush on her for a while now. Jonah always seems so cooly composed, measured and moderate in everything he does. He doesn't ever touch coffee, I've only ever seen him with a cup of decaf Earl Grey tea. Maybe that makes him seem a little distant. Though he is actually my personal editor, I've always related better to Micah.

"Why don't you grab a couple of chairs from next door," Micah says. Jonah shrugs and steps out of the office, returning a minute later dragging a pair of rolling chairs from the boardroom.

As I explain the situation to Jonah, he purses his lips and strokes his chin, but says nothing until I prod him.

"Now would be a good time to offer some explanation," I suggest. "Before I completely lose my shit. As my editor, you're responsible for the final product."

Jonah's gaze jumps from Micah to Mandy to me, and then back to Micah again.

"I'm sorry this happened, Sloane. It sounds like your artistic integrity was compromised and that should never have happened."

"And?" I say, palms out.

"It won't happen again. I promise." Is he taking responsibility or not?

Before I can speak, Micah stands up. "It had better not, Jonah." He points a stiff finger at his longtime senior editor. "Or you can go work at Penguin like you've always wanted."

CHAPTER 9

MANDY

I was down to a single pair of no-show socks, two pair of panties, and an emergency bra. Everything else was in the laundry basket at the foot of my bed. I shake my head, annoyed at my inability to catch up on housework. I'd been in the apartment for a year now and seemed entirely incapable of getting my shit together. It was partly Patrick's fault. I shake my head as I watch him stretch, still half asleep, naked except for his bright blue boxers. Last night was fun, don't get me wrong. We'd enjoyed a movie on Amazon Prime and then he pulled me straight to bed and attacked me. It always feels so urgent when he's here at my place. Like he can't get enough of my body. A nice feeling for sure, but nothing gets done. He stays the night and then we have breakfast – usually ordering out from the diner because he does not want anything I offer to make.

"Hey babe," he yawns. "Why are you up so early?"

"It's nine-thirty, so not that early," I reply. Nine-thirty and I have things to do. I actually want him to leave so I can tackle the mound of dirty clothes that's staring at me.

"It's Saturday, silly," he says, sitting up and scratching his hairy chest. He blinks the sleep out of his eyes, tilts his head, and looks at me just like he did after the movie last night. I'm still wearing just the Gracie Abrams tee shirt he bought me at the concert a few months ago.

"Pat, come on. I have stuff to do," I plead because I know I am two seconds away from being lured back to bed. This is why nothing gets done. He is a nice guy but has zero understanding that my universe could possibly hold anything else other than him.

"I can help you do it," he says with a shrug. It's really the first time he's offered to help me with anything. I suspect we would start cleaning up but quickly devolve into other less constructive activities. Nothing wrong with that normally, but I am so behind it's actually making me lose sleep. I can feel the tension in my entire body, squeezing at my chest and pulsing through my arms. I have to vacuum, and mop the kitchen floor. Patrick is so blissfully unaware siting there and smiling at me. His place is pretty tidy, but that's because he's hardly ever there, between travel for work and spending so many nights here. He doesn't own a lot of clothing so laundry is simple for him.

"It's okay. I'll do it when you leave," I hint, hoping he'll get it. But he doesn't. Instead he changes the subject entirely.

"How's that whole Sloane thing going?" he says. He's been following the story pretty closely. This is like the fifth time he's asked for an update since the uproar began.

"It's turning strange," I say, dropping to the floor and deciding to start sorting the laundry. If I don't do it now it will never get done. "Cabinet is trying to walk back the entire death and turn it into a dream sequence." Note to self, get new underwear, I think as I hold up a pink pair with a big hole right in the middle of the crotch. "And someone changed the ending that Sloane wrote to make Andy's death more violent."

Patrick stands up and cracks his back, twisting left then right. "I read the book. A dream sequence is not going to work."

One of the perks of dating the Cabinet Publishing head of publicity is getting advance copies of books. Though we didn't do ARCs, we had the printed books ready a month early to send to the various newspapers and magazines for reviewing. Patrick's opinion was that the book was great, even with the ending. *I never liked that pompous idiot much anyway*, he'd said when he finished the book. I had to laugh. Sloane's readership was almost entirely women, so it didn't surprise me that he hated Andy. Most men saw Andy as a threat. The perfect book boyfriend – annoyingly too good to be true. While Sloane's biggest fans were grieving, their boyfriends and dads and husbands were secretly celebrating the death of their nemesis. I actually wrote a story for Playboy a few years back where I interviewed a bunch of men who were complaining that they were being compared unfavorably to Andy Creighton – especially in the bedroom. While some took it in stride, the idea of competing with a fictional guy, others were stewing over this valedictorian former star college athlete making them look bad. I even interviewed an actual athlete, former pitcher for the Blue Jays, who told me he would never hold a candle to Sloane's wondrous creation. If the backlash was not so severe and Cabinet had not decided to basically undo the death, this would be the perfect time for a follow-up story. Boy, would they be pissed when they heard that Andy will rise from the dead and continue to be perfect for years to come.

"Yeah, jury's out on that," I answer. "We made it into a contest, and the winner is this girl from Iowa who came up with the theory. We're flying her in and giving her the star treatment."

Patrick shakes his head, pulling on the pair of faded jeans that had been draped over the chair across the room. "I feel like this will go badly and make things worse," he says, as I watch him zipping up.

"Probably" I say, even though I signed onto the idea myself.

He pulls on his black Metallica tee shirt and squats down to talk to me as I wince at the smell of my marinating undergarments.

"You know, they'd be better off saying he was an impostor, it wasn't really Andy."

I laugh but Patrick rolls his eyes. "I'm not joking here, Mandy. The whole subplot where he signed those papers leasing two acres of his land to Home Depot, and Ciara and half the town was shocked he did that, well there's the opening. It was not him who signed the papers, it was his lookalike."

At this point I can't even tell if he's serious or not. I suppose that's as good an idea as any. "I'll tell Sloane," I say, nodding though I have no intention of ever mentioning his idea to anyone else.

"You should," he says, smacking my butt as he walks past me. "If she'd used my idea for Ciara's long lost twin sister in the last book, it would have sold much better." He must be on crack, because I didn't even know Patrick when her last book came out. As if reading my mind, he adds, "I followed her on Instagram for the last four years and I commented on one of her posts asking for suggestions."

"That was me, I came up with that post," I say with a laugh. It was a fun little idea I had to foster a feeling of fan participation and ownership in the creative process, though I knew Sloane would never take any of the ideas.

"Yeah, well the twin sister thing would have…" He turns to me, eyes lit up. "Hey! That's it! Andy Creighton has a long lost twin brother and it's him who was killed. Boom. Problem solved. You're welcome." He takes a mock bow and I shake my head, though that idea is actually no worse than the stupid dream sequence scheme.

CHAPTER 10

SLOANE

When I get home from the Cabinet meeting, there are five women standing in front of my house holding up signs. The least abrasive of them says simply "Bring Andy Back!!" I think to myself, *y'all won*. My crazy fans and my frightened publisher have won. They'll get their wish. I want to lean out the window and shout it at them: "He'll be fine, are you happy now?" But I lock up and quickly duck inside my house as a couple of the women start to yell at me. I bet they didn't go protest at Netflix headquarters when their favorite series got cancelled, or in front of Dean Marcasite's condo when he announced he was retiring from writing novels altogether. Nope, it's just me. There are a million other perfectly viable book boyfriends out there to choose from, to move on to, but they can't seem to fathom that concept. I am highly annoyed that neither Micah, Jonah, nor Mandy could figure out who changed my book's ending to make Andy's death violent and protracted instead of peaceful and quick.

When I get inside my house, I peek out the window just in time to see a police cruiser pull up, lights flashing. At first, I briefly wonder if they're here to take me away for the murder of Andy Creighton, before reminding myself that he doesn't exist. And no, they simply came by to gently disperse the protestors. Mrs. Fennelly down the street must have called them. She gets annoyed by random shit and probably dials 911 three times a week, and they come. They come for her because her late husband was a police captain for thirty years and the name Fennelly still has plenty of pull around town. I watch as the four women give up and leave, getting into their respective cars parked at various spots along my street. I guess the fifth one must have left as soon as she saw the first flicker of the police lights because she's nowhere in sight.

I am frustrated with my day, my week, and generally with my life. This is not what I imagined it would be like to be a bestselling author, a success by any measure of the word as applies to writing. People are protesting me, holding up signs like they would in front of the Supreme Court, and my publisher is reacting by doing backflips to try to reverse the ending of my book. Not only don't I want to reverse Andy's death, I don't even want to write anything anymore. Everyone overreacted. Is this how it was in the sixteenth century when people read Romeo and Juliet for the first time? Did they hold up signs in Stratford-upon-Avon telling Shakespeare he was a murderer? I think not. My readers are entitled little bitches, is what they are. I should have put out a statement telling everyone – hey if you want to commission me to write a book just for you, I will make it end however you like. If you're only paying twenty-five bucks for a copy, then I get to decide how it ends.

I shake my head and trudge upstairs to the bathroom. I start running the bathwater, nice and hot, and add in some scented bubbles just as I'd pictured. I put my phone on do not disturb and set it down on the counter as I strip off my clothes. Just before I do, a text comes in from Micah telling me that our contest winner Dez will fly in two days from now. I'm actually surprised she was able to drop everything and come that soon. I guess the promise of meeting her favorite author was motivation enough. The speed at which Cabinet is moving is unnerving more than it is comforting. They are more motivated to save themselves and my writing career than they are to actually protect me from the maniacs who are taking this too far. Micah, Jonah, even Mandy, they're all the same. I'm an asset and commodity whose success or failure can make or break their company. That's all. Nobody gives a shit about Sloane Rylie herself.

I have this crazy idea to call Ellis and patch things up again, have him come over and spend the night in my bed. But he hasn't called since the whole Andy mess hit the fan, so I feel weird doing that. Well, correction, he hasn't called but he did text, a simple "Hey, you okay?" to me yesterday morning. I responded with a "yeah thanks" and left it at that. He'd be over here in twenty minutes if I asked. I know that and I guess it's comforting that I have that power. Though I remind myself it's not some special exclusive power, it's pretty much something that any of the women he's dated yield. A chance for the pants, is how he once put it when we first started dating and I whacked him over the head with a pillow, and he just laughed. He'd be anywhere for a woman in need with the hopes that it might lead to getting into their pants. At least he's honest about it. And at least he knows he's expected to work for that opportunity. So if I called and said I need to talk, he'd put in the effort and listen. Haha, look at me trying to make him sound great when that's what a normal decent human would do. Guess I am still looking for my own Andy Creighton. Guess I killed him because he was too perfect to keep writing about.

I made Andy Creighton in the mold of my own perfect boyfriend, not even thinking my readers would fall so hard for him. He was mine, but then I got tired of writing about Mr. Perfect. I'd started to try to show some flaws in the last book, and in All Things Must, Andy sold off part of his land to a big box chain, much to the chagrin of the townspeople. And that is theoretically what led to his fictional death, though the readers don't know that yet. I don't just write romance; I read a lot of romance as well. And I was afraid my books were starting to become like those less realistic novels, the fanciful, silly, exaggerated ones with cartoonish covers where things get a little too sunshine and puppies and the characters are too perfectly in love. So Andy maybe wasn't as great as he seemed. I didn't let that sink in for more than fifty pages before I killed him. This has been happening forever in books and television shows. Characters are killed off either because the writers and producers want to change stuff or because the actors leave the show. And maybe some readers and viewers are lost in the process, but maybe it blows up and becomes even more popular.

Guess I'll never find out what would have happened in the end because I'm being forced to change the ending. I just want everyone to leave me alone. I had a plan for the next book and now I have to change it? Fuck that. Fuck everything and everyone.

The bubbly bathtub is mostly full now; the water temperature is hopefully just right. I stick a tentative foot in to test it. Perfect. Holding the edges of the tub, I climb in. God, it's been way too long since I did this. I inhale the rose-scented air and sigh as my shoulders sink deliciously below the warm water. I should have lit some candles too. Oh well, maybe next time. The water is still running, which provides some welcome white noise and feels good on my feet as I lay here. I close my eyes for a moment and try to wipe away everything to do with books. It's a tricky thing to attempt though because my entire life revolves around writing now. Everything about me can be traced back to writing somehow. I think of that vacation I want to take in St. Thomas – one that would be paid for by my writing. One on which I'd seize the amazing scenery to…do more writing. Yeahhh, this isn't the easier thing. I'll just focus on the bath itself, the soothing nature of the suds and the water.

My eyes startle open when I think I hear a noise coming from downstairs. I did lock the front door, right? I always do. I must have. I try to visualize myself doing it but all I can picture is myself closing the door. And then I peeked out the window to see the police cruiser arrive. But beyond that I can't be sure. Oh hell, why would I not lock it when I have thousands of times before? I am being ridiculous, but for a good reason. This paranoia is the direct result of the stress I've been dealing with over the last few days. I turn the water to full blast, and remove the drain stopper to make sure it's both draining and filling at the same time and it won't overflow. My eyes flutter closed again and I manage finally to think of nothing other than the sound of the water. Ah yeah, I should have a bath like this every day. I deserve it. I work hard and self-care is a vital part of being able to function properly. Maybe if I had a daily bath I'd be better suited to rise about the bullshit and tell everyone – Micah and Mandy included, to just leave me alone.

I pour some lavender bath oil into the tub and inhale deeply. I can feel my muscles go limp, finally. After this I know I'll be able to think more clearly. And it's not even late, so I'll be able to get stuff done around the house. The sound of the frothing water is soothing, it brings back childhood memories of my dad taking me to the beach, standing by the water as the waves broke, one after another. I'd write a word in the sand and the next wave would wash it away. Dad liked to just stand there next to me, watching. I have a very vivid memory of those beach visits, even though I was five or six at the oldest. He stopped taking me after that, once he started going to the cabin. Though my cabin memories are fond, the beach ones are even more precious. I picture him picking me up and putting me on his shoulders. I smile, feeling myself start to drift off and the sound of the bathwater transforms into ocean waves crashing; the sparrows outside the bathroom window become seagulls circling above.

I feel a reassuring hand on my head. I'm there on the beach with dad and he's mussing my hair like he loved to do. But that pleasant, gentle sensation is soon replaced with growing pressure. The hand is pushing my head down. A faraway voice says "Bring him back!" Suddenly my face is submerged, and I'm flailing my arms. I startle myself awake and hear a huge splash as my head emerges from the water, scutching my back up so I'm sitting. My eyes fly open as I cough and gasp, trying to get my breathing back to normal. What the hell just happened? There's nobody here. I'm alone in the bathroom. The door is ajar just like I'd left it. I stand up abruptly, sending more water splashing from the tub. Grabbing my towel, I wrap it around myself tightly and hurry out of the bathroom.

"Who's there!" I scream down the stairs. Is that the front door I hear closing? I pad cautiously down the stairs, my feet leaving wet prints on the carpeting. I should have grabbed my phone from the bathroom counter so I could call 911 in case there's an intruder in my house. When I get downstairs, nothing looks out of place but the front door is unlocked. I did forget to lock it? Shit. I grab a fireplace poker and hurry into the kitchen and den — they're both empty. I double lock the front door and peek out the window through the blinds. There's nobody out there protesting. All is quiet now. I release an anxious exhale and wipe a drip of water from my eyes. I must have dreamed it, I convince myself. And then I see a few drops of water on the floor near the door. My pulse quickens. I hear a car drive away, but when I look out the window it's already gone.

I take a deep breath and exhale, spreading my arms outward like my yoga teacher taught me before I got lazy and stopped taking classes.

There couldn't possibly have been an intruder in my house trying to scare me into bringing back Andy Creighton. Nobody would go to those lengths to bring back a fictional character, right?

CHAPTER 11

MANDY

I finally get Patrick to leave after letting him expend his nervous energy doing a few heavy lifts for me around the house. Now it's just me and the remainder of my laundry. Probably another two loads if I don't want to break the washer. Patrick will be coming back later, and we'll get dinner together, which will be nice, but I need a break from him.

My phone buzzes and it's Micah.

"What," I say. I'm used to him calling after hours but I am currently annoyed with him.

"Hello to you, too," he replies.

"Why are you calling me?" Now I'm wishing Patrick is still here. He'd take the phone from me and tell Micah to go fuck himself. Well, not in so many words but he'd say I'm busy and to wait until Monday.

"Just checking to see how the manuscript is coming along." If he hadn't said with such a deadpan monotone I'd think he was joking. He's not.

"How it's coming? I haven't even started it yet. What is wrong with you?" It's been how many hours since I signed the contract, against my better judgment?

"I did say it was a time-sensitive thing," Micah says and I can see that exaggerated shrug of his.

I should have just rejected his offer and risked losing my job. It's not worth the aggravation. And shit, I didn't even get to tell Patrick about the book deal. Not that I am trying to hide it from him, it's just not something I'm proud of. I left the Cabinet office and put the book out of my head. Any other book deal, I'd be gushing over it and ready to go out and celebrate. This book feels like a toxic combination of betraying my best friend, an overall bad idea, and a topic I have zero interest in writing about.

"Yeah. I get that. I just thought I could start it, you know, in a few days."

The silence on the other end indicates otherwise. When Micah finally speaks, his tone is stern. "A few days? Mandy, there are developments happening literally by the minute. I need you to stay on top of them and record them in real time. To make this book feel in the moment journalism. Like Pulitzer Prize worthy."

I have to put a hand over my mouth to prevent a laugh from escaping my lips. Pulitzer Prize worthy? Is Micah high on crack? Is he actually thinking a book documenting the reaction to the death of a fictional character was going to be worthy of any prize, let alone a Pulitzer?

"Yeah okay, I'll start on it later."

"Google Andy Creighton right now," Micah orders.

"Like while we're on the phone?" So bossy. Sometimes I hate this guy.

"Yes, like right now while we're on the phone." I hear him drumming his fingers on the desk. Does this man ever go home? Probably not. I put him on speaker and set the phone down on my kitchen table, and search for Andy. The news story of the moment is that a group of 50 women have gathered at a cemetery in Illinois around the grave of an Andy Creighton who died in 1954 at the age of thirty-two, the same age as the fictional one, and brought flowers and held up signs saying "We mourn all the Andy Creightons of the world who died too young." A video clip shows one of the women leaving a copy of the book at his grave.

"Are you still there?" Micah says after a minute. I'd actually forgotten he was still on the line. I was caught up in the sheer stupidity of the mass overreaction to Andy Creighton's death, the mind-blowing immaturity of it all.

"Yeah, I'm still here." Barely. My mind is somewhere else.

"You see the story? The cemetery story?"

"Yep," I say. "Sure did."

"Well, that's the kind of thing you need to be covering in the book. This is a once in a lifetime cultural flashpoint moment. So get on it!" The book that I just signed up for.

"Don't be rude," I say. If he doesn't like it, tough shit. I'm done pussyfooting around him. "You signed me up. Now leave it to me and don't check on me every five minutes. I do my job, you do yours, which is to shut up and leave me to it." I say it with as much warmth as I can muster so he doesn't think I'm telling him off, even though I am.

"Alright! Now that's more like it!" he says, applauding like I've just finished a flawless rendition of the National Anthem.

An idea pops into my head and I decide to serve it up to Micah. "Well, if you want me to start, I'll start with you then," I say, softening my tone. "When can I sit down and interview you about this whole thing? Or should we do it now over the phone?"

"Me?" he scoffs. "Oh, no, definitely not, I don't think that's appropriate." Did he just reject me? I can't figure this guy out for the life of me. He is so eager to sign me up and then he rejects my request to interview the most important player at Cabinet Publishing – himself. I hear a cat meowing in the background.

"You're not in the office?" I ask.

"No, home office," he says. "What do you want, Charmaine Rose? You don't like when I'm on the phone, do you?"

"You're the man, Micah. If you're not appropriate, then who is?" If he wants a book that anyone could write, anyone without access to key people, then why ask me specifically?

He clears his throat. "Mandy. Mandy, listen. This is the story of what's going on in the Andy world out there. It's not some expose about us over here at Cabinet. Got it? Keep your focus on the news, don't try to make news where there's no news to make." And he hangs up. Wow, this is going to be one fun and informative book of half-truths. I'm not allowed to talk to Sloane, the author, nor her executive editor. I shake my head and slam my phone onto the table. There was probably a paragraph in my contract listing everyone I am not allowed to interview. I should not have signed it so hastily.

I go to my window, throw open the curtains, and watch a pair of squirrels taking turns chasing each other back and forth across a large oak tree branch. I shake my head. If this is going to be my book, then I'm doing it my way. And it will be so good they won't be able to even think about any rules I may have broken. It's time for me to be the chasing squirrel, not the chased squirrel.

I pull up the email from earlier today, the one Micah sent to Sloane and the rest of the gang that was in the boardroom for the meeting. I copy Dez Maxwell's number down and proceed to dial it. I'm not just going to tell a story here. I'm going to become a part of it.

CHAPTER 12

SLOANE

I shut off my car and sigh. Coming here was not a good idea, but I did it anyway.

After the bathtub incident spooked the shit out of me, I texted Ellis and he told me to come right over. I packed an overnight bag and peeled out of that driveway so fast, I would have become a murderer if any protestors had been standing there. Luckily (for both them and me) there weren't.

On the way to his place, I almost turned around three times, but I told myself to keep going and not spend the night alone. As I pull up in front of his house, so many memories come flooding back. A gigantic mixed bag of feelings. We dated for so long, yet things were always slightly on edge. Even the happiest times always seemed to carry a dark undertone just beneath the surface.

I get out of my car and look at the front door. Ellis should be expecting me. I wait for him to come out and greet me, but he doesn't. He's probably playing video games as usual. He used to get lost in them for hours on end, playing with his friends. I don't think that's changed in the last few weeks.

I feel weird about ringing the bell, so I text him again. *I'm here.*

He reads it but doesn't reply. A minute later the door swings open and there he is. Black shorts and a plain white tee shirt, his usual summertime home wear. He doesn't smile when he sees me, but he waves. I wave back. Awkward.

"Come on inside," he says. "Let me get that," he points to my bag, which is small and light. I let him take it anyway, and follow him inside.

There's that scent, maple syrup and breakfast sausages. I've never seen him eat either of those, so I've always been curious but never cared enough to ask why it smells like that. Maybe it's an air freshener?

"You okay?" he asks, setting my bag down next to the coffee table.

"Not yet but I will be," I say, hugging myself. I hate to admit it, but it does feel comforting being here. Disconcertingly comforting, but comforting nonetheless.

"I've been hearing about some of the stuff that's happened," he says, sitting on the tan-colored fake leather sofa and patting the spot next to him for me to sit.

"I shouldn't have come," I blurt, even while sitting and leaning back, trying to get comfortable.

"I told you I'm always here for you." He says it like an admonishment rather than a loving reminder.

"Well, thank you for letting me stop by," I reply.

"You want a drink?" He pops up and glides over to the fridge on his socks. He loves to slide around the wood floors. I'd gotten quite accustomed to it, but now he just looks like a giant man-child. Which he kind of is, to be honest.

"Water is fine," I tell him, glancing around the living room to see if anything's changed, and it hasn't. Sure enough, there's a video game on the TV screen, paused just as Ellis is about to shoot some evil creep wearing a black cape. He opens the fridge and grabs himself a can of lite beer, then fills a glass with filtered water from the faucet, throwing a couple of ice cubes in.

He sits down next to me and hands me the water. "So, what's up? You seem shaken."

I don't tell him about the bathtub. That would be too concerning. I just say I was having a rough day and didn't want to be alone. Fair assessment. But as I sit here, I am not sure how much else I want to confess. This is a man to whom I've spilled some of my darkest secrets, a guy who knows me better than almost anyone — yet I feel odd, not like we can just pick up where we left off. I feel the chasm of distance. I feel like I should be cautious.

"The Andy uproar is starting to get to me. It's gotten out of control." This is not a lie. I kind of want to see how he reacts to that before I go further.

"Yeah well, I told you not to kill him," he says, taking a swig of beer.

"Too late to turn back the clock on that one," I say. Ellis has the darkest brown eyes, and I could never see any emotion in them. His feelings were hidden deep within that darkness. Right now, I think I catch a glimpse of sympathy, but it vanishes quickly.

"You're in charge, you can bring him back. It's not like that hasn't been done a million times in books, soap operas, movies…just look at the Jurassic Park movies for example. People will believe anything." He gulps down the beer like he's been in the hot sun laying bricks all day. I sip my water, which has a funny taste. Ellis never changes his water filter.

"That's what they want me to do." They meaning everyone on the planet. For much of the time I was writing All Things Must, Ellis would keep me company. I'd bring my laptop here and he'd turn the sound down on his game and he'd play while I wrote. Or at my house, he'd sit with me and watch me work. Many writers would find that extremely claustrophobic and creepy, but I never minded with him. The thought of that happening now though, is repulsive. We broke up four times over the course of our relationship, but the other three I kind of knew we'd get back. This time I knew we wouldn't. Yet here I am at his place. Fuck me. And I bet Ellis would want to if given the chance. And to be honest with all the stress that's jolting through me, I wouldn't rule it out, as bad of an idea as that is.

"It's up to you what happens," he says and suddenly I don't think he's talking about the novel anymore.

"I know. And I don't want to do it. If it's up to me then I want to leave it as is, let it die down, and move on with my life. Not give in because of a bunch of crybabies." I used to adore my fans. They are the reason for my successful career. But lately, my opinion of them has collapsed into a heap of disappointment. My opinion of pretty much everyone has shattered.

"Did you ever think about the real Andys out there?"

I blink at him. "What are you talking about?"

"The real guys out in the world named Andy Creighton. What about them?"

"What about them?" I laugh. Once a few years back, I'd scrolled past an article about an Andy Creighton somewhere in the southwest. I really had zero interest in some random guy who happened to share a name with the hero of my books.

He stares at the ceiling the way he used to when he lost patience with me, which was about twice a month. "What they must be going through right now."

"They are probably glad they're not the ones who are dead," I say with a smirk.

Ellis sighs, then gets up and grabs himself another beer and slams the fridge door. "You're not looking at this from all the angles," he says, pulling the tab and eagerly gulping some down while still standing. "You should be worried about them."

"You know what? Bring me a beer too," I say. Being sober with Ellis is torture. I need to have a buzz. Now he smiles and digs in the back of the fridge for the stash of Stella that he always kept stocked just for me. When we broke up, he had six left and it looks like that number is the same today. I won't drink that watered down stuff he prefers, and he won't touch anything remotely full-bodied. He hands me the bottle, and I hold it for a moment, watching it sweat. Hey, pal, we're twinning, I think. It's a little warm in his place. Always was. He's needed a new air conditioner for years now. I should have applied more deodorant before I came over here. Oh well. I finish that bottle way too quickly and ask for another even before I can apply logic to the situation.

After he takes another drink, he looks at me with a raised eyebrow and a mischievous smile. "Hey Sloane," he says. "If you bring Andy back, we can do that thing I mentioned a few months back. Before you wrote the ending. Wouldn't that be cool?" He leans in and studies me like he used to, eyes going from my chest to my lips and back.

I want to shut him up and I don't know how, other than kissing him, so I do.

It hurts to open my eyes. A dull throbbing permeates my brain. Yeah, that's what happens to me when I drink too much. It's been a while. I blink a few times and rub the sleep out of them. Where even am I? The feeling of disorientation sends a shiver of panic through me. I look around and after a few seconds realize I'm on Ellis' couch. Sunlight is streaming in through the living room windows. I am half dressed; my pants, socks, and sneakers are strewn on the floor next to my overnight bag, but my underwear, shirt, and bra are still on. My bag is open; I don't remember touching it at all after Ellis dropped it on the floor. I zip it back up and stand there feeling lost and struggling to remember last night. The last thing I can recall is asking for a third bottle of Stella. Where is Ellis? He must be still asleep in his bedroom. I guess it's a good sign that I'm not in there with him, through the state of my undress leaves me with questions. Part of me wants to go in there and wake him, but I think a quiet escape is probably best for both of us. Usually he snores like a sonofabitch, but I hear nothing at the moment.

I pick my pants up off the floor and a white envelope falls out. It's got my name on it, written in pencil. I pull out the piece of lined paper that's tucked inside and unfold it.

Slo,

I had to leave for a gaming thing that starts at 10 over at the VFW hall. Didn't want to wake you. Let yourself out. Do the right thing, bring Andy back. And thanks for last night.

PS – kidding about the last night part. ;)

Ellis

I read the note twice and feel nauseous. I scour the floor for a condom wrapper, but find none. I have a memory snippet of his hand roaming over my breasts and try to determine if it's from last night or months ago. It would be great to have a shower but my desire to get the heck out of here overrides that. I grab my keys, which must have fallen out of my pocket, put my socks and sneakers back on, and leave, telling myself this is much better than waking up next to him and facing that awkwardness.

CHAPTER 13

MANDY

Calling Dez Maxwell is probably not the brightest idea I've had, especially since I don't even know what I am going to say. My initial thought was to try to ask her some questions about her dream sequence theory, prod a little deeper into that. But as I sit here with phone in hand, I realize this will just backfire on me.

My bell rings, further saving me from making that mistake. I get up and swing open the door expecting to see Patrick, but it's Ellis. He looks and smells unshowered. His hair is spiking in various directions and his eyes are puffy.

"No, Ellis," I say. If this is like the last time he swung by, he wants a quickie. He's been a mess since he split with Sloane.

"I'm not here for that," he says, shaking his head. "Can I come in?" He cranes his neck trying to look past me and into my house.

"Sure, but make it quick," I say. Patrick knows about Ellis and it's a sore spot. They apparently knew each other in college and it's a whole thing.

He follows me inside and plops himself on my loveseat. The very same spot where we…well, where things happened a few months ago. And I'm sure he's well aware of that. He forgets nothing, and everything he does is intentional.

"So what's up? How've you been?"

"I need you to get through to Sloane," he says, ignoring my questions.

"Get through to her about what?" I should offer him a drink but really I don't want to encourage him to stay any longer than necessary.

He leans forward. He looks sexy when he's three days unshaven, the stubble suits his face. That's what got me to begin with. The damn stubble.

"She needs to get in line and bring Andy Creighton back to life."

I roll my eyes and raise my gaze to the ceiling. Him too? It's unreal. "Are you serious right now? What do you even care?" I say. "You're not together. And you don't like her books. You haven't even read any of them, unless you lied to me about that."

"Ouch," he says. "Play nice." He picks up an Aruba is Paradise coaster and rubs his thumb over it.

"Nobody will leave the poor girl alone about this. Why you? Can you support her instead of joining the bandwagon?"

"I am just looking out for her. She's going to put herself in danger if she doesn't do what the fans want. Book people can be pretty psycho." He says it looking right at me. He means me, too. And fine, I'll accept the Psycho Badge with honor. If readers are a little off kilter, so are writers and their entourages. I'm no exception. I force myself to smile at Ellis, the man who was ever so briefly my boyfriend.

"If you are so fixated on that, then why don't you tell her? You still have some pull with Sloane, I bet."

"Yeah, I already tried," he says with a shrug.

"What does that mean? You've been talking to Sloane?" I'm not jealous. Not at all.

"Never mind that. I just need you to get through to her. She's not thinking clearly."

"Look, everyone over at Cabinet is studying the options and deciding the best course of action for Sloane's career and our bottom line." Said with the detached calm of a true professional. I have no idea if he really talked to Sloane or not, and if so, what she told him, but I'm not giving anything away. If he's here to try to pump me for information then he's out of luck.

He seems oddly satisfied with my answer, nodding slowly, studying my face. I force my lips to remain frozen in place, and my eyes unblinking, betraying no emotion.

"Well, that's all I really wanted to say," he tells me. "I've got a gaming thing to run to. You were on the way. Sorry for disturbing you." He stands up and his shoulders sag. I feel sorry for the man. He doesn't look (or smell) good at all. He's nothing like the guy who I was so excited to steal away from Sloane Rylie a few months back.

CHAPTER 14

SLOANE

I swerve into the gravel driveway and kill the engine, glad to be away from both my house and from Ellis. I am actually not sure which is worse, the idea that someone may have snuck into my house and tried to kill me, or that I may have slept with Ellis last night. I hightailed it out of there as soon as possible in case he came back early from the gaming show.

I roll down my window and inhale the fresh country air. Well, it's not exactly country since it's only twenty or so minutes from my house. But it sure feels like country out here. At times like these I'm so glad I didn't sell my dad's old hunting cabin. He'd bought it with a pal when he was about thirty, then bought the friend's half when the guy lost interest in hunting. What I hadn't known until recently was that it had originally belonged to my grandfather, and that was why my dad bought it in the first place. When dad passed, the cabin didn't go to mom, he left it to me. She was not jealous, but she was surprised. "Why would he leave you that musty old piece of shit?" were her exact words. The reason was simple in my mind – because I loved nature and mom always thought of it as a bug-infested horror show. She'd been to the cabin all of three times, while I'd gone with dad dozens of times. He'd take me out on the rowboat he kept by the lake, and we'd grill hot dogs and marshmallows. Though the cabin itself was small and rundown, it felt homey and cozy to me.

Back when I was starting out as an author, I almost sold it to pay my rent. Then my book hit number twenty on the bestseller list and I postponed that decision. Soon after that, visiting Christopher Morley Park on Long Island, I saw the old cabin that had served as Morley's writing retreat and decided maybe I could hole up and write at dad's cabin. As it turned out, I used it mostly to clear my head rather than for writing.

And today, I am definitely here to clear my head.

I stopped spending the night a few years ago, realizing that I'd outgrown it as an overnight retreat but it was still very refreshing to visit for the day.

I get out of my car and slam the door. Looking at the cottage, it makes me sad to realize how much I've let it deteriorate. I've been so focused on my writing that I've neglected to keep up with the maintenance, even though I can afford to hire some people to do it for me. When I try to open the front door, it seems to be swelled shut from last week's rain. I tug and tug until finally it swings free and I nearly go flying. I make a mental note to call in a handyman to assess and do some chores like painting and replacing the windows, which are single pane with no screens. I pop my trunk and grab my overnight bag, toss it into the cabin. I've not committed to staying overnight but I wanted to be prepared just in case. The air inside is especially stuffy because it's been closed up for the six months since I was last here. I open two of the living room windows even though I know that mosquitoes will get in, and I'll be contending with bites in short order. But I really don't care. Bug bites are nothing compared to the ridiculous stress I've been feeling the last few days, and over what? I should have stood up to everyone in that boardroom and just said no dream sequence, contract be damned. Said no and walked out. Instead, I have to make nice with some weirdo from Iowa and pretend she figured out our cute little gotcha.

I am here at the cabin to dissociate with the book, with the harsh reality that awaits me: I have to undo what I very purposefully did. The thought of giving up writing altogether isn't that unattractive. I can live comfortably for a few years, and then decide what I want to do. Change my name and take up some other profession. Hide out here at the cabin until everyone forgets me and my stupid book and Andy Creighton.

I should have brought some food with me. There's nothing here, not even stuff that could last for several months like a jar of peanut butter or a can of fruit cocktail. Nothing. I really haven't been here in a while. I decide to head down to Connie's Convenience Store and grab a few provisions at least for the rest of today and tomorrow morning so I don't starve to death.

I've known Connie since the first time my dad brought me to her store when I was eight. She's always been kind to me. I'm about to climb into my car when I realize that the store is technically walking distance. What is it, like a half mile, maybe three-quarters at most? That's nothing. All I have to do is follow the road and then turn right at Main and I'm there. The road is paved, technically, but it's dusty and littered with gravel, and the asphalt is cracked and big chunks of it are missing in spots. The village is perennially short on funds to make necessary repairs. And that's fine with me; it means this little section of town is pretty quiet. The only sound I hear as I walk is my sneakers crunching on the rocks and the cicadas chirping high up in the trees. Out here Ciara and Andy don't exist. This, this is reality. This shitty road to Main Street is reality. Meetings and books and editors and rabid fans – I left them a million miles away. In this moment, I miss Ellis even though I hightailed it out of his house earlier. I wish he were here walking beside me, fingers interlocked with mine. I am actually tempted to call him; I take out my phone, but blissfully, there is no service on this stretch of the road. I'd forgotten that. Good! Calling him would have been a mistake because he would have come and then we'd get all entangled in our same bullshit push-pull emotional tug of war over the future of our relationship. Lost in thought, I'm already almost at Main Street. The road suddenly improves just as it nears the village proper. I turn right and walk the hundred or so steps to Connie's. The door is wide open as always and Connie is behind the counter as always. She greets me with a big old genuine smile that lights up her entire face.

"Well look here, if it isn't Sloane Jessica Rylie in the flesh!" She runs a hand through her lush mane of gray hair and nods slowly.

"Connie! Good to see you again," I say, and it really is. She's always been kind to me. Do I lean over the counter and try to give her a hug? She answers my internal question by putting our her hand. I reach across and shake it.

"I'm surprised to see you, after everything that's been going on," she says with a raised eyebrow. "Are you okay?"

"I will be. A little fresh air will do me good." Even Connie knows what's going on. And her world is usually quite narrow. She nods at me and goes back to her crocheting. I head down the snack aisle and grab a family sized bag of pretzels and some beef jerky in honor of my dad, who would clean out Connie's supply on the regular. Then I swing by the refrigerated section and take a couple of diet Vitamin Waters. And in case I stay the night, I pick up a box of frosted fruity pop tarts.

I go up to the counter and place the items there, flashing a smile at Connie. She gives me her full attention after she rings up my purchases and gives me my change.

"You need a bag?"

"Nah, I'll just carry it."

"You walked here?" She asks it like she knows I would not normally be caught dead doing anything remotely athletic.

"Yeah, it's really not that far."

"Well, be careful, people take the bends too fast on these roads. We've both seen plenty of squashed deer, wouldn't want to see squashed Sloane." She slaps her palm on the counter and laughs a little too lustily. I manage a weak smile and say okay. Then she leans over the counter as her laugh ends abruptly. "Sloane honey? Why did you kill him off? He was so perfect."

I feel like saying "Et tu, Brutae." I feel like crying. Instead, I just say in a flat voice: "Everyone has their time, it was his time," and it comes across the wrong way because her face pales and she shakes her head slowly.

"Damn. That's your explanation? Well, okay then," she says before returning to her crocheting. "Have a good one. Walk carefully."

I grab my stuff and clutch it to my chest as I walk out the store and head back to the shitty road that leads to my cabin. I manage to twist open one of the vitamin waters and take a much-needed gulp, just in time to be startled by the sound of screeching wheels and a car horn that startles me into dropping the open drink on the ground. "Goddamit!" I yell, shaking my free fist at the dark blue SUV that races past me around the curve, fully believing that Connie put bad juju into the air. I bend over to pick up the bottle and drop the rest of my haul in the process, cursing again. The bottle is still half full, so I wipe off the lip on my shirt sleeve and chug the remains. What was supposed to be a peaceful getaway is already turning annoying. I just want to get back to the cabin and rake some leaves or something physical to calm myself down.

As I round the curve in the road a couple of minutes later, I see that same blue SUV parked in my driveway, perpendicular to my car. What the actual hell? I am definitely not expecting nor wanting any visitors, especially ones who nearly ran me over and scared me half to death.

"Hello?" I call out. "Who's there?" I'm still far enough away that I can't see anyone but close enough that my voice should be heard. There's no reply. Shit, did I leave the cabin unlocked? I might have. Why would I bother to lock it for a half an hour?

The cicadas sound especially shrill as I near my cabin. The SUV's driver's side door suddenly opens, and a man gets out. He sees me immediately and starts waving his arms frantically. Dad's old hunting rifle is in the closet, but that won't do me any good now. I think about turning on my heel and running all the way back to Connie's but for what? So she can scold me some more? Instead I take a deep breath and decide to confront my visitor.

I take a few more steps and see a decent looking guy in his late thirties or early forties, tall and skinny but slightly hunched over, dark mop of hair, wearing faded jeans and a Black Sabbath tee shirt. He doesn't look like a threat; if I'd seen him anywhere else, I'd pay him no mind. Except for the unavoidable fact that he happens to be standing in front of my isolated little cottage in the woods.

"Can I help you?" I shout in as friendly of a menacing voice that I can muster.

I am close enough now to see that he looks genuinely distraught. Worry lines cross his forehead and his eyes look red and puffy. "Are you Sloane Rylie?" he asks.

"I am. Who are you?" And what are you doing here and how did you find me, I want to add. But first things first.

"My name is Andy Creighton," he says. "And we have a problem."

CHAPTER 15

MANDY

If Micah won't talk to me, then I will have to do a little independent research. If he wants a good book, I'll give him one, but it will be a deeper dive than he anticipates. Because what he's picturing will turn out to be a shit book, and I want my first Cabinet book to be outstanding, not a pile of reconstituted crap anyone can find themselves using Google. This is what is going through my mind as I log into the Cabinet server from my laptop, one cat snuggled up next to me and the other on the floor playing with a mouse toy. What Sloane said about her book's ending has been troubling me. Why would someone change the ending to make it worse? Maybe there's a way to get to the bottom of it myself, since so far nobody has admitted anything. I am intimately familiar with the Cabinet filing system. The system is split into five main folders – Accounting, Admin, Prospects, Editorial, and Publicity. It's the last one that I need right now, so I click in as I've done hundreds of times. Each Cabinet author has their own folder in here; I scroll to Sloane and enter Rylie world. Each of her books is in here with its own folder.

As I click into All Things Must, I am not even sure what I am looking for. Though access to four of the five folders has been granted to at least ten key people in the Cabinet inner circle, I don't usually go poking around anywhere other than the publicity folder. I click in there and see all the files I've saved in the last few months, including every major book review from around the country and the various versions of my PR plan. There's a new file in there, one I didn't create, called Dream Sequence Contest. I roll my eyes and open it. Looks like it was created by Jonah and updated by Micah. It contains all the details of the What's the Real Ending? "contest," pre-dated to a month ago, including the fine print of the prize and the legal rights and responsibilities of the winner. Well, I know I can't write about the true story of the contest, so this file is useless.

I skip over the Prospects folder since it is just all the random manuscripts that come in from agents. Editorial is where the various drafts of Sloane's book would be saved. There might be clues about the alternate ending in there somewhere. When I open the folder called Drafts, however, there is only one file in it – Sloane Final Draft. This makes no sense. I backtrack to her previous book and find eight drafts in that folder, along with various files containing notes from the copy editor, the proofreader, and Micah and Jonah themselves. I will have to ask someone where the missing drafts are…but who?

Something tells me to check the Accounting folder next, but when I try I get a pop-up telling me it's password protected. I picture Darlene, the head of accounting. She's only in her late thirties, and her office is decorated with framed photos of Taylor Swift that she took from her floor seats during the Eras tour. Could I possibly guess her password? I think back to conversations we've had about her favorite Taylor song by far – Blank Space. It came out when she had just discovered her boyfriend at the time had taken her great-grandmother's ruby bracelet and sold it at a jewelry store to pay for their trip to Disney. She watched the Blank Space video just after they returned from their vacation and she found out what he'd done. It inspired her to take a golf club to his car windshield, she recounted a little too gleefully. I type in Blankspace into the password field but it's not right. Hmmm. But it has to be that. The girl is nice but she does not have much imagination. I try Blankspace1989 and bingo! I'm into the Cabinet Publishing accounting folder.

Besides a bunch of general administrative, office rent, supplies, and equipment folders, the rest of the files in here are also arranged by author and then book. I am about to go looking for the folder for Sloane's book when a PowerPoint file catches my attention, called Sales Trends 2020-present. It's a ten-slide presentation to the Cabinet Board showing an alarming downward trend for profits such that the current year is projected to be only half of the 2020 number.

Next, I click into the All Things Must folder and study my screen. There are expense Excel files for every month that this project existed, from the day it was signed to present. There's also Sales and Royalties files. I don't need to know how much Sloane has made from her books; that will only make me jealous. But I am curious about her sales. I click into a file that says Sloane Books Five Year Sales. My eyebrows raise when I see the trend of her last three books

– Reduction, the latest one before All Things Must sold only seventy percent as many as the one from five years ago, Intuition. In publishing, a downward trend like this from your best author is definitely cause for alarm. There is nothing in this file on early sales numbers for All Things Must, but I have a feeling they are much higher than her last book.

I keep looking in the folder for All Things Must. There are a bunch of invoices for the production of the book from the printer, the warehouse, and the shipper. And then there is a single Word file called Consultant Fees – Social. Something about that file name seems strange. When I click in first thing I see is the name Brooklyn Davis, a social security number and address at the top, and a dollar amount – $1,500 with an explanation "For services rendered." Below that is a list of about a hundred names with dates and various social media sites next to each one.

I stare at the name up top. Brooklyn Davis. That sounds so familiar, but I can't place it. I quick pull up Facebook and type it in. There are a bunch of people results but I automatically eliminate ones with no profile picture or ones that are across the country. That leaves two in the New York area, an old woman cuddling a dog, and a twenty-something blonde. I click into the young Brooklyn's page and go to her friends list, which is public, and 800 names long. I scroll through, looking for any familiar names – there's Jonah. And then it clicks. Brooklyn is Jonah's stepdaughter. She goes by his last name in real life but on socials apparently she never changed it from her biological dad's name. I'd met Brooklyn at one of the Cabinet holiday parties a few years back. She was smart, but a flighty little thing, as I recall.

I scratch my head, which suddenly feels itchy. I feel itchy all over, like I need a shower.

I should call Sloane. Maybe she already knows about this, whatever "this" happens to be. I try Sloane's cell again, it goes to voicemail. Like straight to voicemail.

On a whim, I go back into Facebook, and type one of the more uncommon names on the list: Kennedy Quantico. A page comes up immediately, and her profile picture shows a pretty young redhead on a boat, hair blowing in the breeze. Her friends list is set to private and her about info is sparse. The name of a high school and occupation just says "accounting." There are a few groups she has joined that are listed, one of them being "(Un)official Andy Creighton Fanclub." Bingo. I click into that and scroll back to May 1, the day after Sloane's book was released, the date listed in the Word file. There are a lot of posts from that day, and a lot of comments on each post. I keep scrolling and then I see it - a post by Brooklyn Davis. "Shocked, gutted here. Crying, screaming, throwing kindles. Seriously throwing it. I think I might have broken it. And good cause I am not sure I can read again after this…My poor sweet Andy ☹" There are 2,300 comments on her post. I toggle back to the Word doc again and check the list of names for another relatively uncommon one – Mikhaela Masterson. Two profiles come up, one is a middle aged woman in Germany and the other a…redhead tossing a graduation cap in the air. I click into the pic and at first glance it sure looks like Kennedy Quantico. I save the photo to my desktop. Mikaela has eighteen friends and is a member of only one group - "Sloane Rylie 4Eva." When I scroll back to May 1, I find her post soon enough. "Words cannot. I am broken. Sloane you took away the baddest, best book boyfriend who ever existed and I am shattered into a million pieces. Am I alone? Anyone else?" Three thousand nine hundred comments. Many of them have sympathetic replies from Mikaehla, which in turn leads to more replies from the group's members. I go back to the list and find a name that has "Instagram" next to it – Persimmon Sassafras, distinct enough that I find her right away and go to her page. She has 4,000 followers but her account was only created a month ago. She has exactly one post and it's a review of Sloane's book: "Five stars – given begrudgingly. Book besties, this is a warning! This book will destroy you, if you haven't already devoured it, go read it now and then come back. Spoilers are below. If you have read it, then you will understand why I say, this is a great book, the best one in the entire series, yet also the worst, the saddest, the most genuinely devastating. I love Sloane so much and I am not sure how she could do this to us other than saying I will have to trust her, trust she has something even greater in store for us all. Maybe Andy was just paving the way for an even greater MMC who will blow us away and make us forget all about him. Or maybe not. So yeah, five stars, five tear-stained begrudging, gutted stars."

I get up, grab a cold Diet Coke from the fridge, crack it open and chug a few gulps. I know I am on to something, I am just not sure exactly what. I scan the rest of the names on the list. Most are far too common-sounding to even try a search. There's one more that might be promising though – Sydney Sighed. Another Facebook account and another group member – this time Book Besties for Andy Creighton. A minute later I am reading Sydney's post, from May 2: "You know what we should do, guys? We should buy up every copy we can, and rip out those last two pages!" A dumb post but it got over one thousand comments, some of them pretty extreme. Clearly, Cabinet has been trying to stoke sales of the book but in the process they probably have contributed to the angry frenzy.

I extract the phone from my back pocket and try texting Sloane but it doesn't go through. I need to reach her as soon as possible.

CHAPTER 16

SLOANE

My first instinct is to laugh. My second instinct is to go up to this joker and punch him square in the face. But I do neither of those. Instead, I decide to tread cautiously, in case he's either insane or armed, or both.

"Andy Creighton? No kidding? Just like the main character in my books. What a coincidence. So, what brings you here?" I get my sarcasm from my mother. She's a pro at that. Like when I told her I was not selling the cabin, that I would keep it and use it sometimes, she said, "Obviously, you need it for all that hunting you do." I want to ask Andy Creighton how the hell he found my cabin. It's still listed under my dad's name. Nobody knows about my connection to this place except my family, and a select few personal friends, Mandy included, but she'd never tell anyone.

He takes a step forward and lowers his head. "I'm sorry. I'm really sorry to just show up here. I tried your house back in town, ringing and knocking for a while and your nosy neighbor came out and said you might be up here, gave me the address, so I took a chance and drove out." Oh yeah. Damn Mrs. Donnelly knows about it because her deceased husband and my dad were friends, and the Donnellys got invited to the cabin on more than one occasion. But what on earth makes her think it's okay to tell a stranger my potential whereabouts; I have no idea.

"Not going to lie, Mr. Creighton, I am tempted to call the cops right now. But technically, you haven't done anything criminal yet. On the other hand, if I wait to find out what you intend to do, then it might be too late. Although impersonating a fictional character might not be exactly aboveboard." Because reasoning with the insane is always a good idea.

The guy seems offended. He shakes his head violently, pulls his wallet from his pocket, and removes his driver's license. He hands it to me. "I really am Andy Creighton. Well, John is my given name and Andy my middle name. But yeah everyone calls me Andy."

The license shows a picture of a man that was clearly the same person who was standing in front of me, only a few years younger. This Andy Creighton is 44 years old, and lives in a small town maybe thirty or forty minutes north of my cabin. So he isn't fully crazy but he's still tracked me down for an as of yet undetermined reason.

"Terrific. So, you're really Andy. That still doesn't explain why you're here. What do you want from me? You can't possibly be upset that I killed him off. It must have been hell going through the last eight years being compared to the fictional Andy. You probably wanted him dead." I kind of feel bad for him, at least for a passing moment before reminding myself that he was basically stalking me.

"I couldn't care less myself, but…" He sighs mightily and takes a folded-up piece of paper from his pocket, unfolds it, and then hands it over.

I open it up to find a handwritten note on a sheet of copy paper.

Dear Andy Creighton,

Sloane Rylie had better bring fictional Andy Creighton back to life within 72 hours! If she doesn't upload a new e-book file with the revised ending to Amazon by then, real Andy Creightons are going to die. Starting with you.

Love,

A Big Fan

I stare at the paper, reading it again, not processing the words on the page. Real Andy Creightons are going to die? What? I look up at the Andy in front of me. He's shaking his head slowly, as if trapped in the same bubble of disbelief I am experiencing. After a minute of stunned silence, my brain snaps into crisis mode. I snap a photo of the paper.

"Okay. Andy. Where did you find this, and when?"

"About five hours ago, it was in my mailbox."

"Just slipped in there? Or mailed?"

Andy Creighton does not like my questions. He seems…is annoyed the right word? Perturbed? Disconcerted? Confused?

"Uhhh. Slipped in there," he says, taking the note back and sliding it into his pocket. "I mean mailed, sorry. The mailman delivered it. I think. I mean it had a stamp. I think? But I didn't look if it was postmarked or canceled. It was with my other mail that came today."

"Did you save the envelope? That's evidence too. Was your address typed or handwritten?"

He holds up his hands and shakes his head. "Whoa, whoa, slow down, you're overwhelming me." Says the dude who shows up randomly at my summer cabin? Okay then.

"Yeah, so we should call the police," I say, grabbing my phone. Andy doesn't like this; he holds up both hands.

"Stop. No. Don't do that. We can't risk it."

"We are risking your life if we don't." I don't know him or particularly care about him but I also don't want to see him get hurt, or worse. I'm an author, not a monster. We are risking more by doing nothing.

"The easiest thing would just be to do what they ask?" He poses it as a question, tilts his head at me and then shrugs. "Can you do it? I mean, is it doable?"

I cover my face with my hands and then drag them down so my fingertips are on my lips. He's asking me if I can rewrite a chapter and upload a new kindle pub file to Amazon. In theory yes, with some help from my publisher. But will I? No, because I've agreed to the dream sequence nonsense. That's what's happening.

"Look. I'm not supposed to leak this stuff, but between you and me, the whole death thing was a dream sequence, okay? There's a whole campaign going on right now at Cabinet Publishing. We're flying in the winner of our contest, the girl who figured it out first." There, I said it. It didn't sound as crazy as I thought it would. Andy looks at me like I've just told him the earth is flat. "So this is a good thing, is what I'm saying. It won't be three days, but it will happen. It's all a plan, you see. There's a timeline for it."

"But the note says…" Andy starts. He hears a bird squawk and almost jumps out of his shoes.

Logic takes over my brain after pausing to think it through. "Look, it's probably some prank. People are mad about the book, but not mad enough to kill random Andys." There was just no way. "There's no way to contact this person. It's clearly a prank."

Andy does not seem reassured. He shifts his weight from one leg to the other and cracks the knuckles on each hand. I enjoy cracking my own knuckles but hate listening to others do it. He speaks now, his voice softer, gentle. "Look, Ms. Rylie, I'm so sorry to have showed up like this but I panicked. I didn't know what to do. I had to ask you to please change the ending."

"Seems like calling the police would have been a better route than coming here to force me do what the note says." The irony was not lost on me that my writing was causing such an uproar; it's making people resort to death threats for me to revive a character I killed. How twisted is that? There was a reason I tried to stay out of the public eye for the most part – people are horrible. People are selfish, crazy, vindictive, mean, and harsh. Put any piece of work out there and someone will hate it. Most of my books have a 4.4 rating on Goodreads. Which still means hundreds of readers rated my writing one or two stars. More than a handful of people read my books and strongly disliked them. I was shocked that the current book, despite the whole Andy controversy, still managed a 3.95 rating. I had 53,000 five-star ratings compared to 3,000 one-star ratings. It was a stark reminder that the vast majority of my fans loved the book, and understood that shit happens in novels. Were readers upset when Rebecca Yarros killed a major character in her Empyrean series? Sure they were, that "they" including me for one. But there was no insanity around that death. Reading a novel, no matter the genre, is willingly risking heartbreak. If everything was all roses and puppies, books (and tv shows and movies) would be boring and just plain bad.

I have often wondered if I had killed off Ciara instead, what would the reaction be? Would my book girlies still be up in arms? Or would they be ready for someone else to take her place as Andy's significant other? Andy is ideal but many readers see Ciara as unworthy.

While I was lost in thought, Andy scuffs the dirt with his left shoe and frowns, shaking his head slowly.

"Maybe you're right. I overreacted. It was probably my neighbor down the street, in fact. I'm always seeing her carting a stack of books to and from the library, muttering to herself along the way. And weirdly, I have the distinct memory of your book in her stack the day after it was released. She was mumbling something about Sloane Rylie being at the top of her TBR, whatever that means."

"TBR is to be read. A list of books people plan to read."

"Oh, okay," Andy says, the corner of his mouth quirking up slightly. "I'm not much of a reader myself."

"That's a relief, actually," I say. "The readers I've encountered lately have been pretty frightening people." I manage a laugh, and Andy smiles.

He lowers his head and his lips curl downward. "I'm sorry I invaded your private space. I shouldn't have even gone to your house to begin with, it's just that I saw it on the news the other day, the people protesting in your driveway, and the street sign was in the shot, so I looked it up. Thought nothing of it at the time of course, until this slipped through my door."

"I thought you said it was in your mailbox," I say.

"Oh yeah. I mean mailbox. Mail slot. In my door. It's been a very stressful few hours." His face suddenly flushes.

I am usually a pretty good judge of character, and this Andy Creighton seems like a decent guy. He isn't here to spook me, he is simply spooked himself. And now that I think about it, it's pretty cool to meet a real life Andy Creighton after all these years of writing about one (even if he's nothing like his fictional alter ego). And though he came here for a very specific reason, now an idea pulses into my brain, a wild one.

"You know…maybe we could use you, Andy."

"Use me?" he blinks a few times like I'm shining a spotlight on his face.

"Yeah. In our whole dream sequence campaign. Like hi, I'm Andy Creighton, and I'm alive. Grab a few other namesakes and stick them in there too. Like a little social media reel or something. Shit, I should call Mandy. Well, if the cell service gods allow me to."

"Who's Mandy?"

"Oh sorry. She's my PR girl. She's great." Though the last 24 hours I am just not sure who I can trust anymore.

"I don't want to be in a video promoting the very book that could get me killed," he says, but he's smiling through it.

"I tend to get ahead of myself, sorry. One thing at a time. Okay, refocusing. The note. Definitely we should get it to the police, and I should tell the folks at Cabinet Publishing that this happened. Even if it just turns out to be the Crazy Library Lady over there."

Andy sighs deeply. He looks embarrassed and defeated. I feel bad for the guy. He didn't do anything except be born with a name that I happened to pick for a book series that would become a bestseller. Nothing is his fault.

Up in the trees above, squirrels squawk, chasing each other playfully (or is it aggressively, I can never tell which), and a few acorns drop to the ground, startling us both. Something tells me not to let Andy leave yet. He came all this way after all.

"Hey, do you want to come inside for a minute? I don't have much to offer except maybe a vitamin water…" I hold one up. "But I've never met an actual Andy Creighton, so you may as well stay a few minutes."

"So, you're definitely going to…alright, I mean I can if you want me to." He bites his lip and takes a deep breath of the forest air. I've always loved the air out here. I find it to be very grounding, calming. Maybe that's why I didn't freak out completely when he showed up with the note. I'm proud of my composure, my logic so far. I look at my new friend and can tell that Andy Creighton doesn't mind staying a while, but he would much rather be sitting watching me rewrite the last chapter, that's what he still has in mind, even after our little talk. But that's not going to happen right now. I came here to escape not to immerse myself even further in the book mess.

"Sure," I say. "We can hang for a few." I walk the few steps to the front door of the cabin and quickly unlock it. As I take a step forward, I feel something sharp and hard poking my back.

"Hurry and get inside," Andy says, desperation in his voice. I've never been prodded by the business end of a gun, so I can't say for sure that's what it is, but it sure feels like it. I do as he says, walking into the middle of the living room, looking up at the deer head on the wall and thinking of dad's old hunting rifle that is a mere few feet away. My mind races. This guy does not look like he could harm anyone, gun or not. I'm just so tired of this bullshit now, I am willing to risk injury just to make it stop.

"Welcome to my cabin," I say, whirling around and grabbing at what turns out to be Andy's pointer finger. "What the hell?" I say.

"Ow!" he yelps. "You're going to break my hand."

"Why did you push me inside? What is actually wrong with you?" I am all kinds of mad now. I want to kick him in the nuts for scaring me like this.

"A car was approaching, and I got nervous," Andy says. He backs away from me and goes to the window. "Shit. They're pulling into your driveway. I knew it."

"You knew what?" Sure, it's not common for people to be showing up here. But it's also not unheard of. Well, okay. Maybe he does have a reason to be skittish. But still. "It's not illegal for people to park in my driveway. If it was you'd be arrested."

"That someone was going to come after me. Like the note says."

"Dude. Has it even been half a day yet, let alone three?" Meanwhile, I'm low key panicking, because I am definitely not expecting anyone here. Maybe it's another Andy Creighton with a note haha.

He hangs his head low. "No, you're right."

"Then chill. Why would someone be after you already? That makes no sense."

I push past Andy and peek out the window. Sure enough, there is another car in my driveway, with a driver and a passenger. The car horn honks, I jump, and Andy yelps "Jesus!" Then the driver's side door opens and out steps…Jonah Carlstadt? What the actual hell is going on. Jonah stretches and looks around, and then the passenger door opens and young woman with close cropped blue hair and two colorful full sleeve tattoos gets out.

"Sloane!" Jonah calls out. "Hey Sloane, it's Jonah, come outside!"

"What's a Jonah?" Andy asks from the corner into which he's wedged himself. "Friend or foe?"

"A Jonah is friend, mostly, but he's my editor so you could classify him as foe. Apparently he seems to also think it's okay to track me down at my cottage like you did. He'd better have a threatening note as an excuse, too." I shake my head and throw open the door. The woman goes around back and opens the trunk, retrieves a camera bag and a tripod. She's pretty young, early twenties at most. "This is great," she tells Jonah just as he sees me in the doorway. "A perfect backdrop."

"Sloane! Hey. I am so sorry to barge in like this. I did try to text you and call you, like five times." I glance at my phone. It is currently not even showing any missed calls. The service up here is terrible. But Jonah already knows this. I should never have told him I was going; I told him so he would not try to reach me, not so he would blow up my phone.

"What is so important that it couldn't wait a couple of days?" I step outside and Andy is right behind me.

"Oh, oh my gosh, I didn't realize I was interrupting…" Jonah's voice trails off. Apparently seeing a second vehicle in my driveway didn't give away the fact that I had company.

"Jonah, I'd like you to meet Andy Creighton in the flesh," I say with a smirk.

Blue hair girl's head snaps my direction and Jonah's jaw drops. "What?" he says.

"This is Andy Creighton, an actual real life one. He's paying me a little visit. Andy this is my editor Jonah Carlstadt and…I look over at blue hair girl. "Oh sorry, this is my stepdaughter Brooklyn."

Brooklyn nods at me and flashes a fake smile and then gives a quick nod to Andy. Oh yeah, now I see it. She's changed a lot since then, but I see it. I met her before, years ago, on take your kid to work day. I happened to be at the office that day for a meeting with Micah, and I remember her nearly destroying the copy machine, throwing a handful of pencils at me just to see how many I could catch, and spilling hot chocolate all over the kitchen floor. That would make her maybe twenty-two or so now, and hopefully not as much of a train wreck.

Jonah walks right up to Andy and offers a hand and flashes his best fake smile.

"This is quite a treat," he says. "So, you're really Andy Creighton, are you?" He strokes his chin and raises an eyebrow. Andy runs a hand through his hair and nods. "That's me. I can prove it if you…"

"No, I believe you. So why are you here?" He pauses and his eyes light up. "Wait. Are you…have you been the inspiration for the book character all along? Is that what this is? This could be good. We could use this. I have to think." He turns to his step-daughter, who's been lurking next to the passenger door with the yet-to-be-explained photographic equipment. "Brooklyn, why don't you scope out a good spot to shoot. Let's avoid using the cabin as a backdrop, cause nowadays image search can be pretty powerful and we don't want anyone identifying this place from some archived Zillow picture or something." Jonah knows this was my dad's cabin and it hasn't been up for sale, but I appreciate the sentiment, for whatever they are planning to do.

"I just met Sloane a few minutes ago," Andy says, mouth still open as if he is about to spill the beans on the note. I decide Jonah does not need to know the full story. Not yet anyhow, so I glare at Andy and hope he gets the hint to shut up.

"Best few minutes of my life," I say, putting an arm around his shoulder and squeezing. Poor Andy is so confused but he manages a weak laugh, nodding his head. I feel bad but I really don't want to tell Jonah about the threatening note, so his explanation is the most logical one to latch onto. He'd probably take the note seriously and make me redo the whole chapter by tomorrow, and I'm just not interested in succumbing to shenanigans.

"You two are adorable," Jonah says. "Now for the reason we're here, Sloane. We need to film a reel of you teasing something big is coming. Dez Maxwell arrives tomorrow, so we need to tease it now, and stop the protests before things escalate even more."

"Tomorrow? What the hell? I thought it was later this week." Tomorrow is way too soon. This is getting out of hand. I am not ready to deal with making nice to some crackhead fan who won a fake contest for coming up with a wacky conspiracy theory.

Though I despise my own voice and have hated anytime I had to make a video announcing an upcoming book, if it will quell the uprising of Andy fans, then I'll consider it. While I am thinking, Brooklyn is setting up the tripod near a tree to the side of the driveway and checking the light. So apparently we are doing this NOW. I don't even have makeup on and my hair is a hot mess. Wonderful. No sooner than those thoughts cross my mind, Brooklyn goes back to the car and grabs a makeup kit and a stool from the back seat. She comes over to me, says "Hey, sit for a sec," very nonchalantly like I'm a Broadway actress and we've done this a million times before. I shrug and do what she says while Jonah strikes up a conversation with Andy just out of earshot. I see the two of them taking a slow walk down the driveway, talking in hushed tones. Andy isn't bad looking, not at all. He's tall and has muscular arms. "Look at me," Brooklyn says, redirecting my attention.

"Whose idea was this?" I ask as she applies eyeshadow.

"My dad's, I guess. He's full of ideas," she says. "Stay still," she gently scolds when I try to swivel my head to locate Andy and Jonah, who seem to have disappeared. After a few minutes of fussing with my face, Brooklyn tells me to stay put while she goes back to the car to retrieve a hair brush and some setting spray. I wish I had a mirror to see what she's doing to me. I'm fine with a professional doing all this, but I have no idea what this kid's credentials are other than being Jonah's stepdaughter. "Okay, stand," she commands. I do so and she looks me over and shrugs. "I did what I could." The corner of her mouth quirks into a slight smile and then she adds: "Kidding, you look great," and turns away from me. "Dad! She's ready!" she yells so loud it startles the wildlife – several birds take off loudly from the tree we're under, and squirrels scamper farther out on its limbs.

There's no answer at first and I feel a twinge of panic rise up from my stomach. But a few seconds later, Jonah emerges from behind some bushes, rubbing his hands together. He looks energized, and as if to emphasize my assessment he takes a deep breath and sighs happily. "Gotta love the fresh air out here," he says. "Let's do this!"

Still uncertain what the "this" actually is, Jonah takes a paper from the dashboard and hands it to me. It's a script, a paragraph of reassurance to my poor readers that all is well and a big surprise announcement is coming tomorrow. And I'm supposed to wink at the end. Anyone who knows me, will tell you that I am a terrible winker. It inevitably looks like I either have dirt in my eye or a nervous tic. Well, Jonah and Brooklyn will soon discover that for themselves.

"Am I supposed to memorize this? I'll need time."

Jonah dismisses me with a wave of his hand. "No, no. Just capture the gist of it. The essence. Be yourself. It's more a guideline than a script to memorize."

I look down at the paper again and look up into the camera a few feet away from me, silently mouthing words that are close enough to what Jonah handed me.

"Ready to try a take?" Brooklyn says, looking bored.

"I guess."

"I'll start the camera, just start talking when you're ready, I can edit out the beginning."

She presses a button and a red light flashes. I look at the camera and a jumble of words tumbles out of my mouth too quickly. Brooklyn shakes her head and stops the recording. Jonah comes over and pats my shoulder. "No need to be nervous. This will be great. This plan is going to work so well."

"If you can edit stuff out why did you stop recording?"

"I can't just leave it running indefinitely, I only have so much battery and only so much space on the memory card," Brooklyn huffs, pressing the record button again.

"Hey, where's Andy? Where'd he go?" As soon as I ask, Brooklyn shakes her head and stops the recording again. I am certain she hates me by now.

"Oh, he had to pee so he went off to do that."

"I do have indoor plumbing. Why would he go in the woods?"

"We were already a ways in and he couldn't wait," Jonah says. "But let's stay focused, shall we? Brooklyn, ready?"

"It's been a bit, shouldn't he be back by now?" It doesn't take that long to pee, or to walk back from however far they wandered off. And if he had to really go, he would definitely have used a real bathroom.

Jonah glances at his watch. "Maybe he had to shit too, I don't know. Or maybe he's picking wildflowers for his girlfriend. He's a grown ass man, I'm sure he's fine. Can we just get this video captured? Then we can go look for him." Girlfriend? Were they talking about that? I want to go look for him now, but Brooklyn is pressing the record button again so I force myself through the little speech again, this time I think it's not bad, but both Brooklyn and Jonah are shaking their heads. "Too fast," Jonah says. "Slow down."

"Did Andy say anything to you?" I ask.

Jonah's eyes widen. "About what?"

"Okay, never mind." He must not have told Jonah about the note, then. So they were just talking about…the picturesque nature of my cabin? I crane my neck to try and spot Andy beyond Jonah's car, but there's nothing. "Andy!" I shout, startling Brooklyn, who jumps back from the camera and throws visual daggers at me. I see she's about to speak but I hold up a hand, trying to listen for a reply. Sure enough, a distant voice calls out "I'm fine." My shoulders relax and I refocus. "Okay, Brooklyn, let's do this," I say with a fake smile, and I get through the announcement perfectly in the next take. Jonah claps and Brooklyn rolls her eyes and sighs mightily, then begins to disassemble the equipment as soon as she checks to see that it recorded properly.

"And that's a wrap," Jonah says.

"Dad." Brooklyn folds her arms and bites her lower lip.

"Hey, I've always wanted to say that." He winks at Brooklyn and turns to face me. "Great job, Sloane. Look for it to hit social media by this evening. Be sure to get to LGA first thing tomorrow to greet Dez. And at that point we'll be doing another couple of reels, one with just Dez, one with just you, and another with both of you."

"Where's Mandy in all this? I thought she was the head of PR?" I really have to go to the airport? This is so dumb. Mandy should have warned me about this nonsense.

Though if she tried in the last couple of hours, my service may have prevented it.

Jonah takes a few steps forward as Brooklyn noisily packs the camera stuff in the trunk and slams it shut. "Mandy's got her hands full right now, but we're running everything by her, don't worry. This is bigger than just one person, Sloane. It's all hands on deck so we're all pitching in to rescue you." He pauses and licks his lips. "And Cabinet Publishing. But don't you worry, we've got this under control."

As if I need rescuing. Well, from the crazy obsessed readers, maybe. But other than that, I'm fine, my book is fine. If I lose some of my following, I don't care.

"Well, I'd offer you something to eat but all I have are Pop Tarts and pretzels." And they're for me, so I hope neither of them wants anything.

"That's okay, we have to get back and get this video edited and uploaded. Again, sorry for barging in on you. We just have to move fast here and turn the tables. Literally flip the script." He laughs at his own joke and gets back in his car. Brooklyn tucks the makeup case in the back seat and gets in as well, offering a slight wave as she does. And just like that, they're gone, backing out of my driveway and gunning it down the road until they are no longer visible.

"Andy?" I call. There is nothing except the cicadas and the birds chirping high above. "Andy Creighton?" I say, louder still. What I want is to go into the cabin and take a nap. I am generally not a big fan of daytime sleeping, but something about the cabin is cozy and nap-inducing. But nope, instead I have to walk into the woods and find Andy. I am not actually going very far in, because I have a fear of both poison ivy and snakes, and these woods are filled with both.

"Andrew Creighton, where in the hell are you?"

But he doesn't answer. Not immediately at any rate. I shake my head and curse under my breath. And then I hear it – a voice in the distance. Faint, but audible. And it's calling for help.

CHAPTER 17

MANDY

Since I can't reach Sloane and have some time to kill before dinner with Patrick, I decide to head into the city and do a little poking around at Cabinet. Then if Micah asks if I started working on the book, I can tell him truthfully, yes. It's Saturday, so I doubt anyone will be in the office to question me. Not that I relish the thought of going into the city on a weekend when I could be home doing more laundry and cleaning. Instead of that, I am here in midtown Manhattan feeling like I might be on the verge of some big discovery without any idea of what that actually means. The empty drafts folder on the server is highly suspicious. I want to see if maybe there are hard copy drafts somewhere in one of the filing cabinets that line the corridor leading from the lobby to the offices and conference rooms in the back. They want me to write a book about this Andy Creighton mess, they will get a damn book – on my terms – and if they won't publish it I'll go rogue. But that's probably just me puffing my chest. I have rarely gone rogue in my life…well, the Ellis thing, but other than that, not really.

I barely catch the subway train that is waiting in the station. Panting, I leap onto the train and plop myself down into a seat just as the doors are closing. I feel people's eyes on me, especially a pair of college-age guys who smile at me lasciviously. I look down and realize the top two buttons of my blouse are undone. Well, that explains that. Good to know I'm still leer-worthy, I guess. I use my time on the train to type some thoughts into my Notes app.

After nearly being knocked over by a blonde family of tourists rushing down Fifth Avenue, I am annoyed and frustrated by the time I get on the elevator to the 33rd floor. Now I'm starting to fear that I won't be alone and therefore won't be able to poke around how I want. Luckily, after swiping my key card, I find myself standing in a completely empty office. After the Metro-North, the subway, and the busy streets, the solitude of this Saturday afternoon in the office is quite pleasant. I smile at the thought of having free reign of the place. I look at the framed publicity photo of Sloane that hangs in the lobby along with a few other bestselling Cabinet authors – Jens Tamkin, Brit Bonnerson, and Stacy Von Slade. Of the three Stacy is the closest I'd say Sloane has to competition at Cabinet. Stacy signed her big contract a year before Sloane and her first book – One Night With My Brother – was a smash, hitting number one on the Times list. There's actually a copy of it sitting on the coffee table in the reception area. Now this, this book was deservedly controversial. It was about siblings who learn after twenty-five years that they are not related after all, and promptly begin a torrid relationship, much to everyone else's consternation. It turned heads and raised eyebrows, but there were no protests or stalkers holding up signs outside Stacy's house, at least I don't think so. Stacy is supposed to deliver her latest manuscript to us in a few months, her first in four years. I believe she's still under contract to Cabinet to produce another book after that too, but we haven't heard from her lately and Micah seems uninterested in following up, which is weird because normally he is a stickler about submission dates. I think Stacy is at least a year past her delivery date, from what I remember.

Stacy's next book did really well, too, a sequel to One Night With My Brother called Sibling Rivalry, but anything she published after that tanked. This was around the time that Sloane was becoming wildly popular with her Andy Creighton book series.

I make my way down the corridor, which features framed images of every Cabinet title that hit number 1 on the bestseller list, with the date on a large brass plaque underneath. I'm not lying when I say most of the pictures are of Sloane Rylie book covers. No wonder they are jumping through hoops to save the day and fix everything; Cabinet's finances are murky at best.

I have never paid so much as the slightest attention to the filing cabinets; they were always just ordinary office fixtures. Now I am bending over to scour the labels on each drawer. They appear to be in alphabetical order by author's last name. I get close to the end of the corridor before I spot the "R" drawers. I pull the first one out – it's Estaban Ramirez, a one-hit wonder whose campaign I did brilliantly but whose second book failed miserably, despite my best efforts. And right behind him is Sloane Rylie. She has the rest of this drawer and the next four drawers. It's amazing in this age of digital everything that they even still keep hard files, but I guess signed contracts and correspondence with translators, copies of foreign editions need to go somewhere. And that's what it is for the most part, until I get to her current book. The files on All Things Must are thick and numerous. And yes, they do in fact contain printed page proofs. "Aha!" I say aloud, clapping my hands together in triumph. I pull over one of the rolling chairs from a nearby cubicle and pull out one of the Pendaflex hanging files. The drafts are each stamp-dated at the top right, and initialed by several people, mostly illegible but one of which looks like MC. Micah. My initials aren't on any of them because the two versions I saw were only PDFs not hard copies. Then again, I work from home half the time so it makes sense that I did not get the office hard copy. I flip to the end of each of the drafts, watching the evolution of the last couple of pages. As Sloane has indicated, the earlier drafts had Andy Creighton dying from the dinner he was eating being poisoned, but his death was instant and relatively painless. When I reach the last one I read, the ending is still the same, just as I'd remembered. But the pass for press final proof ending is different, it's the one in the printed book, where Andy has a reaction to the food he's eating and then falls over onto his fork, impaling himself with it. Between the version I read and this version, there is nothing else in the file cabinet. I must have missed something. I go back to the printed copy of the last version I'd read and look again at the last two pages. I missed something the first time around. At the top of the final page, scrawled lightly in pencil is the word – Make it worse? and then my eyes return to the final passage of the book and notice that the last sentences are faintly underlined, also in pencil.

It's what I feared – Someone at Cabinet didn't think Sloane's ending was dramatic enough and made a change without her knowing.

Only one person signed their initials in pencil – JC: Jonah Carlstadt.

CHAPTER 18

SLOANE

I have no idea how badly Andy might be injured. I almost turn back to the cabin and dig out the first aid kit that dad kept under the bathroom sink, but most of the stuff in there is probably over 30 years old and not very useful or sanitary anymore. What could have happened to Andy? My mind races. I wish Jonah and Brooklyn were still here, but it's just me against the big bad forest. I remind myself this is lower Westchester County and there is nothing either that big or that bad out there. Some deer, and a few coyotes maybe, but they shouldn't pose a threat to a grown man.

"Andy!" I shout, and of course there's no answer other than the coo of the mourning dove that likes to hang out perched on a low branch of the Norway maple behind my cabin. Great. I head into the woods on my side of the chain link fence that separates my property from my nearest neighbor's acres. I don't think Andy would have scaled the fence and wandered over there. The woods to the left of my cabin start off at a very gradual downward incline before getting steeper as you approach the stream bed. Normally the stream is pretty unimpressive, except after a heavy rain when it's more like a miniature river. My land stops on this side of the stream and extends a few hundred feet to the east from there bounded by another chain link fence, and then back up to the cabin. A total of twenty acres. I know the land like the back of my hand, having spent so much time here when I was younger. Most of the trees are young growth, no more than forty years old as the result of a forest fire that miraculously spared the cabin but obliterated much of the woods behind it.

"Andy Creighton, goddammit!" I say, more to myself than to him. The only sounds I hear are my sneakers crunching on the leaves and twigs, and the various birds high above. I've said my main male character's name out loud more in the last week than I have in the last five years. It feels strange, especially now that he's manifested into a real person – who happens to be somewhere on my property in need of assistance.

"Where are you?" I shout loud enough for the Kopeckis down the road to hear me. Dylan Kopecki is a muscular young man, probably mid-twenties, and I've seen him chopping wood shirtless on more than one occasion. Yes, I slow my car down every time I pass, I'm not ashamed to admit it. Each time, I lower my window and say "Hi Dylan" as if that's my excuse for rolling almost to a full stop. Dylan probably looks at me like some weird aunt because he smiles politely, gives me the peace sign, and says "Hello Mrs. Rylie," which hurts me to my core every time and I want to say "That's Ms. Rylie, I'm available!" (even when I wasn't). And confession – it's his chest I used as the inspiration for Andy's in the last couple of books. Having a mental model helped the description be much more accurate. I had Ellis, of course, but no offense to him, his chest is a little flabby and not what ideal book boyfriend stud Andy Creighton would be sporting.

"Andy?" I yell again. "Are you okay? Can you hear me?" My voice sounds strange at such a high volume. I don't think I've ever in my life had to yell this loud. My throat is starting to feel raw already after just a handful of shouted words. Okay correction, at the Taylor Swift concert in Miami, I did scream like crazy and yell-sing – but that was different. My feet crunch deeper into my property, past the stump of the tree that Pop cut down when I was three. I used to stand on that four-foot-high tree remnant and pretend I was giving a speech to a rapt audience. I was a weird kid. Now, it's deteriorated with age and worms and would not hold my weight if I tried standing on it. To my right is the cluster of ferns that has been growing there as long as I can remember. To my left, a rhododendron bush in full bloom, bearing its fuchsia flowers proudly. Every time I saw it I wondered why someone would have planted the bush a hundred feet from the road and out of sight from the cabin, where nobody can enjoy it. I finally asked my dad not long before he passed, and his answer was simple: "That's exactly why it's back there, why your grandpa planted it there, so we'd take a little walk just to go look at it. Sometimes you need to work a little for something pretty."

I haven't been over this way to admire it in at least a couple of years; it's too bad the reason has to be me looking for the (hopefully) alive real-life version of an (unfortunately) dead book character. I read once that rhododendrons are poisonous and that would figure since they are so lovely. I think they are in the azalea family and I know those are poisonous.

My thoughts are interrupted by a voice from behind me. "Hey! Are you okay?"

It does not sound like Andy. I whirl around to see Dylan Kopecki, wearing navy blue shorts, a beat-up Pink Floyd tee shirt, and a broad grin on his face. Is it possible he's even sexier with his shirt on?

"Dylan, hello," I say, thankful that Brooklyn had just done my makeup and hair a little while before.

"Mrs. Rylie," he says and this time I correct him. "Sloane. You can just call me Sloane."

"Okay. Sloane. I heard yelling coming from over this way so I thought I'd check it out. You alright?" He's panting and there is a drop of sweat rolling down his neck. He must have run the quarter mile or so all the way here just to come to my rescue.

"I'm alright, but I'm looking for someone who needs help."

Dylan furrows his brow and points vaguely behind me. "Out there somewhere?"

"Yeah, out there." Dylan's family has the same size property as mine, so he knows it's not a lot of ground to cover. Not counting what lies on the other side of the stream, of course. But why would Andy have crossed the stream and got himself wet?

"Dog?" Dylan asks and I just blink at him.

"I'm sorry?"

"Dog. Are we looking for your dog?" My heart sinks a little that my neighbor doesn't even know me well enough to know that I don't have a dog. I wish I did. I always wanted one.

"No, human. Person. His name is Andy Creighton." I can say this with confidence that Dylan has no clue about the significance of the name. He might not even know I'm an author. His parents still just think of me as Mike's kid.

"What's he doing out here?" Again he gestures. Dylan smells good, like pine trees and musk and I want to get closer to take a deeper whiff, but that would probably be a bad idea since he has given no indication of being interested in me. Yet.

"He went to pee, as far as I know. And then he said he was fine. And then a couple of minutes later he called for help. And that was the last I heard of him."

"He went to pee? Out in the woods?" he gestures. "There's poison ivy in the woods. And ticks. Don't you have plumbing in there?"

"Yeah, of course. Weird, right?"

Dylan nods slowly, as if this Andy could be in grave danger and not just playing a dumb trick on me. After all, what's to say he was telling the truth about that threatening note.

"Well, he's got to be somewhere, hasn't he?" Dylan says. It shouldn't take long to find him. He pauses. "He wouldn't have just...left or anything, would he?"

"No, his car is in my driveway."

Dylan glances back that direction but my driveway is out of the line of sight. His jaw clenches and he cups his hands around his mouth, yelling even louder than I had: "Andy Creighton!"

His voice echoes and we listen. There is nothing. "I'm a little concerned," I say. Dylan steps closer and puts an arm around me and gives me a half hug. "We'll find him, Sloane. Let's go down toward the stream bed." His voice is calm and reassuring even though I can see from his eyes that he's concerned too. You don't just piss in the woods and disappear.

We crunch past the rhododendron and the ground starts to slope downward. "We've always wanted to do something with our property but we have neither the time or money so it looks pretty much like this on our side of the fence," he says, then holds up a finger. "Though we did make a little clearing by the stream and every summer we drag two wicker chairs and a table down there and use it almost never. Except on July 4th when we bring the portable charcoal grill down there and roast hot dogs and marshmallows." He laughs and I join. "Andy!" he calls again, startling me.

We both stop in our tracks after that. "Did you hear something?"

"I think so," I say. Then I notice it. "Hey, look over here." I point to a steeper part of the incline to my right. That's the stormwater gully my grandpa dug out a long time ago to drain the water from the road away from the cabin and down to the stream. Over the years the water made the gully deeper and definitely something to avoid stepping into. We all know to steer clear of it, though at the moment it's partly hidden under the cover of leaves and looks less daunting than it really is.

"Seems like the leaves and dirt are disturbed," he says. "Someone was here. Come on."

We carefully step our way down the incline parallel to the little gully, following the trail of disturbed leaves. Looking ahead, I can already make out the water flowing in the creek. I guess I haven't really explored much since I grew up; now my property seems a lot smaller than it used to. In adulthood, everything shrinks.

"Andy?" I call.

"Help," a voice answers from a little further down. Dylan sprints ahead of me, almost slipping on a large rock but quickly regaining his footing while simultaneously telling me to watch out. I am liking this guy more and more.

As we get to where the drainage gully meets the stream, we see him, sprawled out on his stomach, the fingers of one of his hands actually touching the water that babbles lazily around the new obstruction.

"Oh Jesus," I say.

Dylan is ahead of me, he is already kneeling down next to Andy, trying to assess his injuries.

"Are you bleeding? Where does it hurt? Can you move?" he asks rapid-fire.

"How did this happen?" I say, mostly to myself.

"I think I'm alright. I must have passed out for a few minutes."

"Did you hit your head?" Dylan asks as Andy shifts and turns so he's on his side.

"No, I just, the fall knocked the wind out of me temporarily."

Except for a couple of scrapes, his face looks okay. Dylan extends an arm and cautions Andy to move slowly. Andy reaches and Dylan gradually pulls Andy up. "My ankle hurts, I might have twisted it," he says. "Who are you?" he asks Dylan.

"Sloane's neighbor. I'm going to check you for injuries," Dylan says as he gently presses on Andy's ribs, feels his head for bumps, and then rolls up his pant leg to look at the ankle. "Yeah, looks like the ankle is a bit swollen already. But you didn't flinch when I touched your ribs so that's good."

"I feel like an idiot," is all Andy says. We stand on either side of him so he can lean on us and not put weight on the bad ankle.

"What exactly happened over here?" I ask. "Why did you go so far into the woods?" Apparently the real-life Andy Creighton has a death wish.

"I don't know. I…I stepped into that little ditch and lost my balance and then rolled and slid down to where you found me." That still doesn't answer why he ventured this far to begin with. Maybe the gauze in that old medical kit is still salvageable if it didn't lose its elasticity long ago.

As we crunch back uphill, a car horn honks insistently and a voice calls my name. "What the hell?" I mutter.

"Aren't you going to answer them?" Dylan asks.

"I don't know who it is," I say.

"Probably should answer anyway," he says. Andy grunts with each step, and though I feel bad he fell, I'm annoyed right now. At everything and everyone. Well, except Dylan, possibly.

"I'm coming, give me a minute!" I shout. I am going to need a bag of lozenges from Connie's store at this rate. My poor throat is raw.

"It's Jonah!" the voice calls back. "Jonah Carlstadt!"

Jonah? What the hell? I come to the cabin to get away from the book only to have non-stop reminders of it since I've arrived. We finally make it past the flowering bush and walk more quickly now that the ground has leveled off. Jonah sees us and comes running, Brooklyn not far behind.

"Oh my god, what happened? Is he hurt? Are you hurt?" Jonah seems downright panicked.

"I slipped and Sloane came and helped me," Andy says flatly, almost annoyed.

"And Dylan, my neighbor. I wouldn't have been able to do this on my own."

"Nah, you're stronger than you think," Dylan says with a smile. Is he flirting or is that wishful thinking? Probably wishful thinking. On both our parts. I am definitely not stronger than I think.

"You drove back here…why? You left already," I say, ignoring Dylan's comment. We walk Andy back to his car and lean him against it so we don't have to hold him anymore.

Jonah follows and waves a dismissive hand at me. "Oh that. Brooklyn left the lens cover to her camera on the ground so we came back for it."

"Dad." Brooklyn rolls her eyes in the background.

"Never mind, Brookie," he scolds. He turns to me, smiling. "Sloane, do you realize what just happened?" Jonah's eyes are lit up, and he claps his hands together loudly.

"Yes. I just wasted an hour of my day." Sarcasm comes naturally to me. Anyone who knows me realizes that Ciara has my sassy nature. That's why it's so easy to write her character.

"No," he says with a downward twist of his mouth. "Look over there." He gestures at the injured guy.

"Yeah, okay?" I say. I am not in the mood for games but it seems like Jonah is.

"You just saved Andy Creighton. This is epic. We can use this." He stares at me as if expecting me to understand and applaud. I don't and I won't.

"Use what, for what?"

"Who are these people?" Dylan asks.

"Oh, sorry. My neighbor Dylan, this is my editor Jonah and his daughter Brooklyn."

"Stepdaughter," she corrects, leading Jonah to shake his head.

Dylan smiles and nods. "Cool name. Like the place. That's fun."

Brooklyn scoffs. "I hate my name, but okay. Nice to meet you." I don't really know anyone who loves their name. Sloane bothered me so much I wanted to use a penname for my books, but Mandy advised me otherwise. She thought Sloane Rylie sounded "naturally bestsellerish" as she put it.

"Can you answer me, Jonah?" I say, wishing it was him who fell down the gully. "Use what, for what?"

"We literally just made a promo video right? Well, you've saved Andy Creighton. He fell and needed help and you saved him. We can make another reel about that. It'll be amazing publicity for you." He looks at Andy. "You okay with that?"

"Whatever you want, sure," Andy says.

"Great. Brooklyn, why don't you set up over there. We can get a shot of Sloane helping Andy limping out of the woods." I could see the wheels turning in Jonah's head. Before I could object, Brooklyn was clattering the tripod around and looking for the perfect location to set up.

"I don't get why you had me poking and prodding the socials the other day if now we're doing this," Brooklyn mutters.

"Hey, not now," Jonah growls, glaring at his stepdaughter before turning to smile at me again. Brooklyn rolls her eyes and shakes her head.

"You seriously want to make a fake video?" I ask, trying to understand the little exchange I just witnessed between them. What does she mean by poking the socials?

"Gotta think out of the box, Sloane," Jonah says.

"You're my damn editor, this is Mandy's job."

"Like I said, we're all pitching in. Mandy's not here but I am and this is a golden op we are not going to just walk away from it." He turns to his stepdaughter. "Yeah right there, and aim it to the left a little. The trees over there frame the shot well, we can have them emerging from between the trees."

"Saving a jillion real Andy Creightons is not going to bring back the fictional one," I say with my snark dialed up to a solid 9.5.

"Trust me," Jonah says. "Good will is worth a lot. And you need a big dose of it now. People's brains are rather simple. They will see this and forgive you for the book…in combination with everything else we're planning it will be a knockout punch!"

"The dude is hobbling along, and you want to make him do a retake of his painful walk out of the woods? Are you insane?" I realize I am yelling at my longtime editor, and I don't care at all. I am so done with all this nonsense right now, I am ready to just walk away from it all, lawsuits be damned. Away from my contract, from my books, my fans, Jonah, Micah, Mandy, my writing career. I would say walk away and just live in this cabin, but now the cabin is becoming tainted with book stuff too.

"It really does hurt," Andy finally says.

"Maybe you can manage…" Jonah says, nodding his head and giving a thumbs up.

"Hey, I think the guy fucked up his ankle pretty bad," Dylan says. I inadvertently smile at him.

"I am not sure this is a good idea," Andy says softly, wincing when he tries to put pressure on his bad foot.

"We had a deal…" Jonah starts and his face goes red after he cuts himself off.

"Dad!" Brooklyn hisses.

"Here, just take it back," Andy says, pulling a hundred dollar bill from his pocket and holding it out.

I am trying to process what is happening, but my brain is refusing to believe what I think I'm seeing. Of all the lowdown, sneaky shit.

"What the hell is going on, Andy?" Jonah demands. I've never seen his face so contorted before, his skin blotchy and red, his left eye twitching.

Andy is silent, staring at the bill in his hand, money that Jonah is not taking.

"Put that away and let's do this." Jonah takes a deep breath and smiles, first at Andy, then at me and Dylan.

"What's going on is that I'm actually injured. This isn't pretend," Andy says.

"What did you do, pay this guy to fake being injured so you could get your little video? Are you fucking crazy?" Dylan's fists are clenched and his jaw ticks. He takes a step forward toward Jonah, who retreats accordingly. I'm not ashamed to admit that I enjoy him when he's angry, the way his biceps flex and his nostrils flare. And he doesn't even know the whole context of what's going on here, just what is evident.

Jonah holds out his hand and lowers his head. "I'm only trying to make you look good, Sloane, and make up for…" He stops himself, face reddening as he looks up again.

"Make up for what?" I ask as his eyes dart left and right.

"Nothing, never mind."

"Spill it," I order. Dylan steps even closer to Jonah. "Do what she says," he tells Jonah, who shuffles backward to get away from my angry neighbor.

"To make up for changing the ending of your book," he says, the words tumbling out of his mouth. I stare at him, trying to process what I just heard. "Look, I'm sorry. I thought his death was too…easy. I wanted to kick it up a notch. And I meant to show you the revision but an intern sent it to the printer before I could run it past you. It was too late." My heart is pounding now but I am still silent. Jonah continues. "It was a bad idea, a mistake. I respected your decision to kill Andy, I just wanted it to be more dramatic. And now I feel partly responsible for what's happening. So this video would be a way to resuscitate your reputation."

"You think making a fake video of a fake rescue of a real Andy is going to make up for changing the ending of my book without my permission? Damn you, Jonah Carlstadt.

You're insane." If I could fire my own editor, I would do it on the spot.

But instead of remaining penitent, Jonah is belligerent. "Fine. You know what, never mind. Forget it. Clearly this is a bad idea. Come on Brook, let's go." Jonah waves a hand dismissively at the forest behind him. "Call me later," he tells me. "Have that ankle looked at," he says to Andy.

Brooklyn scrambles to gather the equipment she'd just set up, as her stepdad guns the engine.

"I'm coming, Jesus, Dad," Brooklyn calls out, shaking her head. "Sorry about everything," she says, facing me and Dylan, lips curving downward and I can't tell if it's genuine sympathy or an act. "He gets like this sometimes," she adds on a sigh, as she's getting in the car. The second she pulls her door shut, Jonah squeals out of my driveway and disappears down the road.

CHAPTER 19

SLOANE

I filled poor Dylan in on the entire situation since he inadvertently stumbled into it out of the kindness of his heart, which beats within his extremely muscular chest. He deserved to know the full story. I was correct in thinking he had no idea that I'm an author, nor had he ever heard of any of my books. Well, up until very recently at least. Seems that his girlfriend (when he said that word, my heart sank a little) was obsessed with my books. Devoured them eagerly, including All Things Must. She was so devastated by the death of Andy Creighton that she told Dylan she had to cancel their date because she was too upset to go out. He got all mad and told her that was ridiculous, it was only a fictional character – how could he be worth staying home and crying over when he was an actual boyfriend ready to take her out to dinner and bowling that night? She got mad and accused him of being illiterate and not caring about books, and he told her he only read Stephen King and Michael Connelly. She called them trashy commercial drivel, and he responded by calling what she was reading romantic garbage (hearing him recount this made me scoff and roll my eyes). A big fight ensued, names were called, threats were made, and at the end of the phone call he broke up with her (when he said that my heart sang a little – yes, I am ridiculous).

When he realized it was my book that caused Brittany to have a meltdown, he just stared at me and shook his head slowly, looking at me in a whole new and potentially unflattering light.

"Well now, Sloane Rylie, I don't know if I should be furious at you or get on my knees and thank you," he said.

"I guess that depends on whether you really liked her or not," I answered. The mental image of him on his knees in front of me is not altogether unpleasant, either, and my mind starts to go in a direction unbecoming of my present situation, so I quickly snap it back to reality.

"Yeah, so…" And then he actually got on his knees and thanked me. I grabbed his hand to pull him up and my skin tingled at the touch of his warm, slightly moist palm.

"You've probably caused hundreds of Andy-inspired breakups across the country," he laughed, and I nodded with a smirk, thinking while some books throughout history have inspired people to greatness, inspired entire revolutions or movements – mine's power is to inspire breakups.

That was ten minutes ago. Now we are standing next to Andy Creighton deciding what to do with him. He's now both injured and worried about the threatening note. He still wants me to do what the note says but I tell him we're beyond that point now, that this has escalated in strange and unusual ways, and that I am not inclined even to do what Cabinet Publishing wants me to do, no less give in to some lunatic. I am still fuming over Jonah's shenanigans. Even if he intended to show me the new ending, even if that's true, I'm still pissed at him for wanting to tamper with what I knew to be a perfect close to the book.

"I feel like you are not taking the threat to my life seriously," Andy says. I raise an eyebrow at him and shake my head.

"If you were so worried about the danger the note poses, why did you agree to pull a stupid stunt for a hundred bucks and almost get yourself killed in the process?"

At this point, Dylan nods and jumps in to my defense.

"Honestly, Andy, Sloane is right. That was dumb. And also, I don't think you have anything to worry about. Clearly the note-writer is just someone like my ex – a twenty-something-year-old suburban kindle girlie bawling her eyes out over the book's ending. This note-writer person took things a little too far, yeah. But I highly doubt that they have any intention of killing you. It's just a desperate attempt at trying to undo something they hate. It's probably someone you know, who lives near you and decided to take advantage of your name."

I can't take my eyes off Dylan. He's so much more than just a wood-chopping hunk of a neighbor. He's smart and sensible. And he gives me an idea.

"I am still so angry at Jonah." I turn to Andy. "Offering you money to pretend to get hurt and need me to save you! Like what the actual fuck? I have an idea. It's what Jonah should have been here to do, instead of what he actually did."

"If the idea is me going to urgent care, I'm down. Is there even an urgent care anywhere around here?"

"We're going to make our own little video," I say, temporarily ignoring his need for medical treatment. "Dylan, if you'd be so kind as to help that would be much appreciated," I say to my handsome neighbor.

"Anything for you, Sloane. Now that you've saved me from my girlfriend, I'm in your debt." He bows down in an exaggerated gesture, and I laugh, shaking my head. "Dork," I say. Then I turn my attention to Andy. "There actually is an urgent care about ten minutes from here, once you get back to Route 207. Just give me like five minutes. And we're going to need that note."

CHAPTER 20

MANDY

As I am putting the Sloane file back into the drawer, I hear a voice coming from the elevator bank. Shit, it sounds like Micah. I duck into the break room and hope he walks right past me. But then I tell myself that I shouldn't hide; that makes me look suspicious. I work here, and there's nothing wrong with me being in the office, even if it's Saturday. Micah's voice is getting louder. He's approaching and I can make out what he's saying pretty clearly. He sounds stressed.

"I understand that. Yes, I know how much three million dollars is." He pauses. "I'll make sure it does not happen. It won't see the light of day, and the deal can go through." He laughs dryly. I know that laugh, it's his nervous, scheming laugh. "Yeah, attorneys, let's call it that. But don't worry. I will make sure nothing happens. Honestly, I'd forgotten about it until your call." Another pause. He walks by and I catch a whiff of his cologne. "No leaks, we've had this under tight wraps the whole time. Nobody knows about it yet." He walks away, toward his office. I feel like I have to sneeze so I put my sleeve up to my nose to stop the tickle and prevent being discovered. "We can set up a meeting for as soon as you like, in person, to finish the deal. It will be…"

And his voice trails off as he enters his office and shuts the door. Whatever he's talking about sounds pretty high stakes. I used to be more important around here. I used to know when there was three million bucks at stake. Part of me wants to go in there after he hangs up and ask him what that was all about, and maybe that would have been okay if he'd seen me. But I stupidly hid and now I have to slink out of here. Luckily, Micah's door is still closed, so I can get out unseen.

I'm about to leave Cabinet when my phone buzzes from the depths of my purse. I fish it out and answer only after I am safely in the hallway and have pressed the elevator button, glancing over my shoulder to make sure Micah is not behind me. I look at my screen and see that the caller is none other than Cabinet author Stacy Von Slade. I haven't spoken to her in at least two years.

"Hey stranger, how are you?" I say, stepping into the elevator and pressing the Lobby button, breathing a sigh of relief to be out of the office, but with my mind filled with far more questions than when I'd entered.

"Well hello there, Mandy Jacobsen," she says in the honey-coated southern belle voice of hers. Stacy is all of twenty-eight, and blonde, with a perfect complexion and a generous bust. She'd broken into the bestseller list when she was barely out of college, causing half the publishing world to be jealous and the other half to clamor for blurbs and quotes from her for their authors. She was definitely a hot commodity when she broke out, an internet sensation and a talk show darling. I always wondered if her youth and beauty were the factors that sent her to stardom; if she'd been ten years older and less attractive would she have still caught on the way she did.

"Well hello there, Stacy Von Slade!" I say in my most chipper voice. "So nice to hear your voice."

"Yeah, same here sugar."

"How's it going? How's life been treating you? Good, bad, indifferent?" Small talk is not my strong suit, especially to people who are saccharine phonies.

"It's been pretty alright. And actually, I'm calling to see what you have in store for Ballroom Banter."

"I'm sorry what?" Ballroom Banter? What on earth is she talking about? That sounds like a new Netflix reality series that I will definitely be avoiding at all costs.

"My next book, the one I just finished now? Mandy seriously? I thought you were on top of this. Especially with what's going on with Sloane, and how it affected my book." The honest truth is, with her manuscript being so late, we'd all pretty much given up and thought we'd wait out the contractual period of non-delivery and then void her contract. It's been a joke around the office. But apparently, she was intending to avoid that and deliver just in the nick of time. I stifle a laugh because if she thinks anything she does will have any impact on the Sloane situation, she's deluding herself.

"You know the drill, once we have the draft manuscript is when I can begin formulating strategies for marketing the book. But first I have to see what I'm dealing with." If Ballroom Banter was her proposed name for the book, then that would be the first thing we'd need to fix. It was awful. Not being mean here but the truth is, her working book titles have always sucked. Delusional Deities? That was just plain awful as a title for her second book. We changed it to Sibling Rivalry and had a hit on our hands.

"You're dealing with a pending blockbuster book by one of the top-selling authors of the last ten years," she says through a smile I can picture, a fake sweet grin behind which lies resentment and impatience. "And didn't anyone fill you in?"

"Hopefully so," I tell the Southern belle wannabe, resisting the urge to match her accent with a fake one of my own. "Fill me in on what?"

"Oh, Mandy, such a kidder."

"I'm not kidding," I say.

"You have no idea?" she scoffs. When her question is met with my stunned silence, she continues. "Look, if you're around and have a few minutes, why not stop by my place? Better to talk in person. I'll make us tea."

Stacy Von Slade had moved to New York City about eight years ago and used the money from the generous advance on Sibling Rivalry to put a downpayment on a pre-war townhouse in the Village not far from where Taylor Swift lived. Contrary to her elite sounding name and the fake backstory she made us include in her bio, Stacy had not grown up in an eighteenth century manor house – she lived in a small suburban Atlanta house with three cats and her widowed aunt. I should have put my foot down and insisted we tell her humble true story but she demurred and told me she wanted the fairytale origin story that she's always dreamed about but never had. I want to say no to visiting her, but I don't because I'm intrigued. If there really is something I should know then better now than later. I have an increasingly sinking feeling that there is a lot going on at

Cabinet that I am not being looped into and it's starting to aggravate me. Stacy is an incurable gossip, so maybe she knows stuff – maybe I can get her to dish the tea, over a cup of tea.

Her place is a fifteen-minute subway ride from the Cabinet office, so it's easy enough. I practically grew up on the subway and hung out a lot in downtown clubs when I was a teenager. I get off at West 4th Street and smile. The Village has always been a magical place for me; all the boutiques and fun restaurants, plus the nineteenth century buildings scattered throughout. It's like being in a whole other place and not in the middle of the most populous city in the country.

When I get to her building, the doorman tips his cap. "Miss Stacy is expecting you," he says and lets me in. I bet she makes him call her Miss Stacy. I could see that. A very slow ride on an ancient elevator – the kind with the iron gates that have to be pulled open at each floor – gets me to her townhouse. Uncertain if I'm supposed to tip the elevator operator guy, I settle for a smile and a thank you. I use the elaborate brass lion's head doorknocker and a couple of seconds later, the door swings wide open and Stacy van Slade is smiling at me, surrounded by a rush of lilac scent that is her longtime perfume. She must buy that by the gallon at the rate she uses it. I'd forgotten just how blonde Stacy is, and how bright of a red she prefers her lipstick. She is beautiful, I'll give her that much. I just think she'd be more beautiful if she embraced a more natural look instead of getting herself photo-shoot ready every day.

"Stacy!" I say, leaning in for a cheek kiss but getting a full-on embrace that almost takes my breath away, she squeezes me so tightly.

"Mandy, my dear Mandy," she says breathlessly into my ear like we are lovers. It's a little disconcerting to be honest. Though she's a few years younger than me, she looks twenty-two and acts forty-two.

"This is an unexpected surprise," I say, disengaging from the hug and having a look around her place. I have only been here once before, and it was when she first moved to New York and threw a housewarming bash and invited the entire Cabinet staff along with anyone she knew in the tri-state region. The place has changed a lot since then – the walls are now taken up by framed reviews of her books, citations from her hometown in Georgia (they named her Honorary Mayor and designated her birthday as Stacy Von Slade Day), and a photo of her with Taylor Swift at some promotional event. Sadly, her place looks more like a shrine to the past than the present – by my estimation the most recent thing up there is from at least six years ago. Stacy von Slade is on the verge of becoming a has-been.

"Yes, well, since you don't know what's going on so I had no choice but to invite you over for a little talk. Can't trust Micah or Sterling can we?" Sterling is the owner of Cabinet Publishing's parent company, and I've never actually met him. Apparently Stacy has, though. She gestures to a large old armchair that is upholstered in a rich burgundy velvet. There are two of them, facing each other and separated by a mahogany coffee table upon which is a tastefully arranged spread of Stacy's books in different translations, next to a vase of peach roses that have opened just to their peak bloom. Sunlight streams in through the large double window facing the street and I can hear dogs barking outside and a couple talking about going to the movies. It looks more like a Museum of Stacy in here than her residence.

"So what's up, Stace?" I say. I've never called her that before but for some reason it comes out of my mouth that way, like we're old friends.

"Aw, Stace is what my dear old aunt used to call me." She flashes a smile that has to be fake. "Let me get the tea prepared first," she tells me, heading to the kitchen. "I mustn't be a rude host." She leaves me sitting there and a minute later calls out, "I have Earl Grey, green, oolong, and raspberry herbal…"

"Earl Grey is fine," I say. One particular picture frame catches my attention – it's the feature I got her in the syndicated magazine insert into hundreds of Sunday papers. She smiles broadly in the photo that I took of her standing in a fountain in an Atlanta park. I wrote the whole article myself and sent it to a few dozen media outlets before it was picked up by Parade. Sales of her first book took off after that, and boy was she ecstatic. Memories of that weekend come rushing back. Micah had told me to go fly down there and get some press on her because he felt she was the next big thing. I'd read her manuscript and had to agree. It needed some editorial work, sure, but it was good. So I went. Stacy greeted me at the airport with a kiss on both cheeks followed by one right on the lips. She straight up came on to me during our photo shoot while I was leaning in to turn her head slightly and she pounced. It was all I could do to peel her off me and get her to focus. She was drunk most of the time I was there, so who knows if she was actually attracted to me. And now here I was, alone with Stacy in her apartment. Well not completely alone; a fluffy orange tabby enters the room and approaches my chair, meowing and looking up at me.

Stacy enters with two matching pink mugs of tea and smiles at her cat. "I see you've met Aurora," she says.

"Borealis or Disney?" I ask.

"Neither, I just like the name." She places my tea cup on a coaster next to her book display on the coffee table. "Would you like some banana pudding? I made some yesterday. Secret family recipe."

"No thank you," I say. I can barely picture her making tea, let alone an entire dessert.

"Suit yourself," she says, going to the fridge and plopping two spoonfuls of pudding into a sherbet dish. She sets the dish down on a coaster. It does look good, but too late now.

"It's funny that it's called a coffee table. I think we should rename yours a tea table," I say. She doesn't drink coffee, I remember that now.

"Now weren't you always one with a quick wit?" She says it with a healthy dose of snark, with an undertone of flirtatiousness.

"If you say so," I reply ignoring her tone, taking a sip of tea and almost burning my tongue. "Jesus, that's hot."

"Usually is," she says with a wink, sitting down across from me and biting her lip coquettishly.

"How's Pete?" I ask. Pete was a society page favorite, her long-time casual boyfriend. They hooked up a few weeks after she moved to New York, having met in an art gallery that his father ran.

"I broke it off with him. I found out he had started seeing a Turkish model. Anyway." Pete's been seeing Ana for years, not sure how she only found out now. She averts my gaze so I change the subject.

"So, why did you want me to come by?" I ask, almost expecting something off-color to escape her lips.

"Because you need to know what's cooking over here," she says, leaning toward me. "And things are definitely cooking, boiling over practically, if we are being candid."

"Care to be more specific?"

She winks at me, gets up and walks over to the rolltop desk in the corner of the room. She unlocks it and pulls out a thick manuscript. She click clacks over to me in her heels and hands me the stack of paper. It looks to be about 500 pages double-spaced. A long book by any measure.

"You want me to read this now? I'm going to need more than a cup of tea to sustain me," I say dryly, looking up at her. Her mouth curves into a frown and she shakes her head.

"No, silly. Just go on over to page thirty-eight. Or is it thirty-nine? Anyway, go thereabouts and you'll see."

So I flip to page thirty-eight. Some character named Virginia is in her living room, half naked, when her doorbell rings. She pads over to the door barefoot and swings it open. I read the words in Stacy's southern accent, which is what I suspect most of her readers do, and it adds to the charm of her books. When she opens the door, a young man wearing aviators and sporting a thick, dark mustache is standing there with a broad smile and a bouquet of pink roses. "And who are you?" she asks. "I think you know me," he says in a low voice, pulling off the glasses and ripping the mustache from his face with a wince. "I'm Andy Creighton," he says.

My jaw drops and my eyes go wide. I look up at Stacy and she is smiling like a Cheshire cat.

"So, you really didn't know?" she asks. "You of all people?"

"Didn't know what? That you stole Sloane Rylie's character for your book?" It wouldn't surprise me if Stacy van Slade outright stole Andy Creighton. There was a minor kerfuffle with her third book when a fairly successful indie romance author named Gigi Michaels claimed that Stacy had all but stolen her female main character, made a few minor changes, and thus was born Cora Hartley. The Cabinet Publishing legal team made the threatened lawsuit disappear but I read the Gigi Michaels book and felt like there was a decent chance Stacy had pilfered the character.

"Stole?" she gasps. "What on earth? No! I did not steal a thing. I was given this gift and I intend to live up to the legend, the heritage that was gifted to me."

I wonder what exactly is in the tea she's served us, because it's making her delusional. I flip through the rest of the book, and Andy is on every page – dialogue, exposition, sex scenes. He's the focal point of the book. I look up at Stacy and raise a brow.

"I'm sorry, I don't understand." Let her try to explain this. I'll listen, so long as it's not complete fantasy, which I suspect it is.

She leans over and takes back her manuscript, hugs it close to her chest, and says, "Micah told me to write this book and write it fast."

"He what?" I say, blinking.

"You heard me. A few months ago, he emailed me and told me to scrap whatever I was working on and change it to introduce Andy Creighton somehow and make him the main male character. I mean I kind of had a framework so it wasn't like writing a whole new book, I just had to take out Travis and substitute in Andy. And be a tad creative, which as you know I'm good at. So it was not like writing a whole new book, just half of a new book." She laughs and looks down at the stack of papers she is clutching.

I turn this over in my head. So Micah, reading Sloane's manuscript a few months back, decided to go behind her back and have her competitor resurrect her most popular character and take him for her own? It seems unthinkable, unadvisable, and just plain stupid.

"And you were okay with this? I thought you didn't like Sloane's books much."

"Why would you say that?" she says, raising an eyebrow.

"Because of the article in Books Monthly? Where you literally said, 'Sloane Rylie is not very talented, her books are way overrated and lack depth or sophistication.'" I have that quote memorized because it got me in a lot of trouble with Micah and Jonah. They were both like, "How did this story get published, all publicity is to go through you first." When I tried to talk to Stacy about it she told me a little controversy was great for sales – of both Sloane's and her own books. "There's no such thing as bad press," she told me at the time. My reply was, "There sure as hell is."

"Aw shucks honey, that was nothing. Just me running my mouth and getting a little attention for my fellow Cabinet author, I wish someone would talk trash about me, it might help my sales." She laughs bitterly and flashes a smile. I have wondered how much she spent to get her teeth whitened because they are an unnaturally brilliant titanium white. It's actually a little disconcerting. "But no, I don't love her. But I do love the success she's had with this book series, if we're being totally honest."

"Can I see that email from Micah?" I ask.

"Say what now?" Stacy tilts her head and narrows her eyes.

"The email. Where Micah tells you to change your book."

"Why would you want to see that? You think I'm lying?" I honestly don't know what to think at this point.

"No!" I protest, the wheels in my head turning quickly. "I want to see if maybe he tried to cc me and typed in the wrong address by mistake. That would explain why I don't know anything about this." I can feel the sweat forming on my brow.

"Oh," she says. "Pretty sure it was just me on there. But I'll look." She pulls her phone from her pocket. It's got a pale green case dotted with dozens of flamingoes of all sizes and at all angles. It's very Stacy. "Just give me a sec. I get so many emails, you know!"

So do I, Stacy, and most of them are junk. I watch as she scrolls on her phone, eyes scanning the messages until she finds the right one. I almost tell her she can just type Micah's name into the search bar, but leave her instead to her archaic scrolling method.

"Ah bingo!" she says, handing me the phone. I note the date of the message, and it is three months and a week ago. I read:

From: Micah Curran
Subject: Change of plans
Hey Stacy,

I got your note that you are running late in delivering your next book, which is actually great. Because I have a special secret assignment for you. Sloane's planning to kill off Andy Creighton in her new book, and I want you to change your book to introduce him as your main male character. You will need to deliver the book within two weeks of Sloane's book pub date. We are going to be putting your book on fast track to get it on the shelves within four months – with a huge publicity campaign to make sure we get as many of Sloane's Andy fans to buy your book. It's going to be a big success. But listen – this is super top secret. Don't call me or mention this to anyone. Not what Sloane is doing and not what you're working on. Only call my cell when you have the book ready to deliver. I won't pick up so don't leave a message or anything, I'll call you back when I have privacy. Please reply to this message to confirm you're on board, and then get working!

Yours,
Micah

When I check the email address from which the message was sent, I see that it appears to be Micah's personal email. Not his work one. And no, there is nobody cc-ed on this email. My first instinct is to call Micah right away and demand an explanation, but I suppress the urge. I need to ask Stacy a few more questions.

"What did you reply to him?" I ask.

"Doesn't take a genius to figure out I said yes, yes, by all means yes. I didn't like the idea of it but I liked the potential end result. That I would be the heir to the Andy Creighton empire and carry on instead of Sloane."

"So you're pretty much done with the book? When were you planning to deliver it to Cabinet?"

"Funny you should ask that. I was about to call Micah since I am ready to deliver. What I just showed you is my final draft!"

"This is really quite a shock to me…" I don't manage to say more than that. How does this fit in with the dream sequence and plans for Sloane to resurrect Andy?

"Well he did say it's a complete secret, right? Don't be offended. Publishers can be weird. Anyway, it's going to be huge, Mandy, I just know it. The public is so ready for Andy's resurrection. He's been dead less than a week and they are clamoring for it." That they are, just not in the way that Micah proposed Stacy handle it. I stand up now, having finished my cup of tea and getting anxious to leave and find some answers. "Going so soon?" Stacy asks. "Another cup of tea first, sugar?" She exudes Southern charm, albeit it comes across a little overwhelmingly sweet, like fake maple syrup.

"I'd better be going. I apparently have an entire campaign to plan out!" I say cheerily. Sloane will blow a gasket when she finds out what Micah did. Though I don't understand how the dream sequence contest plan can co-exist with this secret Stacy Von Slade book. They can't both exist, can they? The dream sequence is probably a better idea than having some other writer take over the character and bring him back to life, like in a long-running television show when a lead actor suddenly leaves and is replaced with some other guy; it's just weird. Like the two Darrens on Bewitched. Andy Creighton may live again in Stacy's book but he'll be like some weird cut-rate Southern version of the original. And readers who've spent three thousand pages with Andy will know the difference and reject Stacy's version. I can already predict this. Stacy's book will not only fail, it will produce some major backlash for both her and Sloane.

Andy Creighton is better off dead than as a Stacy Von Slade character.

CHAPTER 21

SLOANE

The real Andy Creighton is a complicated man.

I've learned this over the course of the two plus hours we've spent together, not counting the time he was "missing" in the woods. He stalked me and showed up at my cabin because he was terrified of a threatening note he received – yet just minutes later he accepted a bribe from my publisher to fake an injury just so I could rescue him and make a feel-good video for publicity purposes. That was apparently fine and dandy. But when I present him with my latest idea, having reached my breaking point with all the shenanigans pertaining to my goddamn book, he is hesitant, reluctant, shy, and stubbornly insisting it's a bad idea. I don't get him. I need to try again and make him see it my way, the right way. He stumbled into my lap and instead of being a curse I am going to turn him into a blessing.

"Look Andy, this is exactly what we both want, for this nonsense to stop. Everyone out there needs a good scolding! They need to hear it from me, and from you. Like a misbehaving toddler, if we play into the mass tantrum, we encourage it and feed the flames. Then the toddler cries and throws his juice box against the wall. That's what everyone on my publishing team seems to be doing, encouraging all the toddlers out there to throw shit. And it has to stop. You have a chance to make that happen, Andy. Yeah it will take a little bravery, what my grandma called chutzpah, but so be it. We have to take this into our own hands and stop the madness." I am pleased with my little speech and study Andy's face for signs that it worked. He is expressionless for a few moments before the corner of his mouth quirks down in defeat. He looks like he'd rather be anywhere but here. At least he got to keep the hundred from Jonah.

"But your publisher already filmed you giving the little speech they wanted, didn't they?"

"They did, and that's why I want to make my own, and get it out there first, before they post theirs. In fact, once I post this, they may not post that one." Which would be great, by my estimation. I want to control the narrative here.

Andy thinks for a good long time. He stares high up into the treetops for answers, listening to a couple of bluejays squawking at each other. Then, finally, he looks at me again and speaks. "Okay. I guess. You'd better be right though. I don't want trouble. And it had better be quick, my ankle is seriously killing me!" I feel bad, having scolded Jonah and Brooklyn for trying to make a video when Andy over here can barely walk, and here I am asking him to do the same thing. But my reason is more logical.

"Driving here just to track me down is already trouble," I remind him.

"I meant more trouble. Worse trouble." He looks down at his sneakers and licks his lips, then looks back up to meet my eyes. He thinks someone really is going to kill him.

I do feel badly since Andy did nothing wrong other than be born with a name I happened to choose for one of the most popular romance novel characters ever created. With that comes some unfortunate side effects. It makes me wonder about other popular character names in fiction. Surely there have been real-life Holden Caulfields? Harry Potters? Jessica Fletchers? Then there's the reverse effect, which happened one notable time with the 1980s television show Greatest American Hero. The main character in that show was a teacher turned superhero named Ralph Hinckley – which happened to be the last name of the man who attempted to assassinate President Reagan. After that unfortunate incident, the show's producers changed the character's name to Ralph Hanley.

"Trouble only comes when we lay down and let everyone walk all over us." Not me dragging Andy further into this than he already is. I really should use "me" not "we" but I want to make him feel invested in this mess, invested enough to make the video with me.

"All I did was wake up this morning. I was born with this name. I didn't ask for any of this," he says as if reading my mind, and that only makes me feel worse.

"I'll make it up to you when this is all fixed," I say. On second thought, if I offer this Andy some restitution and word gets out, I may be obligated to offer something to every Andy Creighton in the world, they may start coming out of the woodwork claiming to have been bullied or received threatening copycat notes. But come to think of it, none of them were complaining before I killed him off. A few years ago one of the mid-sized Chicago papers did a study and found that the name "Andy" surged in popularity starting the year after the first book in the series was released. Not Andrew, Andy specifically.

Dylan, insisting on being both hot and helpful, has agreed to stay and film the video for me. There was a Dylan in Book Two of my Andy Creighton series, but he was just a minor character. If I was writing that book now I'd have given him a much bigger role. The more time I spend with him, the more I like him. Is he too young for me? Yeah, probably, but it doesn't matter because he would never in a million years go for me. I take Andy by the arm and prop him up against a tree so he doesn't have to put his full weight on his bad foot. I hand Dylan my phone and tell him to record a video on my signal. And this one I won't need to practice because I know exactly what I want to say.

CHAPTER 22

MANDY

I'm stopped at a red light on my way home from the train station parking lot, sipping the iced latte I'd picked up at the deli near the train when I see an Instagram notification pop up as I glance over at my phone. It disappears before I can see what exactly it is, so I quickly open Instagram before the light turns green. It's a bad habit, definitely. I should not be playing with my phone in the car. But I am addicted to my feed, keeping track of what other authors are posting, what our competitor publishers are up to. When I open it this time, though, I nearly drop my phone. A car horn behind me honks several times and I have to drive. I look for a place to pull over and watch the rest of the reel that Sloane seems to have posted a few minutes ago. We've had an agreement for years now that anything going on her Instagram or TikTok pages gets run by me first. Should I really be surprised, though? It seems lately everyone is circumventing me and doing whatever they want.

I drive a little further and pull over next to a fire hydrant. I start the reel again from the beginning. It's Sloane on camera and it looks like she's up at her cabin because she's standing in front of a bunch of trees. She is frazzled and breathless. This was definitely an unplanned video. I turn up the volume as she starts to talk.

"Hey all you Andy Creighton fans! It's Sloane Rylie and I'm here to thank you for reading my books, especially my latest and greatest one. But also, I'm here to introduce an actual Andy Creighton. Andy?" And into the frame steps a tall guy in his late thirties with a square face and short brown hair. "Hi everyone, I'm Andy Creighton and I live in New York State," the guy says flatly. "I'm one of a bunch of real-life Andy Creightons in the world. This morning, I received this note in my mailbox." He unfolds up a letter-sized piece of paper, holds it up, and reads from it, blocking his face in the process. The upshot is this: Sloane Rylie has three days to write a new ending to her book, an ending in which the fictional Andy Creighton lives. She has three days to put this new ending into the kindle version of the book. If it is not changed by Tuesday, then real Andy Creightons are going to die. Starting with him. Andy steps aside and Sloane is in the full frame again. Her nostrils are flaring and her cheeks are red as she starts to talk. "This is not cool, folks. This and other things that have been happening are repulsive, unfair, and criminal. I will not stand for threats or coercion. Nobody is going to bully or threaten me into doing anything. Behave yourselves, everyone, and be patient or the treat I was planning won't be happening after all. Anyone who sends threatening notes or trespasses or harms anyone in any way will be prosecuted to the full extent of the law. So, behave yourselves and be patient! Love you guys!" And the reel ends. I shake my head in disbelief. How could she just post something like this without showing me first? What is my purpose here? Why do I even exist? I should gather up all my business cards and burn them. I look below the post. It went live seven minutes ago and already has 3,000 likes and 180 comments, pretty impressive by any standard. I scroll through the comments and see that they're about evenly split – half supporting Sloane and her reel, and the other half either fuming about Andy or fuming over the scolding tone in the video.

I try calling Sloane, but it goes to voicemail. She must still be at the cabin, and only had a signal long enough to post the reel. I know how it is over there, you have to stand in a certain spot on one leg with your arm over your head to get service. So she's probably out of range at the moment. I wish she'd find a service window and message me what's going on. If I'd have known there was an actual Andy Creighton at her doorstep, I could have put him to better use than she did. We could have really taken advantage of his existence.

No sooner do I finish the video than my phone starts buzzing. It's Micah. I put the car into drive, get back on the road, and answer the call. I've got some questions for Micah, and I was going to wait on them, but since he's calling me, I'll ask now.

"Mandy!" his voice booms from my car speaker. "Jesus, what the hell is going on with Sloane? I assume you were not behind the post, you saw her post right?" All of us at Cabinet have our notifications set up so that when any of our authors posts on any of the socials, we get an alert.

"I saw it yeah. I'm guessing she's pissed as hell, that's what's going on." I guess I can't blame her. I think I was a little too flip about the whole thing at first. This has spun way out of control – from angry social media comments to book burning to threats of violence? Sloane is right, it has to stop.

"We've got to rein her in. This could be dangerous." Micah sounds worried, but I have a feeling he's more concerned about the company's bottom line than he is about anyone's safety. He thinks Sloane's reel is dangerous, and not what her "fans" are perpetrating? I almost laugh thinking he's probably still in his office, where I was just an hour ago, unbeknownst to him. In his office staring at the photo on his wall of him meeting Stephen King, one of his literary idols. It would have been his dream to sign King to a book deal, but he'd never get King away from Scribner. We have some good authors, but we don't have any of the greats. And that always bugged Micah. Maybe that's why he's so twisted over Andy Creighton; he was the closest we had to a legend and now he's dead.

"I hear you, Micah, but just how do you propose we do that? She's a grown ass woman."

"With an accent on the ass part right now. We have a plan and she's threatening to pull it. She's threatening to breach her contract." Micah is probably fumbling in his desk drawer for a cigarette right about now. I can almost hear him climbing onto his desk to reach the fire alarm and remove the battery while he lights up. "If she breaches hers and does not deliver, then your book deal is off."

"Before we panic, let's think about this. Maybe what she did is good after all. Shakes things up a bit. She needed to get that frustration and anger out of her system, and now she can focus on our plan and it'll all be okay." My first Cabinet book, the one I reluctantly agreed to but am now excited about? What could be the start of a whole new career path for me? I grip the steering wheel so tightly I leave an imprint of the fake leather on both my palms.

Micah scoffs and then coughs as he always does after the first pull on a Marlboro. Those things are going to kill him one day. "This is of her own making, Mandy. Let's not forget that. She killed Andy Creighton."

I honk my horn at an asshole who cuts me off for no reason. "She killed a fictional man and now a real man's life is being threatened. It's a little different. Look, let me talk to her. She's probably at the cabin now and service is patchy. But I can be there in less than an hour and talk her off the ledge she's on."

"Fine. If you think you can. Impress upon her the fact that we have Dez Maxwell flying in tomorrow and we have a whole series of steps planned to deal with this Andy situation and make it go away."

"Tomorrow?" I repeat. "I thought it was Monday."

"She's coming sooner. We want this to happen now, Mandy. And it can't if Sloane backs out. A lot of things will be affected if she backs out. Lives are at risk." A pause is followed by a slight chuckle. "I meant livelihoods. But still."

I signal left and turn down my street. I'll stop home for a few before I go find Sloane. I park, shut off the engine, and the call transfers to my phone. "Leave it to me," I say, getting out of the car. "Leave it to..." and I stop mid-sentence, the phone falling out of my hand and into a hydrangea bush as I see my front door. Someone has spray painted in scrawly, messy red letters: "Bring Back Andy Or Else."

"I'll update you later," I say and hang up before I can get to my questions, rushing up the walkway to my house. The paint smells fresh; and it would have to be since it wasn't there a few hours ago when I went into the city. I fumble for my key and hurry to open the door. I'm startled to find that my television is on; I'm sure I didn't even have it on at all today. Then a familiar voice greets me from my living room.

"Hey babe!" It's Patrick. Shit. I forgot that I told him to come over at four and we'd hang a little and then go out to dinner. He has his own key so he must have let himself in when I didn't answer.

"I am so sorry. I said four didn't I?" I glance at my watch. It's 4:20.

"It's fine. I figured you'd be back soon enough."

"Why didn't you text me?" I ask, trying to decide if I should call the police.

"I did," he says with a shrug. I pick up my phone and see that he in fact did text me. Twice. Oops. I've been a little preoccupied. And I still haven't told him about my book deal, which is now in jeopardy already, just as well that I didn't mention it. And now there's something more pressing.

"I'm so sorry. How long have you been waiting here?" I must have walked right past his car like a dumbass and not even realized it. This is what happens when I'm preoccupied, I zone out and notice nothing. That's why my mom always insisted on driving me to school the day of an exam – she knew my brain was so busy going over test materials I was liable to get hit by a bus or something.

"Oh, I guess about a half an hour." Patrick is habitually early, and that's one reason I gave him a key to my place even though we haven't been going out that long.

"Did you see or hear anything or anyone strange when you got here, or after you were inside?"

"Besides you?" he says sticking his tongue out and laughing.

I take his hand and pull him up off the couch. "I'm being serious. Come with me," I say, leading him outside.

"Whoa, shit," he says when he sees my door. "I definitely did not hear any weird noises."

"Then again, you had the television blasting," I say, shaking my head.

"Had to occupy myself while you were MIA," he says with a shrug. If it was meant as a dig, it hurt. "I told you that you need a security camera." Patrick bends over and looks at the ground next to my shrubs.

"What are you doing?" I ask. "Playing detective?"

"Looking for clues. Hey, maybe we could see if your neighbor across the street will let us review their camera footage." He points.

"She hates me, so I doubt it. But nice try."

"Should we call the cops?" he asks.

"I mean maybe, but it's probably just another angry fan. There seem to be an endless supply of them," I reply. Patrick puts a finger to my door.

"The paint is still fresh. It should come off with soap and water." He goes inside and fetches some supplies and ten minutes later, after I take a couple of pictures for the record, we have the door mostly cleaned off. For a second, a very brief second, I wonder if Patrick himself might have done this. But why? He'd have no logical reason to. He does like to play practical jokes, but this would be going way too far, plus he had to help me get the paint off. This is the kind of thing I'd expect to happen to Sloane's front door, not mine, though. I am well known enough within the circle of her fans, since I post a lot of stuff myself. But nobody knows where I live. Correction – most people don't, but apparently one person does.

CHAPTER 23

SLOANE

I've given Andy directions to urgent care and sent him on his way with my thanks. He gives me his number so we can stay in touch. He was a little skittish about going home, asked me again what my plans are regarding the book and his namesake. I told him it would all be taken care of soon enough. I lied a little, but that's okay. Sometimes the price of reassurance is a lie. The truth is, I haven't decided what to do. I hate being harassed, but I also hate giving in to bullies – even if those bullies happen to be some of my biggest fans and my own publishing team. As I walk back to my cabin, I get a few seconds of service and see that I have three missed calls from Micah, one from Jonah, four from Mandy, and one from my mom. I guess they've all seen my video. I stand there in the spot beside the two young maple trees where a few minutes ago I had a signal long enough to post the reel, debating what to do. I'm kind of sad that Dylan went back home once Andy left. My delusions of him asking to stay were just that – fantasies. Now I'm alone again, which is what I originally wanted when I arrived here, but so much has changed in the…how long has it even been? I shake my head and almost laugh out loud. It's quiet except for the cicadas and in the distance a chainsaw is cutting down a tree, probably one damaged in a recent storm.

I decide to make one call – to Mandy. My mom and the others can wait. I doubt my mom even saw my video. She does have an Instagram account, but she has no profile picture, only three followers, and zero posts. I hold up my phone and my bars disappear. Shit. I take a step backwards and they return. I quickly call Mandy before a leaf falls and disrupts the signal.

"Oh my God, Sloane, I've been trying to get you," she says.

"I'm aware," I say. "I take it you saw the video."

"Dude, are you high? You can't be posting shit like that without running it by me first." Yeah, she's definitely annoyed. I figured she would be. I'm about to speak but she has more to say. "But that's kind of the least of it, there's more. Some weird shit is going on. We need to talk in person, soon."

I look up at the little patch of blue sky where the trees allow it to peek through. I could really use a nap, and if I set up the hammock behind my cabin, that would be so delightful. Even just for an hour. I deserve it. And I need to recharge my mental battery and figure out what to do.

"What do you mean weird shit? Isn't all this already weird enough?" She can't see me gesture at the spot where Andy's car had been.

"You can't trust anyone, Sloane," she says. "There's developments with m…need…talk and you're breaking up…can't really hear…"

"Yeah, okay, I guess," I tell her, wondering what she means about trusting anyone. "I'm going to hang out here a little while more, maybe this evening we can catch up." I pause, waiting for her reply, then I glance at my screen. The call has dropped, and no matter how I position the phone or how many steps I take in any direction, I can't get the signal back. Hopefully she heard that last part at least. I go inside the stuffy cabin and inhale. Though the air is stagnant, this smell reminds me of dad. I miss him a lot. I look at the deer head on the wall and know I could never take it down. I want to keep this place looking like it did back then. I go under my bed and dig out the box with the hammock in it, then remember how long it took me to set it up the last time.

I stand there holding it, feeling the panic of indecision start to set in, and in that moment I decide to set up the hammock after all. The thought of returning to my house yet was unappealing. I deserve to get at least a little of what I came here for – relaxation and tranquility – and there's not really a good place to relax outside other than this. The setup is not as hard as I remembered and within five minutes I am climbing into the hammock (nearly falling right out of it the first two tries until I succeed on the third) and staring up at the birds flitting around the treetops. Though I don't want to sleep, it's too easy to close my eyes and just relax. Life has been exhausting lately.

CHAPTER 24

MANDY

I try to tell Sloane I am on my way to her cabin, but the call drops before I finish my sentence. Now I don't know what to do. Maybe she's already on her way back home. I do need to talk to her in person, but I'd rather not waste a trip to her cabin if she's not going to be there. Besides, Patrick is here. At least Sloane called me, even if briefly. I've left Patrick inside to finish watching the last ten minutes of the episode of the classic car restoration reality show he'd started while waiting for me, and now I'm standing in front of my house trying to figure out my next move. I have to trim the hydrangea, I note, they're getting out of control.

A pale green Beetle races around the corner and pulls up across the street from my house, blocking my neighbor's driveway, and in my peripheral vision I see the driver's side door open. I am still looking at my flowers and wondering if you're even supposed to trim hydrangeas. Roses, I know you are, but something tells me it might be a bad idea to cut these plants. They were pretty expensive, to be honest.

"You!" a female voice yells from across the street. I look up to see Stacy Von Slade marching toward me, fists clenched and eyes narrowed, I must have missed something because I left her on quite good terms just a couple of hours ago.

"Stacy, hi, nice to see you again. Dropping off some banana pudding?" I say, hoping she will break out laughing and give me a hug. She did tell me she was going to pack a container for me to take and then forgot. I didn't want any in the moment but now I'm kind of craving it. Instead of bearing a container of dessert, she's bearing a scowl as she click-clacks right up to me in her high heels. I forgot that Stacy keeps her car in a garage, pays the 500 a month just so she can have a vehicle in Manhattan. I tried long ago to no avail, to convince her of the benefits of using mass transit. Or even Uber.

"What did you say to Micah?" she demands.

"I'm sorry?" I did talk to Micah. How does she know about that? And what does it have to do with her? I did not mention her name once.

"You talked to Micah. Made him change his mind. You fucking traitor!" She stomps her feet like a toddler.

"Uh what? I'm not following." My neighbor emerges from his house and yells at Stacy to move her car. "I'm not staying long so just chill out!" she yells at him and he grumbles something and goes back inside, slamming his door.

"Micah called me not long after you left," Stacy says. "Like ten minutes later. And he cancelled my book. Just fucking completely cancelled it! Said something about a clause in the contract that gave him that right. And it was for important reasons, but he had to pull the plug because Cabinet's plans changed. They don't need my Andy book after all. And it was you who caused it." She spits the words (and some saliva) out at me in a Southern-accented torrent. The carefully constructed image she's worked so hard to maintain has shattered before my eyes. She looks old and bitter. Washed up, actually, which (not to be mean, but) is kind of what she is. Her makeup is smudged from crying and her hair looks like she'd been riding with the window open. I can see the dark roots that I'm sure she tries hard to hide between hairdresser visits.

"Why on earth would I mention your book to Micah?" I ask knowing full well that I was about to ask when I hung up because of the spray painted message on my door. I am the head of publicity at Cabinet, I should have ripped Micah a new one for making a secret book deal behind my back. But I am being honest with Stacy, I didn't say a word about her book.

"It had to be you! Who the hell else?" I can almost see the steam coming from her ears. Her typical southern composure is gone.

"Listen, I am sorry about your book. Publishing is an odd business. As I told you, I knew nothing about your revised book to begin with, and I am still processing all of what you said and showed me in your apartment." I gesture at the car. "How did you make it here so fast, wasn't there traffic?"

"I drive like a maniac when I'm mad! And don't change the subject."

"Look, Stace, this sounds like a further conversation you need to have with Micah. Or with your lawyer. Leave me out of it." The things I'm supposed to be involved it, I'm not. And stuff I want nothing to do with I am somehow dragged into. It's been a highly annoying day.

"Don't Stace me. It's you who pulled the rug out from under me." She pauses, studying my eyes, then lifts her chin and smiles smugly, nodding slowly. "Hmmm, or maybe it was Sloane. Maybe you spilled the beans to her, and she complained to Micah. Yeah, I could see that happening. She was always your favorite Cabinet author. Maybe you two teamed up to screw me over. A couple of sneaky bitches!"

"Let's try to calm down, Stacy," I say, watching her nostrils flare uncontrollably. "What were Micah's exact words?"

"I already told you. What I said a minute ago, those were his words."

I debate how much to tell her about Sloane and Cabinet's plans to defuse the Andy Creighton situation. I hesitate but then realize two things – this would be great material for my book, and second, if Cabinet is keeping secrets from me, then my loyalty in keeping secrets is going to be compromised.

"Look, I'm not supposed to say anything," I start, lowering my voice, "But I can tell you that the backlash from the Andy Creighton death has made them rethink their plans for her book." I am careful to say them instead of us. She's already mad at me and I don't want to add any more fuel to the fire.

She stares at me for a moment, then spins around as if to make her way back to her car, then turns suddenly and slaps me across the face.

"I hold you responsible!" she seethes. "You and Sloane both! I don't care what you say, you did this. You killed what was going to be the best book of my career." The anger morphs into tears and she starts sobbing uncontrollably. I don't know whether to step away or pull her in for a hug; she solves this question for me by laying her head on my shoulder and whimpering an apology.

"It's fine," I say even though it isn't fine at all. How am I supposed to ever work with her again after she smacked me hard enough to leave a mark – I can feel the sting of the assault burning my cheek. She must have slapped plenty of people in her life, I can't help but think.

"If you really didn't say anything to Micah, I need you to now. I need you to go run interference and find out why he cancelled my book."

"I told you why, he is trying to squash the terrible backlash that's been happening."

She takes a step back and wipes her eyes on her sleeve. "And my book would have solved that. Andy would have had a brand new life." I want to tell her that it wouldn't be the same, but then again, nothing we do with Sloane will be the same either. In a way, Stacy is right; giving Andy new life in a new book series by a different author would be a cleaner way to go. And Stacy is still a well-known name even if her last few books didn't sell.

"Look, I'll call Micah right now if that will make you happy. See if he'll talk to me. I'll take the angle of why didn't I know about this?"

She sniffs and nods, takes a handkerchief from her purse and blows loudly into it. When she's done, I hit Micah's name on my speed dial and wait as it rings.

"Mandy," he says. "Hello."

"Have a few?" I ask.

"I am in the office now and will be for another two hours, then I have…book business to take care of. Maybe after, I can call you, later on." Something about the way he says that seems odd. Book business to do out of the office? Micah is usually very blunt and descriptive. He's an over sharer who will take ten minutes to explain how he marinated his pork chops if you ask him what he had for dinner. Makes me wonder if it has something to do with that phone call I overheard.

"Okay talk to you later then," I say and disconnect the call.

"He'll call me back later," I say to Stacy. "Go home and pour yourself a drink, it'll be okay," I tell her, not even caring that I am encouraging a habit that led her to check herself into rehab for three weeks a few years back. She nods and apologizes again, touches my cheek where she'd slapped me and says sorry again, then heads back to her Beetle. And throughout this whole confrontation, Patrick has remained inside glued to the television. Apparently he didn't hear someone shouting right outside the front door. Or heard it and didn't care. Men.

I hate to have to break our date, but I am going back into the city. I am going to spy on Micah and find out what this "book business" is that he needs to do, because I suspect it has something to do with Sloane Rylie and Andy Creighton.

CHAPTER 25

SLOANE

I must have passed right out in the hammock. Something about the way it cradles the contours of my body is just so relaxing and womb-like. But instead of just being able to wake up on my own, I am startled out of a lazy summer slumber by the repeated woop woop of a police siren. My eyes pop open and I am completely disoriented as I struggle to get myself up and out of the hammock. Where am I again? What day is this? I hear a car door slam and a few footsteps. A gruff voice says, "Easy there, don't fall."

When I manage to finally get up and orient myself, I see a black sedan with a single flashing light on the dash. A stocky, tan guy probably in his early forties, wearing black pants and a plain black tee that reveals his bulging biceps flashes a badge at me. From what I can see through my half-asleep eyes, he's not bad looking.

"Rylie Sloane, I presume?" he says.

"Sloane Rylie, actually," I say, my mouth dry and my voice hoarse.

"Oh, Jesus, how did I do that?" He shakes his head with a smirk, seemingly amused at his mistake. "I'm Detective Lenovo of the Pleasantville Police Department."

We shake hands. "Nice to meet you. Can I assist you with something?" Pleasantville is the closest town to my cabin.

"Hopefully. Scarsdale PD had a report of a threatening note come through their tips line, they visited your house and your neighbor said you were here. So they called us since this area falls under our jurisdiction. We watched your video, and decided to come talk to you. You record it here?" He looks around and gestures broadly. My damn neighbor needs to stop telling everyone where I am. She's probably annoyed at me over Andy Creighton, too.

"Yeah. Right over there between those trees."

"Hmm," he says, studying the backdrop I've pointed out. "Can I see the note please?" he asks, putting out a hand.

"Oh, I don't have it, sorry. Andy has it."

"Well, I would definitely like to talk to Andy." He folds his arms and stares at my cabin.

"Oh, no, he's not here. He left."

The detective flashes a fake smile and says, "Can we talk inside?"

"It's not air conditioned," I warn.

"I don't care about that, I'd just rather sit down. My back's been killing me."

I lead him inside, and it feels even warmer and stuffier than before. We sit on the only two chairs in the living room; they're made of wicker and they crackle with the brittle nature of their age when we put our weight on them. The detective is no lightweight so I pray the chair stays intact while he's sitting. Having him fall through the seat would be embarrassing.

"Rustic in here," he notes. It's not a compliment.

"Yeah, it dates to the thirties." And it's showing its age.

He looks around, eyes taking in what little there is to see in the cabin. His gaze lands on the deer on the wall and he nods. "Hunter?"

"My dad," I say. The condition of the deer head does not indicate that it was shot anytime recently, so perhaps the detective is just making conversation.

"You have a gun here?" he asks.

"No," I lie but I'm not sure why I do. I guess it's because it was not my gun, so I still don't see it as me having a gun here. It's my dad's; I didn't put it here. It came with the place. And I have no idea if it actually even still works.

"Tell me more about this Andy Creighton in your video." He's suddenly taken out a small notepad and a pen and starts jotting something down in script.

"There's not much to tell. He lives about 40 minutes from here. He got the note in his mailbox earlier today. Through the postal service. But other than that I don't really know anything else about him."

The detective nods and jots more notes down. "Did he show you the envelope?"

"No, he didn't." Which is odd, since that would have maybe had some clues on it.

"I see. So you'd never met this Andy character before today?" He shifts in his chair and it crackles and creaks. I wince and hope it holds.

"Correct." I'm so thirsty now and want a drink of my Vitamin Water but I don't want to act suspicious.

"Interesting." He pauses, tapping the top of the pen on his upper lip. He looks me up and down and I feel a little violated. "So Ms. Rylie, are you heavily involved in promoting your books?"

"I mean, as much as any popular author, I guess."

"Are you willing to do whatever it takes to sell copies?" He makes another note and circles and underlines it.

"What are you implying?" I ask.

He smiles broadly and leans forward. "Planting fake death threats is a crime," he says in a low voice. "You realize that, don't you Ms. Rylie?" It takes a second for my brain to process his words. Did he just accuse me of sending Andy Creighton that note as a publicity stunt to sell more books? I mean, publicity stunts to sell books are not unheard of, but not the kind that cross the lines of criminal behavior.

I stand up, place my hands on my hips and tilt my head. "Detective, I cannot believe what I just heard. Why would you even propose such a thing?"

"It's just a question. Easy does it, Ms. Rylie. If the answer is no, then it's no. It would help if that Andy guy was here for me to talk to. But he's conveniently gone." I dislike the detective's tone but I have to be careful how I answer. He cranes his neck as if Andy might be hiding in the bedroom. I note that my overnight bag is within arm's reach of the detective. I don't want him getting his hands on my underwear or anything else, but to get up and randomly move it would seem suspicious.

"He doesn't belong to me, Detective. He's not my responsibility. He was inconveniently here, so yes I am glad he left. I had no reason to ask him to stay." I don't want to mention he wound up going to urgent care. Getting into that whole story of Andy hurting himself while pretending to be hurt is a very bad idea. I would definitely seem shady and make me look worse than I already do in his eyes. "Look, I have his number. I can text him and have him talk to you. He wanted to call the police when he got the note. I persuaded him against it."

"Oh, did you now? That was the wrong decision." He stands now, too, and licks his lips. "Warm in here." He fans himself with a hand and then slicks back his hair, a few strands of which have fallen into his face.

"Like I warned you," I say. It seems worse with him in here. One person's body heat and exhalation is plenty; two makes it unbearable. Unless it was Dylan in here with me, I'd bear that just fine.

"You never did answer my question. Did you plant a fake death threat?"

"No! No I did not. Seriously, that's ridiculous," I scoff.

"No question is ridiculous. It's only answers that can be considered ridiculous." He says it as if it's some ancient piece of wisdom. I know better; he made it up just now. He leads the way back outside and takes a deep breath. "You should get some air conditioning, it's brutal in there," he suggests, gesturing with his thumb. He bends over (despite his back), and picks up a pine cone, holds it up and studies it, then chucks it across the road.

"I'll make sure it's installed for your next visit," I say. I am being sassy and I know it, but he seems to bring it out in me. I don't like his insinuations. Or the way he's ogling my breasts, to be honest.

He smirks at me and then keeps walking to his car. He opens the door and stands there, staring at me. Neither of us speaks. This is fun. He gets a notification on his phone and glances down at it then nods. "So, Ms. Rylie…" he begins. I could have told him to call me Sloane but he doesn't deserve to. "I had Patricia back at the station search for an Andrew Creighton within a one-hour radius of here, she looked in Westchester County, Putnam, Orange, Rockland, and Duchess Counties and could not find one. Not a single one. Different spellings, too."

"Okay?" I say.

"You said he was from forty minutes away."

"That's what he told me." Maybe he drives really fast, how the hell do I know? God, I wish Dylan would come back and save me from this goon with the badge. I bet a few choice words from him and the cop would be on his merry way. It's my fault, though. I should have grilled Andy Creighton more. But why would I have thought to do that?

"Well, we come up with nothing."

"What does that mean?" I ask.

"You tell me, Ms. Rylie. You tell me." He leans on the open car door and raises an eyebrow at me. His wife or girlfriend must have read the book and been upset with me. Seems to be an epidemic of that going around.

"Actually his legal name is John Andrew Creighton, so maybe that's the problem with your search," I say. I need to text Andy and see if he's okay. But not while the detective is here.

Detective Lenovo comes around the front of the car and hands me his card. "Call me if anything comes up, please. We just want to make sure this does not escalate. For now, my department will handle this investigation. But if it turns out this death threat goes across state lines, we might have to bring in the FBI." Jesus, the FBI? Really? Have things gone that haywire with my book? He strokes his chin for a moment and opens his mouth, closes it, and then finally speaks. "Are you going to do what the note says?"

"I haven't decided." Everyone wants to know my intentions. It's fine, no pressure or anything. Getting into the inner workings of Cabinet's brilliant dream sequence idea seems pointless and will only lead to the detective staying even longer and asking more annoying questions.

"Hmm," is his reply, with an impish grin beginning to form on his mouth.

"Well, thank you for stopping by," I say. He nods and walks back to his door, opens it, and gets inside the car. I follow him and add, "I am concerned about this, Detective. I just want it all to go away. All of it. That's why I posted that video. It's probably just some grumpy reader."

"Maybe so," he says. "Maybe so." He takes another of his cards and hands it to me with a pen. "Why don't you write your number on there so I can contact you if we find anything."

I do what he says and he smiles and shuts the door. A minute later, all that's left of him are his taillights disappearing around the bend in the road. Should I have mentioned that I was almost drowned in my own bathtub? Maybe, but I am still not sure it wasn't just me falling asleep and slipping under the water. I move to the spot where I get intermittent service and fire off a text to Andy:

Hey it's Sloane how did it go at urgent care?

I stand there and wait five minutes, but there is no reply. I try calling the number but it goes straight to voicemail.

Looks like I'm heading to the urgent care place, because right now, that's my only hope of finding Andy Creighton.

CHAPTER 26

MANDY

At first, Patrick was not upset when I told him I was going back to the city, because he thought he was invited to come along. He thought we could make a city date of it, have dinner at this Mexican place in Hell's Kitchen he's been wanting to try. I mean, he's not wrong to be mad since we were planning to have a date tonight and I cancelled it very last minute. But in my defense, I just don't feel like having him along with me in the city when I'm trying to stalk Micah is a great idea. He'd just distract me, ask too many questions, try to change my plan, and complicate everything. He huffs and pouts and asks me why I need to go, but I don't want to tell him what all I'm doing so I lie and say I left some important files in the office and need to go grab them and if he wants a late dinner I should be back by nine. It's not a complete lie; I am looking for some important files. I just don't know exactly which ones yet. He says we'll see when the time comes, he may not be able to wait that long. He gives me a begrudging kiss, then insists on driving me to the train station. Which means he will probably pick me up too and we'll get dinner and everything will be fine in the end.

The train ride takes way too long, I didn't bring any reading material, and I'm grumpy and tired by the time I get out at Grand Central Station. I am hoping that Micah didn't finish his office work early and leave before I get there, or this will have been a wasted trip. I have not really thought this through. I can't very well go into the office and have him see me; he will want to know why I came in when he told me we'd just talk later; it'll be a whole big thing. But I also told Patrick I needed some files, so if I return home empty handed, it'll look very strange. Though I do have the flash drive key chain I always carry in my purse. Who said they had to be hard copy files? Patrick doesn't know that I can access the entire computer system from home. Okay one problem solved. I find a spot to wait for Micah to emerge from the building, in front of a CVS that is two doors down from the office, and I buy a copy of the Daily News so I can stand there with an open newspaper looking very much like the stereotypical movie spy. Perfect, except for when a pigeon drops some very runny poop that drips down page 7 while I wait. Of course, I have no way of knowing if Micah came out before I arrived, but I did get here in an hour and twenty minutes, well before the two hours he mentioned he'd be in the office. But after I have been standing for thirty-eight minutes I start to both lose hope and feel like an idiot for doing this. And my feet hurt. I should have changed into sneakers. Testing my boyfriend's patience so I could stalk the executive editor of Cabinet Publishing just because he said two words seems like a foolish endeavor.

I tell myself at the forty-five minute mark I will leave, cut my losses and salvage the evening with Patrick. Then at forty-four minutes after I arrived, the revolving doors finally move. I raise the newspaper slightly and watch carefully. It's Micah alright. Now I feel a renewed sense of purpose. Luckily, he does not come my way, he turns right and starts walking north. I decide about a third of a block is the right distance to keep, and I stay on his tail as he walks uptown. I have no idea what I will do if he goes into another building, like one with a doorman or a security guard. I'll be stopped before I can figure anything out. So I just hope it's an open public place where I can easily watch him. Though for all I know he's heading to a bookstore (is there one up this way anymore?) and that is the "book business" he mentioned.

It's late Saturday afternoon so the sidewalk is crowded with tourists. It's getting hard to keep up with Micah and for a minute I think I've lost him. But then I spot him again, still walking north on Fifth.

I'm getting tired; this is more than I bargained for now. He crosses Central Park South and heads right into the park. Maybe his "book business" is simply to lay in on the grass and read a book. He does have his briefcase with him, and I know he likes to read the competition's latest offerings to help us better decide who to sign and how to compete. I want to text Patrick and apologize again but decide to leave it until I am on my way back. Because that's the first thing he will ask: Are you done there? Can we finally eat?

Well, Micah does not go lay on the grass but he finds a bench not far from the entrance and sits himself down, briefcase on his lap, hands folded on top of it. It feels like a scene from a movie. I find another bench about twenty feet away and quickly erect my newspaper shield, and wait. This time, I don't have to wait long; within five minutes someone sits down next to Micah and they start talking. Though there are interruptions from passersby talking way too loud, a kid carrying a boombox on his shoulder (is this 1987?), and various chattering birds, blaring car horns, and a passing musician who plays the trumpet as he walks, I still manage to hear most of the conversation that ensues.

"Thanks for meeting me here, Daniel," Micah says.

"I enjoy the park, no worries," the man replies. "I wish I got up here more often, to be honest, if Jessie wasn't such a bitch then I would." Micah laughs so he must know how much of a bitch Jessie is. I can't get a good look at Daniel, but he's about ten years older than Micah, he's wearing a suit, and he too has a briefcase.

"Same here. So I took care of it. The other book is dead. It's only Sloane now."

"Good. And how are you handling the rest of the situation exactly? Because we're ready to proceed if everything is copasetic."

"Dream sequence," Micah says, clearing his throat. He always does that when nervous. The dream sequence idea sounded good behind closed doors at Cabinet, but out in the wild it comes off weak. And Micah's friend senses this.

"Dream fucking sequence? To explain the death? That's what you came up with? I was hoping for better than that."

"What do you suggest?" Micah asks. "Should we ask Jessie?"

Daniel scoffs. "I suggest something more creative. Maybe it wasn't Andy at all, it was an impostor. Something. Dream sequence is the biggest creative copout," Daniel says. "That won't go over well." I want to laugh because Daniel is saying the very same thing that Patrick said about the dream sequence. I should hire Patrick as a storyline consultant.

"I mean we were going with that, we already created a contest…"

"If you do that, the deal's off." The guy stands up and Micah pops up too.

"No, no hold on. We will do better than that."

"Good." They both sit back down again.

"Deluxe hardcover edition with bonus chapters, sprayed edges, and color inserts. It can be ready in three months if we are lucky. I have a Chinese supplier who can expedite things." I peek around the newspaper and see Micah remove an 11 x 17 paper from his briefcase and hand it to Daniel.

"Then we'd better be lucky. That sounds wonderful, a great tie-in to our planned early promos. Congratulations, you just saved the deal. I brought the contract for you to look over." Daniel takes some papers from his briefcase and hands them to Micah. He catches me looking his way and for a split second I think he's going to say something to Micah, but he just flashes a quick smile at me and turns his attention back to Micah, who is leafing through the papers. "You'll see the clause on page four, where we have to approve the changes before printing, for the deal to go through." Daniel looks glances around and then says, "There are a couple of clauses we are not putting on paper, just between you and I." He leans over and speaks practically into Micah's ear.

"Okay, well, I'll have our legal team take a look," Micah says flatly. I roll my eyes. Cabinet has a part time attorney that we share with two radio stations and a dentist's office. He doesn't even have a cubicle in our office.

"Nah don't do that. I need this signed now. I need to take this back to Drake. We want to start production immediately."

"But…" Micah starts.

"Listen, we have another project lined up at a rival publisher if this falls through. We're hot to trot on this." Daniel takes a Ziploc baggie of bread crumbs from his suit pocket and starts feeding the pigeons, whose numbers grow exponentially as they see the food offerings.

"Another project? That won't get nearly as much attention as this," Micah insists.

"People are like pigeons, my friend. They will eat up whatever's thrown to them. And we intend to throw them something by early next year. Whether it's this project or someone else's. You decide, we want Andy Creighton, not Thomas McAllister. But we'll throw Thomas to the pigeons if need be and they will flock to him." With that, Daniel stands up abruptly and shoos the birds away and they flap their wings and distance themselves from their benefactor turned chaser.

CHAPTER 27

SLOANE

The last time I was at Help Yourself Urgent Care was ten years ago, when two bees stung my face. I was starting to swell up so bad that it was getting hard to see the last couple of minutes before I pulled into their parking lot. Luckily, it just took an epinephrine shot and I was fine. I have carried an epi pen with me ever since.

Back then it was early in the morning and the lot was empty; today it's almost full. I figure there must be a lot of summer-related accident victims moaning and groaning in the waiting room. Surprisingly though, when I walk in, it's empty. I guess most of the spots are taken by people at the nail salon and the fitness center next door. I head straight to the desk and the woman there directs me to the self-check-in kiosk before I can speak.

"No, I'm not here to be seen, I have a question about a patient."

"Your child? Parent? Someone you brought in?"

"No, just a friend."

She sighs and says as if reciting this for the hundredth time, "All patient records and information are private,

HIIPA regulations, sorry." And she goes back to tapping away at her keyboard.

"This man is wanted by the police," I say, hoping to grab her attention back.

"Are you the police?" she asks, bored with me already.

"No, but I want him too," I say. Okay that sounded weird.

"Then sorry, I can't help."

I lean over the counter and glance at her desk. There, next to her purse, is my book. I smile. Sometimes being me comes in handy.

"You reading that?" I say, gesturing.

"Yeah. I love her books. Why?" She raises an eyebrow. "Are you one of those crazies who's been posting shit and complaining?"

I laugh. "No, I am the author."

"Yeah right," she says, rolling her eyes. She goes back to typing and then her gaze redirects to me suddenly. "Wait…" She grabs my book, opens it to the back flap of the dust jacket. "Holy shit. You are her."

"Sloane Rylie at your service," I affirm. "So, if you help me out I'll sign that book for you," I say with a wink.

She leans across the counter and smiles. "Deal!" She grabs my book and slaps it down. I see by the bookmark she's about halfway through.

"I'm not thrilled that the fuss over this has made it impossible to read it without knowing the ending," I say, and it's the first time I've voiced the thought that's been rattling around my brain for the last five days. Book spoilers are a big problem on all the social sites, but with this one it's been even worse since it's become a news story, almost impossible to avoid.

"I'm still enjoying it anyway," she says. "Now what do you need? Is this for a new book you're working on? Will you mention me in the acknowledgments? My name is Sandy!"

"You're going to laugh, but I need to know if a guy named Andy Creighton was here in the last couple of hours to be treated for a busted ankle."

"Is this some publicity stunt?" she says, wide eyed.

"Not quite." I hope. "Long story but it's important."

"I think I'd have noticed if Andy Creighton walked in here, Ms. Rylie," she says, her lips curving into a wry smile. "Or a Ciara Barnes, for that matter." I should have killed Ciara. There's been a lot of chatter lately that Andy deserves someone better than Ciara. I happen to disagree, but that's just me, the author of the damn books. She types something into the computer and shakes her head. "Nope. There's been nobody by that name here today." I'm about to dig a sharpie out of my bag when Sandy holds up a finger. "Wait a minute. There was a John A. Creighton here this afternoon. Diagnosis, strained ankle."

"Well, that's him. And he's long gone by now, I bet."

"Not necessarily," she says. "I remember him now. He had an x-ray done of his ankle and our machine was being wonky so it took longer than usual to get the results. When he was done, he talked to my coworker for a minute, saying he wished he could just go home and rest but he had business in town to take care of first."

"That's all he said? He didn't say what he needed to do?" What business could Andy possibly have here? The only reason he came out this way was to find me. But still, this is good. If he is in town I can find him.

"No, he didn't. Looks like he left here about twenty minutes ago."

I thank Sandy and sign her book. She wants to keep talking about my writing, but I politely extract myself, telling her it's urgent I find Andy Creighton.

Pleasantville is like most small towns in Westchester County, a few main streets with shops and eateries, surrounded by residential neighborhoods. If Andy has business in town, then he will be parked within a small radius and I'll find him. I hurry to my car and peel out of the parking lot; it's only two minutes to the center of town. I drive slowly along Bedford Road, looking for his SUV. What am I even going to say to him if I find him? I am so good at plotting my books, yet my life, not so much. I need to plan better and stop improvising. I remind myself that I was supposed to be relaxing at the cabin and not driving around trying to find the namesake of my dead character.

Now that I have service again, my phone is going bonkers with notifications of missed calls and messages. Micah and Jonah both called me again, and Mandy tried me as well. So far, no sign of Andy's car. I turn off Bedford and try a few other streets. No sign of Andy's car. I am debating whose call to return next when my phone rings. It's Jonah. I sigh and answer.

"Jesus Christ Sloane, what are you trying to do?" is the first thing he says. I pull over in front of a pet grooming salon and close my eyes.

"I am trying to make it stop, man. I just need the nonsense to stop."

"And we have a plan for that, my dear." He's just annoyed that I beat him to posting.

"Nothing I did interferes with that plan. I wanted to send a clear message to everyone, to stop being little bitches over an ending to a book. Seriously, this is just silly." I am practically yelling into my phone now. I've reached my boiling point. Anyone else tries to question what I did, I may punch them in the face, and then kick them in the nuts, if they have any.

"Calm down, Sloane."

"I will not! I stand by my post." As I am talking, I pull it up on Instagram. "It's already got 30,000 likes and 2,500 comments. Publicity is a good thing."

"Have you read the comments?" he asks. I hear Brooklyn whining about something in the background. "Brookie, come here. Read her a few."

"That's quite alright, you don't need to read me comments. I'm sure the comments run the spectrum from supportive and loving to vile and hateful. As usual. So that's a big whatever. I've got people's attention."

"I'm still annoyed about the post, but I guess you're right. It is getting attention, and your new edition is going to sell like crazy. We'll hold the video Brookie filmed until tomorrow. And don't forget Dez Maxwell arrives at 10 o'clock and you need to be at the airport to greet her."

My life has become so complicated because I decided to kill off a character. I just want to hide. I am going to be the most reluctant, miserable host on the planet. What am I even supposed to talk to Dez about? The dream sequence that I have not even written yet? Maybe I can get her to write it since she came up with the stupid idea to begin with, and I am actually half serious about that. I hang up with Jonah, and pull back onto the main street, about to give up on locating Andy Creighton when a block ahead I spot his SUV. He's parked near the bookstore, which has a line of people out the door and down the block. There are no spots left on the main street, so I pull onto another side street and hurry out of my car.

I squeeze my way past the line and into the store, where I am greeted by a chalkboard that has in hastily written blue letters: "Now until 7 pm at Pleasant Books! Andy Creighton is Alive and he's signing copies of All Things Must."

I have to read the sign twice to comprehend it. Andy is signing my books?

I storm my way to the back of the store where the line leads to a table with a stack of my books, not just the latest but the others in the series. And sitting there in a chair with a big smile plastered across his smug face, is none other than Andy Creighton. He's holding a Sharpie and listening to a woman's dedication request before setting the pen to the title page and putting his signature down in big, broad strokes like he's John Hancock. On a mini easel on the table next to him is a blown-up copy of his driver's license with personal details blacked out, to prove his identity. I am about to blow a gasket.

When Andy Creighton sees me, the smile vanishes from his face and he drops his pen to the table. "Oh, hey, Sloane," he says, "What are you doing here? Did they tell you to come?"

"Looking for you, that's what I'm doing here, especially after you didn't answer my text."

"What text? I did not get a text." He tilts his head at me.

"Yeah okay, whatever. Anyway, I stopped by urgent care and they said you were headed into town. I thought maybe you'd be in the drugstore getting supplies for your ankle, but instead I find you at the bookstore signing my books? Like what the hell, man?"

"Hey, wait, so you don't know about this?" His reaction seems to be genuine but that does not quell my fury.

I lean into his face, seething. "I most certainly do not. Besides, what's there to know other than you're sitting here autographing copies of my book?" He has a large, bold signature for the shy guy he seemed to be a couple of hours ago.

One of the bookstore clerks who monitors the line glares at me. "Excuse me ma'am, you'll have to pay for a book and get in line like the rest of them if you want to talk to Andy Creighton. No cutting."

"I wrote the damn goddamn book, you idiot!" I yell and the whole store goes quiet.

At first, she's taken aback, but then she takes a better look at me and her jaw drops. "Oh my God, Sloane Rylie is here in person?"

"Nice to meet you," I growl. Whispers and gasps erupt along the line and among the regular shoppers in the store as people point and stare at me.

"What on earth is going on here, will you please explain?" I demand of Andy.

"That guy Jonah called me," he says. "Just a few minutes after I left your cabin, while I was waiting to be seen at urgent care. It was his idea, he said he'd pay me a thousand bucks to do it. As soon as I said yes, he sent the money and called the bookstore to set it up. They posted it on their socials and boom, an hour later by the time I got here, there was already a line of people waiting!"

Why does Jonah have Andy's correct number, but I don't. This is too weird. I pull out my phone and call up the Pleasant Books page. Sure enough there's a post and a story, it's just a green background with big white letters and it says "Andy Creighton is Alive! Meet Him Now at the store and get yourself an autographed copy of any book in the series."

I want to laugh and cry and punch a hole in something all at once. Jonah is a backstabbing bastard but he's also a marketing genius. I go back to my video, and it's now got 300,000 views. It's what I wanted, yet this thing is now taking on a life of its own and spiraling out of control in directions I have not anticipated. The real version of my fictional character is sitting here signing copies of my books because Jonah wants to seize the momentum, yet I just had him on the phone and he mentioned nothing.

The next woman in line pushes her way forward and has Andy sign her book to Ashley. When he's done with her, he looks up at me in earnest. "Hey Sloane, I'm sorry about this, I thought you knew. I thought he told you. That's a shit thing for him to leave you out." Earlier today, Andy was freaking out about a threatening note and lamenting his association with my famous character; now he's embracing it to the point of making a public appearance. Money will do weird shit to people.

"You should probably go home and rest that ankle," I say.

He winces as if me mentioning it has made the pain worse. "They wrapped it and it feels better now. And I have to get to everyone in the line first. Jonah was asking if someone could take video and send it to him. The store already live streamed the first twenty minutes of this on Facebook. Since you're here, would you mind? Like pan along the line and then over to me signing for someone."

Look at mister fraidy pants suddenly coming out of his shell and giving me orders. I apparently killed the wrong Andy Creighton. I shake my head but agree to do the video. I will deal with Jonah later. I'll deal with everyone later. I run my hands through my hair and turn back to the line. I'm glad I'm not the one on camera; I'm sure between my nap and being grilled by the detective, I look like a hot mess. People are now smiling and waving to me and taking their own videos of me talking to Andy. I manage a weak grin and a slight wave to them and then an idea hits me. I am going to beat Jonah at his own game. I raise my phone and start to record the video, but with a little added narration.

CHAPTER 28

MANDY

So Micah has a movie or television series production deal going and that's why he's so insistent on resurrecting Andy Creighton, and pulling the rug out from under Stacy Von Slade. It all makes sense now. My sleuthing was not for naught. Of course, being in the business, I know that while it seems very shady, publishers are free to negotiate for book rights on behalf of their authors. In this case, since Sloane does not have an agent, they can do whatever they want and then pay her the percentage from the deal that her contract says, in this case I believe it's 40%. I've been on her for years to get herself an agent (who would have got her 50% for sure), but she's extremely stubborn on this point. "So, I somehow managed to get my first book deal all by myself years ago, and I've been a bestseller every time on my own, and you want me to hire someone to serve as a go-between so I can give them fifteen percent of my money? How much better than #1 on the New York Times bestseller list can you get? No thanks." And I mean I can see where she's coming from. But having an agent is a level of protection and negotiating power that you just can't accomplish on your own. I think she's been getting twenty percent less than she should be. Plus, if she was agented, she'd already know about whatever deal this is going on with Micah and that shady Daniel guy.

For a moment I wonder who they will cast as Andy and Ciara. I guess it depends on their budget, but assuming this is a big ticket production, I'm thinking it'll be a couple of Hollywood A-listers, one of them will likely be an Oscar nominee. While this news is very exciting — as far as I know it would be only the second time a Cabinet book will have been optioned (Stacy's debut was but the movie is yet to be made) — it's still shady that the deal was done on a park bench. Like what the actual hell?

I let Micah and the guy leave first. They walk right past me without a second glance, and I breathe a sigh of relief. I toss my ad-hoc poop-stained newspaper disguise into the trash can next to my bench and stand up. I have nothing else to do in the city; I can go home and figure out how to apologize to Patrick for my impulsive (and repulsive, to be honest) behavior. And yeah, I think I can come clean and tell him why I was here and what I found. I start walking toward the 59th Street entrance to the park so I can get the subway. Part of me wants to ask Patrick to come in and meet me here, now that I am a little calmer. But as nice as being here might be, he will just scold me for not having him accompany me to begin with.

I need to call Sloane. I need to sit down with her and tell her all the things. She might actually be excited about the movie deal, though it's not something that's come up in our conversations. I have no official word about this new development other than overhearing the two men talking and watching Micah sign a piece of paper, but I still think it's worth telling her. She can still feign surprise when Micah tells her, but she'll thank me for giving her the heads up. It may sway her permanently in the direction of compliance, which would be good for all of us. I don't get why Micah just didn't tell her what's going on; it would be a pretty safe bet that she would be fully on board knowing there's a movie deal at stake.

If I hurry to Grand Central, I can make the next train in thirty minutes. I walk faster on my way out of the park, but just as I hit Central Park South I'm forced to stop suddenly, because Micah is standing in front of me texting someone. I fall back a few feet and wait, pulling out my own phone and scrolling TikTok until he's finished.

The second reel that comes up is a guy in a bookstore signing copies…of Sloane's book? What the hell? It's Pleasant Books in Pleasantville and the reel was posted fifteen minutes ago. Andy Creighton is alive and signing books! is the text that runs across my screen. I squeeze my eyes shut and then inhale deeply. I may as well just hand in my resignation on Monday since I am apparently in charge of nothing anymore.

When I glance up, Micah has disappeared. I am free to go, but I am momentarily stuck in TikTok hell, scrolling among the recommended videos. Just one more, I tell myself, and then I'll go home. The next one I pull up is at the same bookstore again, but it's not from the bookstore's account. It's from Sloane's author account. She's showing us the line in the bookstore, and then turning the camera onto Andy Creighton, all the while, narrating the reel.

"Hey guys, it's Sloane Rylie here in Pleasant Books in beautiful Pleasantville, New York. And yes, the real Andy

Creighton is signing copies of my books! Talk about surprises! I think he's going to be here another thirty minutes, so get your butts down here. Because while this Andy is alive, the fictional Andy Creighton is very much dead and will remain so. Y'all have to just accept it. My next book will be great anyway, so stay tuned."

Well, I now have even more material for my book. Maybe I can't exactly write about following the executive editor to a secret meeting in the park, but I can describe the rest of what's going on. Including Stacy's cancelled book.

I think about the success Sloane has had and how this is now my chance at a bestseller. Though I was so reluctant at first, I am now ready to see my book on the Trending on TikTok table by the entrance to Barnes and Noble. I should tell her about my deal, of course, but for now there's much more pressing stuff to talk to her about. Like the fact that she would be losing out on a major movie deal if she refuses to bring Andy back.

I text Patrick to let him know I'm on my way back, and then I call Sloane. She answers quickly, barking into the phone, "Mandy, I am so done!"

"Hey bestie," I say. "Bad day?"

"Stop the world, I want to get off," she says. "I'm so over it."

"From your two posts in the last few hours, I can see it's been a day."

"Worse than a day. It's entered the realm of ridiculous. I can't even keep up with this anymore. And tomorrow that Dez Maxwell girl is arriving, winner of the made-up contest, and I am supposed to be her cheery host for three days." I can hear an announcement in the background; she must still be in the bookstore.

"Eh, it'll be alright. Hang in there. Once you get the writing done for the new ending, you'll feel better. And it won't take you long once you get on a roll. You know how it goes with you, a few solid hours and you will be finished." Of course, the dream sequence is out, but she probably doesn't know that yet. Dez is going to be one disappointed fan.

"No, you don't understand, Mandy. I am done as in finished. I'm not doing it. I'm not changing anything. Let them sue me. I don't even care. What happened to artistic integrity? Why do I have to bow to corporate pressure? I won't. They can't force me to write." I hear someone say, "Can you sign the book too?" and Sloane says an impatient, "Sure."

I walk down the grimy subway steps, aware that I am about to lose service once I descend to platform level and get on a train. "Look, why don't we talk in person. Can I come by?"

"I guess so. Not really in the mood for visitors, but I'll be at the cabin until about ten, unless I decide to stay the night," she says. "Just warning you though, I'm not changing my mind. Everyone can fuck off and leave me the hell alone. My book, my decision. Andy Creighton is dead." Either she hangs up or my call drops because of the sketchy service underground, but the line goes dead. All I can think as I board the subway for Grand Central is that Micah and Jonah are not going to like this one bit.

CHAPTER 29

SLOANE

Andy Creighton is dead.

I refuse to be pushed around and told what to do. I got into writing for one reason: so I could create my own worlds. To be told that the world I created isn't good enough was a gut punch, but to be told to fix it, change it to please everyone else, is like a dagger through my heart. Nobody realizes how lucky they are to have had Andy for this long. I was originally intending this to be a one-off book. I had so many ideas for my follow-up novel, but the popularity of Dangerous Hearts in Love led Micah to reject anything other than a sequel. And just like that I was pigeonholed. At the time I accepted it with a shrug and the dollar signs of the three-book offer he made me. Mandy says I should have agented up at that point, and maybe she's right, but I preferred to handle things myself. Like I always have in life. Which is why I'm not calling mom back yet. She will literally have nothing helpful to say.

I've been back at the cabin for an hour now, and new questions keep bubbling up to the surface of my brain. The latest one being – how did Pleasant Books manage to have so many copies of my books on hand? I mean, yeah I get it, I'm a bestseller, but still. They must have moved two hundred of the various titles. No bookstore would keep that many on hand, they'd monitor stock and replenish as needed; they wouldn't be stockpiling ten cartons of books.

It's getting dark now and I decide to sit outside on a tree stump, with one of my Vitamin Waters, now freezing cold how I like it, because my old fridge has only one setting and it's Arctic. The chatter of the cicadas is waning, giving way to the trill of the crickets. God, I used to love coming up here and spending time with Dad on warm summer evenings. Some nights we'd roast marshmallows over a fire. I can still see the outline of the rocks he'd placed twenty-something years back.

I've put my phone on Do Not Disturb for a while even though with this spotty service I probably didn't need to, but I want to clear my head and actually get some of the peace I'd come here for to begin with. I was so steadfast on my video and in my call with Mandy. Will I come around? I don't think anyone knows what to believe right now. And even if Jonah and Micah are furious at me, the minute I change my tune they'll laugh and tell me the flip-flopping was actually good because it kept my fans' attention.

I am tempted to spend the night, though this bed is not very comfortable and the sheets could use a washing. Home would be much more cozy, but if I pull into my driveway to more protestors I will lose my shit. For now, I'll just sit here and sip on my drink and watch for deer and rabbits, maybe even a fox, as the light fades. I thought I wanted complete silence, but instead I've turned on the old cassette player and loaded up an 80s mix tape that my dad had made for me. As Howard Jones tells me things can only get better, I have to agree with that assessment.

The stump is okay for a few minutes but then it starts hurting my butt, and also I could swear I feel ants crawling along my thighs. I stand up just in time to see headlights approaching. Please let them go right past me. But nope, that would be too much to ask. It's that detective again, and he's pulling into my driveway. Maybe he has a lead about the note. Or maybe he wants to ask me why Andy Creighton's signing books. I shake my head; in all the commotion at the bookstore, I completely forgot the whole reason I was trying to find Andy to begin with – to ask him more questions about himself and the note. Instead I was asking him why he was signing my books.

The detective shuts off the engine and gets out of the car. He is wearing a frown and sighs when I stand up to greet him.

"Didn't think I'd see you again so soon," I say. "I didn't get a chance to install air conditioning, sorry. Did you forget something?" Like leaving me alone? Did you forget that?

"Have you heard from Andy Creighton since we spoke?"

"I went and looked for him, and I found him. So yeah, we spoke." My dad gave me unsolicited advice once, no idea why, but when I was sixteen he took me aside – in fact it was here at the cabin – and said, "If you ever get questioned by the cops, answer exactly what their question is and nothing more. You are much safer if you limit your answers, no matter if you've done nothing wrong."

"Oh did you? How long ago was this?" He looks at his watch.

"I'd say…" When the hell was that anyway? Oh, yeah. "About an hour and fifteen minutes ago, give or take."

"And you've been here since?" Out comes the notebook again and he's scrawling away furiously.

"After driving back from town, yeah."

The detective looks around and nods. "That flavor any good?" He gestures to my half empty drink.

"Eh, it's okay. I don't love the zero ones but they're no calories so I deal with it."

He comes around his vehicle and approaches me. "Ms. Rylie, we have a little problem."

"And what's that?"

"Andy Creighton is missing." He watches me for a reaction. I have none. I am worn out and nothing anyone says can surprise me anymore. He could have told me the earth is flat and I'd be stone-faced.

"I told you I just saw him recently." I am really so very tired of hearing that name.

"I know what you said. And I saw the bookstore video. I know he was there." Trying to trick me, that's cool. I have to watch it with this guy.

"So then he's not missing?" I feel like this is a trap.

"Oh he's missing alright." He takes out his phone, pulls something up, and hands it to me. It's a pic of Andy's SUV. The driver's side door is open.

"Where was this?" I ask, though it looks familiar. It looks like it's around here.

"Half a mile down the road. Dispatch got a call about an abandoned vehicle. We get those calls occasionally, usually it's just they ran out of gas or had a flat tire and wandered off in search of help. So I take a ride out this way, run the registration, and come to find out it's that Andy guy's car."

I start to hand the phone back but he tells me to swipe to the next picture. It's another note. This one says "Last warning – fictional Andy lives or real Andy dies." At first glance the lettering looks similar to the other note, but I can't be sure. I swallow hard and hand the phone back.

"Well that's not great," I say. "Did you look for him?"

"I did a cursory look, no sign of him, but then I called for backup; a couple of my officers will be arriving any minute now and searching the woods. Meantime, I decided to come here and talk to you, see if you had any insight into this mystery." He keeps such a straight face I can't tell if he suspects me or is just hoping I can help.

"Well, all I can say is hundreds of thousands of people have seen the videos that were posted. So anyone could have written that note. Not necessarily the same person as the first one."

"I'm aware," he says. He kicks at some rocks with his boot and looks me in the eye. "Of what you've been doing. You and him, pretty clever marketing stuff. I took some business classes back in college. You guys are pretty savvy at getting attention. I read some of those comments. You have all kinds of reactions going on." I don't love what the detective is insinuating. But it's better than him accusing me of kidnapping or murder, I guess.

The darkness triggers the outside light, which flickers on and casts the detective's face in an eerie glow, making the stubble on his cheeks look extra sharp and ragged.

"The bookstore thing wasn't even my idea," I shrug. "It was my publisher's. Have you talked to them yet?"

He laughs. "I literally answered the vehicle call twenty minutes ago and then came straight to see you. How would

I have talked to them yet? Or known who to talk to? You can give me that info later."

"Take me there," I say, not knowing what else to do. Standing here in front of my cabin certainly isn't going to solve anything.

"Take you where?"

"To the car. Andy's abandoned car."

He blinks at me. He was not expecting this. Or was he? What is that saying? The criminal always returns to the scene of the crime? In this case I just want to see it for myself. Up close. Maybe there's a clue he's missing. I take my phone off do not disturb but I have only one bar.

"I guess," he says. "If you want to see it, I guess that's okay."

He gestures with his head, for me to get into his car. Not thrilled about it, but if I insist on my own car that will look suspicious. The ride isn't too awkward because it's actually less than half a mile. Andy's car is on the side of the road in front of Dylan Kopecki's property, and the hazards are on.

"Now that's strange," Detective Lenovo says, scratching his chin.

"What?" I ask.

"Those hazards were not on a few minutes ago…"

"I put them on," a voice chimes in from the darkness up ahead. "Didn't want the car to get hit, but didn't want to touch the door either." It's Dylan, and as he slowly jogs toward us, he turns on a flashlight that momentarily blinds me. It's not even that dark yet. "Oops, sorry!" he says, lowering the beam to the ground. "Hey Sloane."

"I'm Detective Lenovo of the Pleasantville PD." He reaches out a hand and Dylan shakes it.

"Oh yeah, you helped my mom when our ATV was stolen a few years back."

The detective nods, eyes gleaming with recognition. "Ah yeah. You were younger then, a teenager," he laughs. "I didn't recognize you."

"So what's with this Andy? Can't he stay out of trouble for more than a few hours?" Dylan turns to me and asks with a smirk.

"Huh?" the detective says.

"Inside joke," I quickly reply, waving my hand dismissively while shooting a look at Dylan.

"Well, my guys seem not to be here yet." Lenovo glances down the road, then goes back to his car and radios to the station. I hear the detective speak and then a garbled voice over the radio and some static. Lenovo comes back and says, "They'll be here in about ten minutes. We could start searching for him in the meantime, if you don't mind helping."

Dylan shrugs. "May as well," he says.

"What are you even doing outside?" I ask. His family's house is a good 200 feet further down the road.

"I came out when I saw the flashing lights stop here. But by the time I got over here, the cop car was gone. I realized whose car it was, turned on the hazards cause this stretch of road can be pretty dangerous, and started to walk back."

The detective considers this statement, rubbing his chin and narrowing his eyes.

I glance in the car and see the key still in the ignition. This can't be good. Detective Lenovo pulls a flashlight from his belt and starts to walk into the woods. "You guys coming or what?"

I turn on my phone flashlight, which momentarily illuminates the ground right in front of the open driver's door, and see a splotch of red on the ground. I want to scream but nothing comes. I take a breath and simply look at Dylan and then back at the ground. His eyes follow mine. He kicks at the dirt a little until the red spot is covered up.

"You know what?" I say, not really exaggerating, "Suddenly, I don't feel good. All this stress is making me dizzy. Dylan, can you drive me home?"

"Oh jeez, Ms. Rylie…er, Sloane, I'm sorry, yeah sure I can. Gimme a sec to get my car."

"You writers have a sensitive constitution, don't you?" Lenovo says, turning toward me, flashlight shining into the tree branches above, where I can see a bat hanging from a limb. A shiver runs down my spine and I look away.

It's no lie, either. I don't feel great after seeing Andy Creighton's blood on the ground. But I don't want to tell him about it. He'll see it soon enough. I shut my flashlight off and just stand there. The new note is on the passenger seat, lit by the car's dome light. I lean in for a better look, careful not to get my sneakers in the blood. The paper smells strongly of fresh permanent marker. "I guess so, as sensitive as the next bestselling author." I almost said guilty as charged but that would not have been a wise choice of words.

I run through the possibilities in my head. One – Andy is pulling another prank, either on his own or paid by someone; he just accidentally hurt himself along the way. Two – Andy is in trouble, and the note is real. Either scenario brings up more questions than I can answer, more questions than my brain can handle right now.

I hear Dylan revving his engine. My escape is imminent. I'll leave the search for Andy Creighton to the professionals. Before I can see Dylan's car, though, another vehicle speeds down the road. When it reaches me, the car squeals to a stop and the driver's window rolls down halfway.

"Sloane," Mandy says. It feels like I haven't seen her in years, she seems like a stranger to me.

"Mandy! You decided to come after all. I had given up on you," I say. The detective is out of sight now. In the distance I hear sirens. His backup is approaching. Dylan's head jerks in the direction of the approaching police cars.

"Get the fuck in the car, Sloane. Now," Mandy says and rolls up the window.

CHAPTER 30

MANDY

Patrick broke up with me when I got back to my house from the city and told him I needed to go talk to Sloane right away. He ranted for ten full minutes about how I am all distracted lately and he feels like a third wheel, and we have no future if this is how it is going to be. In a way, I don't blame him for being frustrated, but then again, far worse sins have been committed to deserve breakups. And if I've been ignoring him, it's only been a few days. So, he'll come to his senses and we'll probably make up at some point, but right now I can't worry about that. So I don't stay and argue and plead with Patrick and stretch the discussion into an hours-long tear-filed marathon that would probably result in a reconciliation. I just say okay and leave. I knew I had to find Sloane, so I drove over here. And right now I know I have to be decisive and grab Sloane's attention, and make her listen to me. And that means being bold.

Sloane was so annoyed and taken aback when I ordered her into my car. She looked at me like I was crazy, and with good reason; that's not like me to be so demanding. Any other time I would have tried that, I'd have been unable to maintain a straight face. I'd have broken down and laughed until I was in tears and unable to breathe. But this time I was serious. And then she refused, told me not to talk to her like that, and also that she already had a ride from the neighbor dude, and he's kind of hot. At first I thought she was joking around, but now a Jeep pulls up behind me and the neighbor guy gets out. I see what Sloane means. This guy is jacked and has a pleasant boyish face.

"You ready?" he asks her with a smile, ignoring me. I wait for Sloane to introduce us but she doesn't.

"Listen, I'll meet you at the cabin, wait for me there," she says instead, waving her hand impatiently in the general direction of her place. Not sure what the point of this is, since it's literally a one minute ride down the road, if I remember correctly. I guess the point is that's one minute alone she gets with her hunk of a neighbor. But I've collected my thoughts and I'm finally ready to tell her all the things (well, most of them at any rate). I've waited long enough and I don't want to wait much longer. Too much is at stake for both of us.

I don't even know what's going on, but the fact that there's a car with its door flung open on the side of the back road can't be a good thing.

While Sloane gets into the Jeep, complimenting the vibrant green color, I put my own boring car into drive and head down the road to her cabin. When I get there, I crunch slowly into the gravel driveway, pull up next to her car, and kill the engine. After a few seconds, I get out and inhale the forest air. The setting sun filtering through the trees makes for a pretty scene, so I snap a picture. I can post this on my personal insta later and then Patrick can be even angrier at me for going off to watch a pretty sunset without him. Sigh.

They should be along any second now. I wonder what's keeping them? He's probably demonstrating all the cool features the car has and she's oohing and ahhing appropriately. She took the latest breakup with Ellis hard, and I know I played a role in that so I'll keep my mouth shut about who she flirts with and why.

I take a good look at her little old cabin. It's quaint for sure, but in need of a good restoration. The paint is peeling badly, and the window glass is cracked in several places. The screen in the front door has a few big tears. Still, I see the appeal of this place. I see why she ran here when things got crazy with her book. It's a nice escape. I wish she'd invite me to stay over one night. Maybe after this Andy storm dies down I can hint at it. We could use some girl bonding time in this serene setting, and get back to where we once were. Ellis doesn't have to come between us. A girl can dream, can't she?

I turn my attention to the road now. Why is it taking so long? Where can they be? I glance down at my feet, comfy in the sandals I slipped on after I returned from the city, except for the piece of gravel that's slipped its way in. I lift my leg and pull off the sandal, shaking the rock out.

As I return it to my foot, I see headlights. Finally!

I watch and wait as the Jeep approaches. Should I have left more room when I parked? No, it's fine since he is just dropping her off.

The Jeep approaches but it doesn't slow down. It picks up speed as it gets near, then it passes by with a quick honk of the horn. Before I can react, the car has already disappeared around a bend in the road.

CHAPTER 31

SLOANE

As soon as I close my door, Dylan's vibe changes. He fiddles with the air conditioning for a moment, then tells me to buckle up. I remind him I'm just down the road, but he insists. The sirens get closer. I don't know what I was trying to accomplish by insisting that Dylan take me home, once Mandy showed up I should have just gone with her. But she was being kind of a bitch ordering me into her car. And though it seemed like Dylan had a reason for whisking me away, he's silent as we head down the road. As my cottage comes into view, I see Mandy standing there, waiting for me. It's been so long since I saw her in person, going back to just before I broke things off with Ellis.

Okay, confession time.

I know I said I killed Andy for the money, and because I was tired of him. But there's another big reason. I killed him because it was causing tension between me and Ellis.

It took me a few books before I was ready to admit to him that he was the inspiration for Andy Creighton. And I'm not at all saying that Ellis Jenkins is perfect. Or even close to perfect. He's not. But somehow, he fired my imagination into creating a more perfect version of him. So it's him but not at all him. I knew it would be a mistake to ever mention it to Ellis, and I was right. I opened my fat mouth one night when we were sharing a bottle of wine, and he never let me forget it. In fact, in the last few months he started to come up with crazy ideas. I could never be sure with him if he was serious or not, probably because he was always at least partly serious. One time he said in passing, "Maybe you should pay me a royalty for the use of my likeness." I ignored it because it was utterly ridiculous. But then a week later he came up with a scheme where we'd go on a book tour together with me billing him as "the inspiration for Andy" and he'd get a cut of the take since he'd be a huge draw. I just looked at his scrawny-ass body and laughed. Even if I signed a sworn, notarized statement, nobody'd believe that he was the genesis of Andy Creighton. It'd be taken as a big joke and would backfire completely. Of course, his inflated sense of self didn't help things. It was one of the reasons he broke up with me a few months back and slept with Mandy, then came back to me one last time before we split again.

I saw the final breakup coming and could envision him doing something stupid like filing a lawsuit or some nonsense if I let Andy live. So, I killed Andy Creighton and along with him, any chance of us getting back together and him trying to persist in glomming onto Andy's popularity. He was so mad when he found out what I'd done.

These thoughts are zipping through my head as we approach my cabin, and then pass it as Dylan honks his horn at Mandy, who looks as bewildered as I feel.

What the hell?

"Hey, that was me back there, you know," I say, trying not to sound like I think he's secretly a serial killer who plans to murder me and leave my body in the woods.

"I know. But I need to talk to you somewhere private." He doesn't look at me, keeps his eyes on the road and accelerates.

"My cabin is plenty private." Well, not at the moment with Mandy there. But whatever he needs to tell me he can say in front of her. I don't care.

"Just give me a few minutes," he says.

I have no idea where Dylan is heading, but I'm not scared. He wouldn't hurt me or anything. I hope. About a mile past my cabin, he turns left at the sign for Starling Lake. I suppose that's pretty private. It's supposed to only be open until dusk, but nobody ever bothers to lock the gates. Horny teenagers used to hang out there by the water, but I guess they found a better place to go where they would not get eaten by mosquitos.

Dylan drives slowly down the access road and into the parking lot which fronts the lake. He parks next to the boat ramp and dock. We're alone. The last of the sunlight is glinting off the still water. Starling Lake is small but all of us in the near vicinity had rights to use it. My dad had a rowboat for one season then sold it to the Kopeckis. And there it is, tied to the end of the dock, a little aluminum boat painted deep blue, the same old wooden oars resting on either side. The sight of it makes me smile. I never come to the lake, but I really should. It offers a whole other level of tranquility than my cabin does. Dylan leaves the car running and turns up the air conditioning almost to full blast. He turns to me and offers a weak smile.

"Hey," he says, looking into my eyes.

"Hey yourself. Why did you drag me down here?"

"It's pretty isn't it?" he says, but he's looking right at me. I feel all tingly in my chest and I feel my face flush.

"Sure is." I glance at the water. At the far end of the lake, I see a family of ducks swimming along slowly into the sunset, parents and three ducklings.

I am still looking at the lake, when I feel Dylan's hand on my knee. Is this really happening? It might be. I face him, expecting him to lean in and kiss me. Instead, he speaks.

"Sloane, I have to tell you something," he says. The hand is still on my knee for another second, but then he withdraws it.

"Okay, shoot," I say. Yes, I'm still half expecting him to make a move, though my hopes are dwindling. This does not sound like a confession of amorous intentions, it sounds ominous.

Now he's the one looking out at the water. "Can we get out of the car?"

"Sure," I say.

We do so silently. It's so quiet here. The sound of our doors closing is jarring. I'd swear I can see ripples in the lake water because of it. Dylan walks up to the dock and stops there.

"I hit Andy Creighton," he says, and his confession hangs heavy in the summer air. "I hit him with my car." I cannot believe what I am hearing. The words refuse to sink in.

"Sloane did you hear me? I said I hit..."

"I heard you," I cut him off, turn to him as my heart pounds in my chest.

"You killed him?"

"I didn't mean to," he says. "That's the thing. I was coming around the bend and he was standing there with the door open, and I tried to slow down and it was too late and he went flying and landed and Jesus, I didn't know what to do."

This is not happening right now. This can't be happening. I can't handle this.

"Then where is he?" Maybe he's kidding. I don't know Dylan that well. Maybe he loves practical jokes like Ellis does. He pranked me with some good ones, cruel but good ones including the time he pretended that he was giving up gaming and taking up crocheting. He even bought hooks and yarn and taught himself the basics just to fool me.

"Nobody was around, and I panicked so I dragged his body into my storage shed. I didn't know what to do, Sloane." His eyes are tearing up.

I bury my face in my hands. "Into your storage shed?" I cringe at the visual. "Oh Dylan. That was a big mistake. Now it's going to look like you killed him on purpose." And I am not going to escape suspicion. This is looking very, very bad.

He picks up a large rock and hurls it into the middle of the lake. It sinks with a plunk and scares the ducks, who take flight immediately.

"It was an accident. I made a mistake in judgment," he says.

"That's not the only mistake. You left the scene just now. If they find him while you're here, it'll look like you fled." My mind races through all the possible outcomes, and none of them are good. "What was your plan, for God's sake? What was your next move?" I am still trying to understand why Andy was stopped in front of the Kopeckis' property, standing in the road with his door open. It makes no sense. But then again, little that's been happening in the last few days makes much sense.

"I don't know. Maybe drag him out and drop him in the woods somewhere remote. Then they can find him later."

"So he's got trauma injuries and internal bleeding consistent with being hit by a car, but he's lying in the woods? How does that calculate? How did he get there?" The poor kid is delusional. He won't look at me now, he's just staring at the ducks. Right about now I wish I was a duck. They don't have to worry about books or fictional boyfriends.

"Yeah, I don't know," is all he can say. Because he knows I'm right. "I didn't think of that."

"We should go back." I think that through. "Correction, you should go back to your place but drop me off at my cabin first like you were supposed to. It's probably already a red flag that you've been gone so long. It's been like ten minutes now." More actually. Detective Lenovo is probably getting very suspicious. They may well have found the body already.

"Shit, I don't want to be arrested," he says, starting to cry, and in that moment he seems like a kid, which he really is. He's just an innocent neighbor boy caught up in nonsense that I inadvertently initiated.

"Everything will be fine. Just come clean with the cops, tell them exactly what happened and leave nothing out. You had no reason to run him down. It was an accident. And tell your parents, too. It'll be okay, Dylan." But deep down, I know it won't be. For either of us.

CHAPTER 32

MANDY

Sloane and the neighbor guy drove right past me, didn't even slow down. But I'm not going to worry. She's a big girl; she knows what she's doing. And she won't dare keep me waiting here too long. That would be rude and even if she's ticked off about me ordering her into my car, she'd still not just leave me here indefinitely. I listen for a vehicle, but there's nothing from either direction. This road is pretty dead. Would she mind if I waited inside? Probably not. Considering she blew right by me, I think she'd be hard pressed to call me out for waiting inside.

She left the door unlocked, so I let myself in and immediately my lungs are assaulted with warm, stagnant air that smells of wood and dirt, with a touch of whatever's getting moldy in the dusty satchel of potpourri that's been left on the windowsill for God knows how long. Delightful! The cottage has clearly been closed up for months if not longer. I sit down in one of the wicker chairs and drum my fingers on my knee. The seat starts to crackle and groan under me, and I spring up, afraid to wreck one of the prized chairs that her dad bought in 1978 at a flea market. Sloane's laptop sits on the small end table in front of me. She brings that thing wherever she goes.

May as well have a look around while I wait for her. I walk past the creepy old deer head (it needs a good vacuuming, and a little restoration – one of the eyes is missing) and into the bedroom. There's a small walk-in closet on the interior wall, and a double bed in the middle of the room. It's got a mahogany Art Deco headboard and matching nightstands on either side, and that's it. I sit on the bed and the springs rise up to meet me. On the wall is a framed crayon drawing of a man and woman, with the words "Once upon a time…" scrawled on top in dark blue. A little brass plaque on the bottom proclaims, "Sloane's First Story." I have to smile. Her dad must have put this up right around when her first book was published. He was always so proud of her and encouraged her writing. Too bad he didn't get to live to see how successful she became, though I'm glad he's not here to witness this particular hot mess she's in right now. Seeing all the spiderwebs in the corners – some of them occupied – makes me doubt she will spend the night here. This place needs a deep cleaning before it's worthy.

I come back to the living room and turn left toward the kitchen. The old 1960s fridge's motor kicks on and it hums loudly. Inside is a half-empty bottle of Vitamin Water Zero. A small, low mid-century aluminum kitchen table with a painted red plaid top and matching chairs are nestled in the corner. Two boxes of Pop Tarts and a bag of pretzels are laying on the table. The dates are current so she must have brought them with her. The vintage stove has not been used in a while; a couple of upside-down pots are atop the front burners. In the corner under the table is an unsprung mousetrap. A feeling of sadness and loneliness washes over me. I guess to some this might seem like perfection, but to me it just feels desolate. Or maybe it's just Patrick ending things. Dammit, I really did like him and I messed up. I ran over here only to be stood up by Sloane. Why do I even care so much? I start to cry despite my best efforts to hold it in, and soon the tears are cascading down my cheeks and my nose is running. I go into the bathroom in search of tissues. I usually carry a pack in my purse, but I used them and never replaced them.

The bathroom is surprisingly the most updated room in the cottage. The walls have been retiled and the sink looks new, the faucets a shiny chrome. I turn on the cold water, feeling in need of some cooling off. It sputters and spits for a few seconds and then issues a highly aerated stream of pale brown water. I scoff, shutting the water off. Country living indeed. But there are no tissues in sight. I poke around under the sink but all that's there is a plunger and some drain cleaner. Behind the mirror, the medicine chest is mostly empty save for some expired ibuprofen and a bottle of cough syrup that looks like it's from the 80s. She must have a few tissues somewhere. I go back to the living room and stand before her overnight bag. Would it be awful if I looked inside, just felt around for a tissue? I don't think that's terrible. I sniff, wiping my eyes with my sleeve temporarily, and unzip the bag. I listen for a car but hear nothing, so I reach my hand in. Sure enough, there's a travel pack of tissues. I take them out and grab a couple. Once I'm done I go to put them back, and then remember what I brought with me. Oh, how tempting this is. I know I should just close the bag and move on, but something pushes me to pull the paper from my pocket. I unfold it and stare at what it says. The letters are in neat block all caps. She'll never realize it's my writing in blue permanent marker that says:

BRING ANDY CREIGHTON BACK

I wrote that a couple of hours ago and stuck it in my pocket not even sure what, if anything I would do with it. I just figured one gentler nudge, another outside reminder, might push her over the edge and bring her around. I'm not usually selfish but my book depends on her acquiescence. A note mysteriously left for her, in her own damn bag, is something that will hit a little closer to home than one received by a stranger. I forgot that I had it with me to be honest, but her ditching me here in the cabin rubbed me the wrong way and in my growing resentment, I remembered it. And besides, this seems like the perfect opportunity, an excellent place to leave it. I tuck the note into her bag on top of a folded bra, and zip it closed again.

I walk outside again and take a deep breath of the earthy-pine scent. I use the extra tissue I grabbed to blow the cabin dust from my nose, and inhale again as a breeze wafts the delicious country air toward me. I take back what I'd thought about her inviting me to stay over. I wouldn't stay in that cabin unless it was aired out for a solid week and scrubbed top to bottom.

The sound of a car engine gives me hope, but it's a dark sedan with a flashing light on the dash, coming from the direction of the neighbor's house. Thankfully, he does not stop, he just keeps going. Maybe he's after Sloane. At this point, who knows?

It's getting darker now. A mile from here I'm sure it's much brighter, but in this wooded area, the light fades faster, and the same trees that bring welcome shade on summer days, usher in nighttime earlier. I am not sure how much longer to wait for Sloane. I really do need to talk to her, but I don't feel safe either inside or outside the cabin. I pull out my phone and try to get a signal. I see what she means; it's awful here. I walk in circles watching my bars and stop when I finally see a sign of life. I pull up TikTok; thankfully no further reels from anyone related to Sloane. But there is one, posted an hour ago, from an account I follow, a teen girl who reviews a ton of books and posts about them all day every day. She's holding up Sloane's book, so I let the video play.

"So besties, if you've been following the whole All Things Must saga closely like I have, here's my two cents. Sloane killed Andy. It was a stunt, and everything that has followed it is a stunt. Way to go Cabinet for keeping life interesting. What's the bottom line, book babies? Well in my humble opinion, Andy will rise again in fulfillment of the golden rule – you don't mess with something good, and you don't mess with a bunch of distraught kindle girlies. This is no Liam Mairi in Fourth Wing, this is much more serious. So buckle up buttercups, but I think you'll see the ending to this mishegoss will be happy. If not, then…" And she throws the book against the wall and the video ends.

Well, that's interesting. A text comes through from Patrick and my heart leaps out of my chest even before I see what he said. I open the message:

Hey. Can we talk. Maybe I was too rash. How about a late dinner in the city?

I look to the sky and breathe a sigh of relief.

Yes. Let's do that. I glance at the train schedule and type more. We can catch the 9:10 train. Meet at the train station?

The message does not send. "Argghhhh!" I yell to nobody. I shift a few feet and try again and it sends. Whew. It's currently 8:10. If Sloane gets back soon, I'll still have time to talk to her and make it to the train easily.

Just as I am thinking that, Dylan's Jeep comes out of nowhere and pulls up right in the driveway, scaring the crap out of me. The passenger door opens and Sloane hops out. She's flushed and breathing heavily. Before I can question Dylan, he pulls her door shut and drives off, leaving me standing here facing Sloane.

"What happened? You look awful." Best friends are allowed to say that, though I'm not sure we still qualify as besties after the whole Ellis thing.

"I can't really talk now," she says, face red and sweat beading on her hairline. "I don't mean to be rude, but can you leave?"

"Uhh what? I've been waiting here for you for like…" I glance at my watch. "Twelve minutes. Where were you?" First she drives past me then she asks me to leave?

"Please. I need to be alone for a little bit." She's shaken. By what, I'm not sure.

"I just wanted to tell you, I know it's been rough with everyone pushing you to bring back Andy. But as your publicist and friend…" As I am speaking she's holding up a hand. She turns away and runs off behind the cabin and I wince as I hear her getting sick.

She comes back, white as a ghost and teary-eyed. I feel bad for her, but so much for my Ted talk. I'll have to just finish my sentence and go, even though there's a lot to update her on.

"So what were you saying?" she asks.

"Hey, babe are you alright?"

"Not really, but go on finish your thing you were saying and then I need to be alone." She closes her eyes for a second and takes a deep breath. "I'll be okay," she says. "But yeah you should go. I think the detective guy is going to come by any minute and bother me again."

"His car passed by a few minutes ago, going that way," I say, gesturing.

She looks perplexed. "Really? That's weird. I was sure he'd stop by here."

"Anyway, what I was saying – I think once you just get that stupid dream sequence done you'll feel a lot better. I overheard something earlier…"

"My stomach hurts. I'm sorry. We can talk later. I'll probably wind up going home and I'll fill you in then." She wants to fill me in? I'm the one who has filling in to do. The note. Shit. I feel really bad now having left it in her bag, but there's really no way I can take it back. I'll have to hope that, since she isn't planning to spend the night after all, she won't open the bag this evening.

CHAPTER 33

SLOANE

Fifteen minutes on the toilet seems to help me feel better. That and the fact that the detective has still not returned. I think of poor, dead Andy. I really wonder what Dylan did. Has he confessed to the police? Is his bloody, broken body still in the shed? I cringe and shiver at the thought. So awful. Then my mind starts to veer off as if I'm a thriller writer and not a romance queen. What if Dylan was lying and hit Andy on purpose? But why would he do that?

I fire up my laptop and watch the computer come to life. The only reason I'm doing it is to play my favorite game — a world building Western town game that for some reason helps keep me calm. Over the months I've played, I built two saloons, a hotel, a mining company, a stagecoach line, and a general store. I've also had a shootout with the Harlan boys from the next town over. I'm on the verge of expanding to buy a huge plot of land from the railroad and starting a new town. When I'm in here, I get lost in the world I've created and forget about life. Right now, there's going to be a square dance in the town square and I have to watch out for pickpockets while also selling my wares at the beef jerky stand. Yes, I said beef jerky stand. Hey, we all have our distractions, and this is mine.

Darkness has descended now and I pull the chain on the overhead light in the living room – basically just a single incandescent bulb behind a small yellow tinted glass shade. It gives the room a warm but slightly eerie glow. It's been a long time since I've stayed late enough to need the light. Flashes of childhood visits, playing cards with dad, dance in my head. Warm and happy memories for the most part. Especially those evenings when the weather was bad and we were stuck in the cabin, the rain pattering down on the roof, me feeling all cozy and protected in here sitting on the very same wicker chair, dealing the cards for another round of Crazy 8's. Sometimes, if dad was busy, I'd build card houses and see how high I could make them before they crumbled. And when a severe storm cell passed through the area and a flash of lightning would be followed by a deafening crack of thunder, I'd flinch and dad would tell me the lightning would never strike the cabin, it would always go for the much taller trees, so we were safe. Then me, being a smart but wiseass kid, would ask what if it strikes a tree and the tree falls on the cabin. "Then we're dead," he'd say with such a straight face that we'd both crack up.

I'm glad it's not storming or even raining right now. I'm creeped out enough as it is. I wish Dylan would come by and update me. I figure I'll wait a little longer and then leave. I guess I'm just hanging around just in case. I have to pass by his place anyway on my way home, and I'd rather give it enough time before making an appearance.

But my plans are foiled by a pair of headlights blinding me through the curtains as a car crunches into my driveway.

I've had more visitors in one day than this cabin ever did in thirty years. Before I can speculate as to who it is, Detective Lenovo's voice calls from outside: "Ms. Rylie are you in there?"

I reluctantly leave the townspeople of Indecision, Wyoming and get up to open the door.

"Thrice in one day, this is quite a treat," I say, though with far less snark that I'd have liked. I'm still nauseous and nervous. "Well, I still have no air conditioning. You're not really giving me a chance to get it installed. You have to space your visits out a little more."

"I don't need to come in, Ms. Rylie. Just wanted to give you an update. We searched the property and could not locate Mr. Creighton, but now that it's getting dark, we're giving up for the night. So let me remind you, if this is some cockamamie publicity stunt, you need to tell me now." I like the word cockamamie and make a mental note to use it in a future book. Looks like Dylan has not said a word to the police, against my advice. This is going to be much worse when they do find the body. I guess for now I have a reprieve, and I can leave here before anything further happens.

"I have no idea what's going on. The last I saw Andy he was at the bookstore signing my books."

His tired eyes study my face, though I'd swear they stray for a second to my cleavage. "I'm asking you nicely, because I don't want to find out from TikTok that this was all just a prank."

"I'm actually worried about him, Detective." Sort of true, I suppose. But I'm not worried about him being okay.

I know he's not. I'm worried about what will happen when he's found.

"One reason we are not searching through the night is that I am counting on this being a prank," he tells me.

"Don't you normally wait 24 hours to declare someone missing and start searching?"

"Normally yes. But abandoned vehicles are a different story."

So much for that tactic. I suppose he's right. Abandoned and with the door wide open no less. I'd hope people were searching for me if they found my car like that.

"Well, I've got your card so I'll let you know if I hear anything. And you do the same please."

"Have a good night. Stay safe," he says with a grave nod, retreating to his vehicle.

Twenty minutes of wild west bliss pass. I've made the square dance a huge success and won over a rival family by having one of the men in my clan propose to one of their daughters. It's a story that's unfolding, one I can participate in but don't have to write. It's about time for me to get back to my house now. I should close the laptop and grab my bag and leave. But a loud bang on the door startles me. Lenovo apparently won't leave me be.

"What now?" I yell. "You already said goodnight!"

"Open. The. Goddamn. Door," a male voice demands.

I am tempted to get out the shotgun, but I realize it's probably just Dylan having a freakout. I need to scold him for not taking my advice. I get up and open the door and gasp when instead of Dylan, I see a wild eyed Andy Creighton, face lined with scrapes and cuts, hair matted with blood, standing there with a tire iron in his badly bruised right hand. His lip is swollen and his shirt and pants are torn.

"I thought you were…" I blurt. His left hand clutches his side. He must have a busted rib.

"Dead?" he coughs. "I thought so too but woke up in a shed. My car is gone."

"Police must have towed it," I say. "Come inside. Please."

He limps into my cabin and drops himself into my chair.

"What happened?" I ask.

"I was trying to find your cabin, after the book signing. I wanted to talk to you. I got lost, so I stopped and got out of my car to try and get my bearings. I heard a car and felt an impact and have a vague memory of being pulled on the ground by my feet. Then I woke up in a shed and here I am."

This is not the frightened, meek Andy Creighton who first showed up at my cabin earlier today, nor is it the confident and cocky one who was at the bookstore. This version is…scary. He has a fiery gleam in his eyes and the combination of dried and fresh blood all over his body makes him look like a newly resurrected cast member from the Walking Dead. I am responsible for turning him into this. All he did was be born with the name I chose for a character, and now he's been threatened and run over.

"What was that note in your car? You got another one?"

"It was there when I left the book signing. Did you put it there?" It's an accusation, not a question.

"Andy, apply common sense. Why would I put a note in your car?"

He says nothing for a minute. I run to the bathroom and dig out the first aid kit. Though I was reluctant to use it earlier, now it's a godsend. If I can cover a few of his scrapes it's better than nothing.

We are silent as I dab his face with one of my dad's old tee shirts that I dipped in water, then place a couple of old bandages on his cheek. Next I move to his left arm, where there's a pretty bad gash near his elbow. I use some gauze to wrap that, though he will need medical attention. Urgent care closed at eight so he may have to go to an ER. After I finish with his arm he says "Enough! Just leave it," and waves me away.

"Just trying to help," I offer. "You look pretty bad."

"Thanks to you. This has to stop," he tells me, shaking his head. I am still in shock that he's alive. Relieved but in shock. Dylan will be happy too.

"Look, it was Dylan who hit you, it was an accident, it had nothing to do with the book."

"You heard him before. His girlfriend broke up with him on account of me. Everything has everything to do with your book."

"That doesn't mean he hit you on purpose, and it wasn't you she broke up with him over, it was a character in a book."

"We share a name. And I'm tired of this," he says, lowering his head.

"It's been a lot for one day," I admit. To think that twenty-four hours ago I was bemoaning how rough things had become. If I could go back to then, I'd gladly do it. "Say, what's with the tire iron?" I ask.

"Have to defend myself," he says with a gleam in his eyes. "I don't trust anyone anymore."

"You're safe here." But am I safe here, I start to wonder.

"You and I both know that I won't be safe until you write the new ending and send it to your publisher and upload it to Amazon."

"Yeah well, that's not happening," I say with a shrug. "I can't bring myself to do it, I've made my decision."

He raises his eyes to meet mine and there's a fire, a gleam in them that frightens me. "You should do it."

"I mean, I will keep that in mind."

He stands up and brandishes the iron. "I mean, you should do it. Now." It's not a suggestion, it's a demand.

I take a step backward and look around the room for a weapon. There's nothing in here other than the deer head, and by the time I'd get that off the wall and try to maul him with its antlers, he'd have bashed me in the head with the tire iron. "Look Andy, I'm sure that note was nothing, I mean both of those notes were like I said just frustrated fans. Someone at the book signing got all bent out of shape and left the second note. They're unrelated. Nobody will be hurt." It's okay to lie to protect yourself, right?

"Someone will be hurt if someone doesn't change the ending. Do it."

"Andy look…" I start, but he swings the iron and smashes it into my little wicker coffee table, bashing a hole in it. It lodges in the mesh for a moment before he yanks it out. I need to get to that rifle.

"Sit. And start writing."

I need to stall him but I don't know how. I sit down and open Word on my laptop. The blank screen taunts me, cursor flashing expectantly. I cannot write on command or demand. That's not how this works.

"Don't you have the file with you?"

He swings the tire iron over my head and into the living room window, sending glass fragments everywhere, including in my hair. For a split second, he looks shocked at what he did, but then his face hardens again.

"What the hell!" I yell.

"Do it now!" he orders. "Write. I have to save myself."

"Stay calm. I'm not prepared for this. It will take a minute for me to gather my thoughts."

"What else do I have to smash?" He's shaking. This is not who he is. I know that. He's been transformed into some kind of frightened, vengeful monster, and he's about to take his wrath out on me if I don't act quickly. So I start writing. I pick it up from near the end of the novel, from the penultimate page. He hasn't read it so he won't know if this works or not, it just needs to look like it does. He may have forgotten, too, that the service here is terrible and I'd be hard pressed to send an email or to try to upload any changes to the e-book version. I'm just stalling, is all. I write a paragraph and then another, but it's slow going. I'm too nervous. Now I feel the cold metal of a sharp blade against my neck. "You're not going fast enough," he says, tapping my neck with the knife. "Yeah I found this in the shed also, figured I should borrow it."

"Look, the new ending has to be right or they will reject it and then your whole idea is for nothing," I say, wondering if I picked up my laptop and whirled around, would I be able to throw it at his face and stun him. I'd have only one chance and it probably wouldn't work.

"Then make it good." He coughs, and spits on my floor. It's blood. Not a good sign at all. For all I know he could still be mortally wounded and slowly dying here instead of trying to get saved in a hospital. But arguing that point will probably only make him angrier.

"I'm trying…"

Another swing of the iron against what's left of my window. "Hurry up!"

If Dylan were here he could talk some sense into Andy. I type some more words and pray for a miracle, some divine intervention, and my prayers appear to be answered, because in a minute there are headlights in my driveway once again. Probably Dylan!

"Get up and move away from the window," Andy hisses. The iron is cold back on my neck.

"Ms. Rylie?" It's Detective Lenovo. Even better than Dylan. I manage a weak smile and wait for Andy to instruct me. When I say nothing, he adds: "You in there?"

"Answer him," Andy whispers. "Open the door and tell him you're okay. Any false moves and I'll bash your head in." I don't really believe that he will attack me, and I also think I could pretty easily disarm him in his weakened state. But I'm not about to take any chances.

"Okay," I whisper back. "Coming!" I say with fake cheer. I open the door a crack and smile at the detective.

"I was passing back in this direction and noticed you have a broken window. How did that happen in the last twenty minutes?"

"I got frustrated and I smashed it. I'm dumb." I say it and have no idea how convincing it sounds, but I'm proud of myself for coming up with a plausible lie so quickly. I debate flinging open the door and making a run for it; what's Andy going to do, throw the knife at me? But I do nothing. I just stand there and talk meekly to Lenovo.

"So you broke your own window?" He raises an eyebrow.

"Sure did. I am just having a day, Detective. As you can imagine."

"May I come inside?" He tries to get a foothold with his boot in my door, but I rebuff him. I stick my face as far out into the gap as I can. "I am really not feeling well, I'm sorry. My stomach hurts. I just need to rest." For what it's worth, I'm not lying.

"You're going to get some critters in through that broken window," he says with a gesture. Maybe a fox or even a bear. It's not unheard of. "Definitely mosquitos."

"It could even become like Jurassic Park in here and I'd get some dinosaurs. Just like Jurassic Park," I say.

"Funny, very funny. You probably would have a rough go of it against a velociraptor."

"Look, I've got an extra sheet and some duct tape, I'll cover it." I need to make him go away. "You did ask for air conditioning, I don't suppose this counts?"

"You missed your calling as a comedian, Ms. Rylie. You're sure you're okay?"

"As long as there are no raptors in these woods, I'm fine. I'll check in with you in the morning, Detective."

"Okay, very well, have a good night." He nods at me and retreats to his car. I close the door and when we hear the car start and the engine fades into the distance, Andy prods me with the knife back to my seat.

"If you hurt me then you won't get what you want," I remind him as I type some more words.

"I'll use AI if I have to, then," he says. "I refuse to be a pawn in this game anymore."

"You're the one who took the bribe from Jonah, may I remind you?" I am feeling sassy and I am not sure why. Maybe sheer exhaustion and exasperation. Or maybe the hope that this new, ruthless Andy will crack and bring back the old, frightened and shy version. I try to ignore that fact that this man has shattered my window and smashed my dad's wicker table. This is not who he is. The irony is not lost on me that Andy Creighton has become the very thing his note-writer was — a maniac driven by my book to threaten violence. Only difference is, as far as I know, the note-writer hasn't harmed anyone while Andy here has caused actual damage.

"Write!" he yells, whacking the back of my chair with the tire iron. "And then this can all be over," he adds.

All is silent as I write more, tears starting to stream down my cheeks. For a few minutes the only sound is my fingers against the keyboard. Then, a loud noise breaks the relative silence. It sounds like a rock hitting the other living room window. And then another rock. The window doesn't break but by the crackling sound I bet that cracked it. Great, just what I need, more damage to repair. What the actual hell?

"Shhhh, stay there," Andy says. "I'll check it out. Probably just a squirrel."

He stalks over to the other window and peeks out from the side of the curtain. I almost scream when a face appears in the void left by the smashed window. It's Detective Lenovo. He places a finger to his lips and gestures for me to duck down. Andy is still peeking out the other window as Lenovo leans through the broken one, gun drawn, and tells Andy to drop the tire iron. He whirls around and complies, but then pulls the knife from his belt and makes a move for me. He gets halfway to me when the detective fires a shot at the floor.

"Drop that too, and step away from Ms. Rylie." The tone of Lenovo's voice gives me a shiver and he's not even directing it at me.

Andy freezes, and his face changes in an instant. Suddenly he's the old Andy again. He drops the knife and it clanks to my floor. He starts to cry, hands reflexively coming to his face as the tears morph into uncontrollable sobs.

"I'm sorry," he says through the tears. "I didn't mean to scare you."

Detective Lenovo steps into my living room through the void where the window used to be, and grabs a pair of cuffs from his belt. "Sorry or not, you're coming with me." He strongarms Andy's hands behind his back and clicks on the cuffs.

"I was afraid you wouldn't get my hidden message," I say. It was admittedly a long shot.

"I didn't get it immediately but as soon as I left, it sank in. Michael Crichton is one of my favorite writers. I drove off a little ways, parked my car, killed the engine, and walked back here. Sure enough, you had a raptor in your cabin."

"Am I going to be in trouble?" Andy asks, trying to stop crying.

The detective looks highly amused at that question. He considers it carefully, then answers. "I guess that's partly up to whether Ms. Rylie here presses charges. Regardless of what happened in this cabin, we still want to question you about what happened earlier, who hit you and why you parked there by the Kopeckis property to begin with. And from the looks of you, there may be internal bleeding or something broken, so we need to get you checked out by a doctor as well."

Lenovo opens my door and leads Andy out. "You have my number, Ms. Rylie. Don't be afraid to use it. And stay safe."

I wait a minute or two, and watch them walk off into the darkness lit only by the detective's flashlight. I can see the beam of light hit the chrome of his car not too far up ahead. I shut the door and go back inside. Well, as much of "inside" as it is now that there's a gaping hole in my living room. Already, a few moths have found their way in and are fluttering around the ceiling bulb.

I am definitely ready to get out of here. I sit down and stare at my laptop screen, at the words I wrote while Andy was breathing down my neck. It's pretty bad, worse even than I thought in the moment. I can't write well under pressure. Though I am tempted to just delete the file, I save it anyway. Maybe this can be special bonus material to the new edition – revised text that real-life Andy Creighton forced me to write. I start to laugh in spite of myself, and it sounds a little too maniacal for my liking. I need a drink, a good hard one, but all I've got is Vitamin Water. It'll have to do in the moment.

The guy was just frightened, like he said, I try to convince myself. He would never have actually hurt me. He was afraid that the threat in the note would come true if I didn't comply with it. Being hit by Dylan sent him over the edge. I mull that over and it doesn't calculate. While it was a horrible accident, it was exactly that, just an accident that had nothing to do with my book.

I should really tell Dylan that Andy is okay. Well not okay exactly, but alive. I pull out my phone but realize I don't have his number. What I do have is his parents' old land line saved to my contacts list. Worth a shot, so I dial them.

After six rings, a frail female voice picks up but I recognize it right away. Mrs. Kopecki. She and my dad had a few conversations in front of the cabin on days when she'd come by with a paper bag full of heirloom tomatoes that she'd grown.

"Hello, uh, Mrs. Kopecki, it's Sloane Rylie. Sam's daughter."

"Sloane Jessica Rylie, oh my, it's been so long. How are you?"

"Okay I guess, and we need to catch up soon, but for right now this is kind of urgent, is Dylan there?"

Mrs. Kopecki calls her son's name out loudly, and again. "Yes honey, just a moment," she says and I hear rustling as the phone receiver is handed over.

"Hello, who's calling?" His voice cracks with anxiety.

"Dylan, it's Sloane. Can you come by the cabin for a minute? We need to talk."

CHAPTER 34

SLOANE

Dylan just stares at me when I tell him the news about Andy. I thought he'd be thrilled, ecstatic to find out he didn't kill the guy after all. But instead, he starts pacing around my cabin, looking like it's the end of the world.

"Maybe you misunderstood what I said? I said he's alive, he's okay more or less."

Dylan whirls around to face me. "Oh, I heard you alright. This is terrible though. He's going to tell the cops what I did."

"Were you seriously never going to tell anyone? Were you going to bury him in the woods?" I raise an eyebrow at my neighbor. He's gone from the hunk next door to a morally gray character in the space of a few minutes.

"I don't know what I was going to do. I hadn't got that far yet." He's wringing his hands, pacing back and forth in my tiny living room.

"Hey, did you bring the duct tape like I asked?" I'm not trying to change the topic but another six moths have entered my living room and I want this hole patched up. I figured a full roll of silver tape would be enough to cover it for now, about ten rows worth would do it. He pulls the roll of tape from his denim jacket pocket and puts it on the damaged wicker table.

"You didn't answer me, he's going to tell the cops what happened, isn't he? That I tried to kill him."

"Did you try to kill him?" I mean, the question needs to be asked.

He gets right in my face, his bright blue eyes wild with a combination of fear and anger. "Why the fuck would I try to kill him? I don't even know him."

"Yeah. Sorry. I just wanted to…" I don't finish my thought. He's right, there's no logical reason he'd run Andy Creighton down, even if his reaction after the fact was bizarre.

"But regardless, he's going to tell the cops I ran him down. And then dragged him like a corpse into my shed."

"I mean, yeah I'm sure he will." I pull a length of tape and span it across the top of the window frame, then rip it. I head back the other direction with the next piece. This is going to take more time and tape than I'd estimated. Especially without Dylan's help.

"And you don't see that as a problem?" He stops pacing and watches me tape the window. I don't want to be rude and tell him I've got my own problems.

"There's literally nothing we can do about that. Anyway, I think he's in enough trouble as it is for breaking my window and threatening me with a tire iron and rusty knife from your shed. I highly doubt they'll be interested in coming after you, considering what he just did over here."

I finally get Dylan to sit down. I pour us each some Vitamin Water and empty half the bag of pretzels into a giant bowl. We sit there quietly, munching on the salty twists and swigging our drinks, each of us considering our own rotten luck and poor decisions. I do feel bad for the kid. He started off just trying to help me and ended up running Andy Creighton over. It's a pretty awful turn of events.

As I sit here, contemplating what to say next, here comes another pair of headlights in my driveway. For real, it's been a non-stop parade of visitors to my cabin. I told Mandy to leave so it can't be her. Unless it's the detective again, but he should be busy questioning Andy right now. Nope, I'm out of guesses.

"My stomach hurts," Dylan says, placing a hand on his belly. I'd guess he was making that up except his face is contorted in that special misery caused by digestive issues. Just as he hurries into the bathroom, I hear a car door slam and there's a knock at my door. A rather friendly and melodic one, if that counts for anything.

"Who is it?" I ask in a singsong.

"Sloane Rylie, you are here! Amazing!" The voice sounds familiar but I can't place it. Almost like Blanche Devereaux from the Golden Girls, a honey-coated southern twang.

I open the door and there is Stacy Von Slade wearing a floral print dress and flashing the biggest smile I've seen in a long time.

"Oh how sweet it is to see you again!" she says and pulls me in for a heavily perfumed hug.

"Uh hi," I say. "What brings you here?" I did have a Cabinet authors picnic here four years ago, so she's known this place exists. But still, why is she barging in uninvited on a Saturday evening?

"May I come inside?" She says it as she notices my window. "Good Lord, what happened here? Undoubtedly the work of some uncouth vandal!" She shakes her head.

"It's fine, I was just in the process of taping it up when you pulled in."

She nods and practically pushes me into my cabin. I just now notice that she's carrying a tote bag. She places it on the table next to the bowl of pretzels and pulls out a bottle of red wine.

"For you," she says through a protracted smile that is seeming less and less genuine. "We have to celebrate. Do you happen to have a couple of wine glasses handy?"

"Glasses yes, wine glasses, no." I have literally no idea what she could possibly want to celebrate with me. I'm also surprised she has not mentioned the second car in my driveway or the fact that there are already two glasses on the table. She thinks I'm alone, judging from the look on her face when she hears my toilet flush and the bathroom faucet turn on. I bet the water is brown since I've not used that sink in a few months.

"Oh," she says, attention focused in the direction of my bathroom. "You have company."

"That I do," I reply staring at her and giving her back the same fake smile. At that moment, Dylan emerges from the bathroom and if I didn't know better I'd almost say he's instantly enamored of the blonde peach who's staring back at him.

"Well hello and how-do-you-do, who might this be?" She steps forward and extends a hand toward my neighbor.

"Dylan Kopecki, and I was just leaving," he says.

"Nonsense!" She holds up a hand and her seven bracelets jangle together as they fall down her wrist. "I brought wine. Stay. Share. We're here to celebrate, Dylan Kopecki. Sit."

He shrugs and takes a seat. I go to the kitchen and grab one of the chairs and drag it into the living room so Stacy can sit too, and bring another glass to the table. My unwelcome guest pops open the wine and pours us each half a glass.

"You still haven't told me what it is we're celebrating." I sniff the wine. I'm no connoisseur but it smells expensive.

"You, my dear. You, standing up to the man, putting your foot down and refusing to be ordered around like some kind of publishing puppet! You killed Andy Creighton and you told the world he will stay dead. Bravo, girl. Bravo to you. An excellent decision. We authors have to express solidarity with each other, don't we?"

"I mean, I suppose…" I say, still unsure where this is leading.

"And I will bet you a pecan pie from Magnolia Bakery that no other Cabinet authors have reached out to you and expressed their support." She raises her chin and looks at me expectantly.

"Not yet," I say. Nor do I expect them to. They're generally not the friendliest bunch, as I learned at the little shindig I threw here. Britt Bonnerson was downright rude, complaining that her burger was undercooked and she was going to die and I was trying to poison her and eliminate some of the competition. She was half joking, but still, she said it so dramatically I wanted to give her an Academy Award for Best Performance by a Jealous Fellow Author.

Of all the bunch, Jens Tamkin was probably the most sympathetic. As the lone male author at my party, he overcompensated for feeling out of place by flirting shamelessly with me – right in front of Ellis, no less. But Ellis was too busy enjoying Stacy's short skirt to really notice that Jens had picked some wild flowers out back and handed them to me. Never mind that they were Queen Anne's Lace and highly poisonous, I'm sure Jens didn't know that. They looked pretty in a vase at any rate.

I study Stacy's face as she raises her glass and then sips some of the wine. "Mmm, I always did have excellent taste in wines. This one is from Austria. Who knew they had wine there? I thought it was all mountains and Mozart. M&M haha!" She laughs at her own alliteration and then encourages us to drink, too. "Come on guys, this stuff isn't cheap. Bottoms up!" And she gulps down the rest of her glass as fast as I've ever seen anyone drink wine.

"Well thank you for the sentiment, but why do you care enough to track me down at my summer cabin?" It's a legit question and I'm not going to just sit here and pretend this is normal. Then again, nothing about the last six days has been normal so should I be that surprised?

She refills her glass and swallows half of that. "Because this benefits both of us. We're celebrating for two, my dear. Cheers!" Dylan shoots me a look and I give him a slight shrug. I sip the wine and put the glass on the table. Drinking on a mostly empty and already questionable stomach is not the best idea.

"How does it benefit both of us?" I ask.

"Does it benefit me, too?" Dylan says on a laugh. I roll my eyes.

"Maybe so if you play your cards right," she replies, totally not brazenly flirting with my neighbor.

"Mine was the serious question," I say, trying to pry her eyes off Dylan and back onto me.

"Oh gosh I really shouldn't say, in fact I'm legally bound not to say." She leans forward, face completely serious, and then she breaks into hysterical laughter, face flushed. Well, it certainly didn't take much for her to become tipsy. I have to admit, when I read One Night With My Brother, I was really impressed. I thought Stacy was going to be huge. We all did. And then, well, then things kind of petered out for her. The next book sold okay but everything since then kind of flatlined. Now some in the press (and Mandy herself) have been quick to point out that Stacy's demise coincided with the rise of my star in the book world. This may be true, chronologically speaking, but the rest of it is pure coincidence. We're not a couple of soft drinks where it's one or the other. There's plenty of room for multiple authors on everyone's To Be Read list; it's not like a new one comes along and pushes out an old one. Yet I read the article a few years back, where Stacy basically trashed me. I remember sitting at my kitchen table with Ellis, I read the whole article out loud to him. *Not very talented*, she said. Not sophisticated. Pedestrian, yeah that was one of the words she used to describe my books. Ellis' exact words after I finished reading were: "That backstabbing little bitch." He said that because just a month or two before, I was interviewed for a newspaper article feature where they asked me some of my favorite books and I listed One Night With My Brother among them.

Stacy wasn't wrong in what she told me a minute ago; there's an unspoken agreement among all of us at Cabinet that we support each other, no matter if we perceive some among us to be the competition. Solidarity is good for sales throughout the entire Cabinet front and backlists, as Micah once said. The Stacy article was a big misfire. Her sales declined further after that and mine shot up. And this time, it was no coincidence. We share a good percentage of readers, and I think hers were taken aback by her bitterness against me. Of course, she sent me a card and a container of homemade banana pudding by way of apology. It was good pudding, I'll give her that, but the apology sucked. "Sloane honey, Don't believe all the negative fluff that's floating in the air between us. I have nothing but the highest respect for you and your books. Love always, Stacy VS."

So now suddenly she comes to my cabin to celebrate with me, but there's something she can't or won't tell me? That tracks. She always did seem like a little bit of a sneak to me. When rumors emerged that she'd plagiarized One Night With My Brother from a memoir by a self-published author in Louisiana, they went away just as quickly, and the word in the publishing back alleys was that Stacy sent Codey Cartwright a nice big check in consideration for her "mildly similar" life story. It was all unofficial of course, and Cabinet never even acknowledged the plagiarism rumor to begin with, but there are still some, myself included, who take everything Stacy says and does with a grain of salt.

"Well if you can't you can't. But me alone, I'm not sure this is worth celebrating." I pause for a moment. I want to add more, I want to burst her bubble and deflate whatever good thing she thinks she's getting over my decision.

"Besides, despite my video, I'm not a hundred percent sure about my decision yet. I just wanted to throw a wrench into everyone's gears."

Her smile rots on her face like a peach that's shriveling and turning moldy in the hot sun.

"Don't say such things, Sloane. Stick to your guns. Keep your resolve steadfast and don't change your mind. Show everyone who's boss." She pours herself yet another half glass of wine. Unlike me, Dylan has finished his glass of wine.

Stacy has had so much to drink that I'm worried she won't be able to drive herself home. And I definitely do not want an overnight guest; I was hoping to be leaving by now and getting cozy in my bed at home, not watching a fellow author get drunk. I grab a handful of pretzels and scarf them down, chasing it with the rest of my glass of wine.

"Now that's more like it," Stacy nods. All I can think is how I hate having to wash lipstick stains from drinking glasses, a flashback to my childhood when my parents threw parties in their pre-dishwasher days and it was my job to wash the dishes. Finally when I was sixteen they gave in and bought a dishwasher, but also they stopped having parties by then because Dad was spending more time up here at the cabin and things were not going well between them. I glance at the smashed window and chuckle to myself. Dad would be so mad if he saw this! He'd tell me *This place is sacred, you have to take care of it and not allow freaks and weirdoes inside.* Too late for that, Dad, sorry!

The wine hits me hard and fast, it goes straight to my head. It's both a good and bad feeling at the same time. I don't mind being a little lighter but not in the present company – almost murderer neighbor and a plotting fellow author. Haha, plotting, that seems appropriate. I do wonder sometimes if thriller and romance writers are always scheming in real life, since their books are filled with twists and turns. I can see how it might become hard to separate reality from fiction; today was a prime lesson in that for me with my fictional character coming to life and almost killing me. I reach over and grab for the wine bottle and in the process knock over Stacy's empty glass, which in turn hits the keyboard of my laptop, jolting it back to life from sleep mode.

"Always working, aren't you?" Stacy comments, then leans in for a closer look. Her smile vanishes when she reads some of what's on my screen. "Sloane! You lied. You are working on bringing Andy back to life." She shakes her head with a level of disappointment that is customary from my mother.

"I didn't lie," I say, drinking more wine and crunching another two pretzels.

"Oh, he's back to life alright," Dylan says unironically and I shoot him a look. I think he's tipsy too, though he shouldn't be because his bigger body should be able to handle a glass of wine better.

"A word to the wise," Stacy hisses through a forced smile. "Let the dead rest in peace and everything will go much better. For all of us."

"Thanks for the advice, but I'm a big girl. I can handle this fine," I say as politely as my brain will let me. I really want to reach over and strangle her across the table, but I keep my hands folded in my lap. No more wine for me; I'm already feeling both feisty and sleepy at the same time.

"I don't think I trust you," she says, reaching for my laptop before I can react.

CHAPTER 35

MANDY

Bright and early Sunday morning someone is blowing up my phone non-stop. I missed the first few calls because I was still asleep, and my brain incorporated my Kelly Clarkson ringtone into my running out of hot water in the shower dream (I have those more often than I care to admit). Then it finally jostles me awake and I grab my phone from the charging station and blink myself into semi-consciousness before I attempt to answer it.

"Hello? Hello," I blurt, not even sure which end of the phone I'm talking into.

"Mandy!" Someone is exasperated with me. Great way to wake up.

"Who is this?" My eyes are not awake enough to see the caller ID, but from just the one word, the voice sounds familiar.

"It's Micah, Jesus. Why didn't you answer sooner?" Haha, Micah Jesus would be an apt name for him, and I think everyone at Cabinet would agree with that assessment.

"Uhh, it's Sunday morning at nine and I was asleep as I usually am Sunday mornings at nine." I yawn and sit up in bed. Patrick's not here, right. We broke up. He broke up with me. And my efforts to reconcile last night were inconclusive. He wanted to meet in the city but I didn't get back from Sloane's cabin in time for the train. So he came over here. I am trying to remember what all happened last night. I know there was a good amount of wine involved. We talked and drank, and drank more. I can recall him throwing his hands up in the air at one point and saying "I give up." And now I'm alone in my bed and it does not smell like him. He didn't stay. Or even lay in the bed at all. He's a very fragrant boy so I'd know if he was anywhere near my bed. Okay, at least that much is clear.

"You're always on duty with this job, Mandy. You know that. Emergencies happen."

I don't know everything, but I do know that publishing emergencies do not in fact happen at nine am on Sundays. Very few emergencies of any kind happen this early on a Sunday. There is pressure in my head, right behind my eyes, front and center, the usual spot where it hurts when I've had too much to drink. I want to get up and go to the kitchen and look for the evidence of my get together with Patrick, but I also don't want to move yet. Sitting up was hard enough.

"Okay then, what the hell is the emergency now that you woke me up?"

"Have you heard from Sloane?"

"No. Why?" I rub my eyes with my palms. I would have slept at least another hour if not for Micah.

"Me neither and I can't reach her."

"She may have spent the night at the cabin." I know she wasn't planning to, and we were supposed to see each other and talk in person last night, but I got distracted by Patrick coming over and then the wine and then the passing out and forgot about Sloane and Andy Creighton.

"Great, but she should be on her way to the airport by now. Dez Maxwell is arriving at ten."

"Who?" I ask on a yawn.

"Really, Mandy? You already forgot?"

"Oh. Oh yeah, her." Dez Maxwell, the Dream Sequence Girl. The Fake Contest Winner Girl from Iowa. That is weird. Why would Sloane not show for that? I know she was all kinds of hesitant to go through with the whole change the book ending thing but she was still at least supposed to go be the welcoming party for the girl from Iowa.

"I just texted Sloane," I say, having typed out a quick message. Except it doesn't send. "Nope it didn't go through. She must still be there." I suddenly remember that we are still sharing each other's locations. I got to my maps and check – it says she's offline and it was last updated twelve hours ago, at the cabin location. "I can drive over there," I offer, though I was looking forward to a lazy morning of doing nothing.

"No time for that. I'm going to need you to go meet Dez at LaGuardia."

"Me? Why me?" Micah lives closer and so does Jonah. It makes no sense for me to go. Going to the airport right now is the very last thing I want to be doing. Going anywhere is the last thing I want to be doing.

"It makes more sense if you go, it won't seem weird to her. You're the head of publicity, so it will just look like you are in charge of the contest or something."

Doesn't feel much like I'm the head of anything the last couple of days, I want to argue. I really do. But I also want to keep this book contract. And this meet and greet with Dez could be great material for my book. I just hope Sloane is okay, I'm honestly getting a bit worried about her.

"Fine. I'll go. But I'm not sure I'll get there in time." Getting my sleepy ass in gear will take more than a few minutes.

"According to the arrivals board, she lands at 10:08, and by the time she gets off the plane and through the terminal it'll be at least 10:30. You have plenty of time." People who are giving others instructions and marching orders are always so confident, because they aren't the ones who have to execute the plans. I hang up and then unleash a torrent of curses at Micah and life in general.

I jog from the parking garage into Terminal B huffing and puffing at 10:27. Micah sent her my number and she texted me at 10:20 saying she was just getting off the plane. We arrange to meet by the passageway to the parking garage. I stand there catching my breath, trying to call Sloane to no avail, it goes to voicemail again and I leave my third message. My patience is being tested. Sloane dropped the ball and now I am stuck dealing with Dez Maxwell. I'm not doing this for her, I remind myself, I'm doing it to protect my job at Cabinet, same reason I agreed to write that book.

In my rush to make Micah happy and get here, I forgot to ask what I'm supposed to do with Dez Maxwell once I retrieve her. We only got as far as me coming here to meet her. I don't even know where she's staying or what she's expecting to happen. If she loves books then maybe I can take her to the Strand downtown and let her gawk at all the shelves. Sure, she will get a shit ton of Cabinet books for free, but to be honest, besides Sloane and a few others, Cabinet doesn't have that great of a catalog.

Looks like another plane has landed, because there is a sudden rush of travelers heading toward the exits and the garage. I should have brought a sign like a limo driver. I will just have to go by her Facebook profile picture.

Finally, after ten minutes pass and two more crowds of people descend on the exit points, I see someone who might fit the bill. She pulls her luggage behind her and has the same short pink hair as the picture, and part of a tattoo is visible on her upper arm. Something about her screams Iowa, even though I don't know why I think so. I call out "Dez Maxwell!" as the woman approaches and her face lights up. She waves frantically, then breaks into a sprint and barrels into an embrace collision with me.

"That was the worst flight ever," she breathes into my ear. "I sure do hate flying."

"Welcome to New York," I say in my best Taylor Swift imitation as she squeezes the life out of me. She smells like a mix of menthol cigarettes and a pleasant floral perfume.

"Where's Sloane Rylie?" she asks when we disengage from the embrace, craning her neck around me for a sign of her favorite author. "I thought she was coming?" Girl, you aren't the only one, I think, trying hard not to roll my eyes.

"For now, I'm the welcome committee, as the head of Cabinet publicity," I say with a forced smile. "Sloane will join us later." How much later, if at all, who knows. I'd rather still be in bed stretching and yawning under the covers. But no, I had to rush and get ready. I did note as I walked into the kitchen that there was one empty wine bottle and two glasses on the table; one empty and one almost full. My guess is the full one is Patrick's. I was drinking myself into a sleepy stupor while he mostly watched.

"Well, lead the way," Dez says, grabbing her luggage handle again. "Let's get out of this nightmare." She thinks it's a nightmare now; she has no idea how bad it was before they modernized LaGuardia. We are silent as we walk to the garage and take the elevator to my level with some genuine tourists as opposed to fake contest winners. I should have been able to turn on my bubbly public relations persona but it's simply too early. I haven't even had more than a few sips of coffee yet. I am relieved when I spot my car. For a moment I'd forgotten where I parked it. I press the key fob as we approach and the car beep echoes in response.

"So where are we going?" she asks as I load her overly heavy suitcase into my trunk and slam it shut. I have a feeling she brought a bunch of books with her to get signed, which is quite unnecessary as we were planning to give her as many as she wanted. We keep a stockpile of signed books from our most popular authors just in case.

"Well it's too early to check in to your hotel, so let's go into the city and see some sights?"

"Like the Cabinet offices?" she offers as she opens the passenger door.

"Well since it's a Sunday, not sure that will be very much fun." Especially since I was just there yesterday, digging through files. "I say we do that tomorrow. I was thinking more like Rockefeller Center and St. Patrick's." I have no idea how long she's here for, or what the itinerary was supposed to be, and it's starting to rattle me. "I am surprised you're here so soon," I admit, starting my engine and trying to follow the signs and navigate my way down the garage ramps to the street level.

"Me too. I thought I'd have way more time to plan and pack. But the guy who was emailing me said it had to be today. I really hope I don't get fired for taking off work on such short notice!"

"Weren't you bringing your boyfriend?" I get to the gate at the exit and it lets me through once I scan the prepaid bar code on my phone.

"I was but he couldn't get off so soon. So it's just me. Unfortunately."

I sure hope that in his haste, Micah didn't turn a hit into a miss by rushing this. If this backfires, it will be impossible to recover. Dez Maxwell needs to feel like the luckiest and happiest Sloane Rylie fan in the world and I'm sensing she's a little miffed to start her prize package vacation in New York. It definitely doesn't help that Sloane is missing in action.

"You know," she says, "I would really like to see Cabinet. And it's okay if nobody's there. It'll actually be cooler like that, a little private tour just for me."

I almost tell her no but then figure at least we can kill part of the day that way and maybe by then Sloane will appear, maybe even in time to meet us at Cabinet.

As we head into Manhattan, I remember why I don't drive in New York City. It's Sunday morning and yet the traffic is still horrid. Dez doesn't seem to mind; she's fascinated with the highways of Queens and the weird urban-industrial vibe this part of the borough exudes. And of course, she's excited every time a glimpse of the skyline comes into view. She asks a lot of questions and I have few answers, even though I've lived in the area my whole life. When we enter the Queens-Midtown Tunnel, she reaches into the carry-on shoulder she insisted on keeping between her legs, and extracts some papers.

"I brought the story, like I was told to," she says, holding the papers out.

"I have no idea what you're talking about and I'm driving, so I can't look at that now."

"You know, the new ending." Dez waves the papers in the air. "To the book. It was part of the agreement I signed, I had to write out the ending I envisioned and bring it with me." I definitely need some caffeine, because I can't be hearing this correctly.

"I'm sorry, what? You were asked to write a new ending?" I think Micah is on crack or something. Maybe he needs an intervention to set him straight because lately I swear his judgment is clouded. Secret rights deals in the park, weird requests to a contest winner. He's off the rails lately.

"Between you and me, I wrote most of it on the plane," she laughs. "It might be a little hard to read. I looked over the instructions carefully and it didn't specify that I had to type it."

"I guess I can take you to Cabinet. Just don't be disappointed. There's really not much to see over there." It's not like I'm giving her a tour of NBC studios or something. It's just a publishing company office, and not even a big one like Penguin Random House.

"Shucks, Mandy, you just say that 'cause you get to be there every day. You're used to it. But for me, a girl from Iowa getting an inside look at my favorite romance publisher's offices, that's way cool." She pauses to take a pic of the tunnel through the windshield. Weirdo.

"Is Sloane the only Cabinet author you read?" I ask, just trying to find anything to talk about.

"I also read Stacy Von Slade. And some Jens Tamkin too. I loved Stacy's debut book."

"I know them both well," I say.

"What's Stacy like, is she the super polite Southern belle she sounds like in her reels?"

"She is…" Until she gets mad and slaps you hard across your face. We emerge from the tunnel. "Well this is Manhattan," I say, changing the subject. "Publishing headquarters of the world, home of Cabinet."

"This is so amazing," she says, gawking out the window as I head toward the Cabinet building. "I can't believe I am going to see where the magic happens."

I want to tell her that not very much magic happens in that office. If she wants to see where the magic happens she should take a tour of Sloane's house. Speaking of, I still haven't heard a peep from Sloane, and Micah has given me no further instructions on what to do with Dez. I'm flying free here. Meanwhile, I still can't stop thinking about Patrick, partly because I have no idea how we left things last night. Would it be in poor taste to call him while Dez is in the car with me? Oh fuck it, I don't even care anymore.

"Hey, would it be okay if I called my boyfriend? We've been fighting and I kind of want to know where we stand right now and it's bothering me."

She puts a hand on my knee. "Oh absolutely honey, I've been through the ringer with mine a few times so I know what you mean. Plus we all lived through that time in book three when Ciara and Andy broke up for two months. That was brutal!" Ah yes, the big breakup. That one was a shocker but they got back together by the end of the book, thankfully. If it had ended on a cliffhanger where they were still apart, then the fans would have caused a ruckus, though not quite as severe as the current one.

I press Patrick's name in my contacts list and the call rings through. By the sixth ring I start to lose hope, thinking after watching me get drunk he probably hates me and never wants to speak to me again, but on ring seven he finally picks up. He sounds groggy and I remember that he loves to sleep in on Sundays, even later than me. Oops.

"I didn't think I'd hear from you after how we left it last night," he says flatly, voice crackling. How exactly did we leave it. Shit. I shouldn't have called. "Are you in the car?" he adds.

"Yes, you're on speaker. I just picked up Dez Maxwell, the winner of the dream sequence contest," I say, hoping he'll remember our conversation and not blow it.

"Oh yeah. You mentioned that. Hello Dez," he says warmly. "Why are you calling me then, if you're busy?"

"Look, Patrick," I start, glancing over at Dez, but her eyes are focused on the window and everything we're passing. "I wanted to apologize for…"

"An apology," he interrupts, "means nothing if you're still going to let Sloane and her stupid book take over your life, no offense Dez. There's no room for both me and Andy Creighton. You have to pick." And he hangs up.

273

CHAPTER 36

SLOANE

For the fifth time, I repeat my story to Detective Lenovo. I'm in a small interrogation room, sitting on a metal folding chair, a cup of water in front of me. I've talked so much in the last half hour I need to sip on it to prevent my mouth from getting dry and my throat from being sore. This is getting old really fast. It's so late now and I'm exhausted. This is the last thing I needed to happen.

"Look, Ms. Rylie. I believe you, just let's go through it one more time, please. Ms. Von Slade was sitting across from you after you both had some wine, and then what happened?" Dylan was nice enough to come with me and give his account, which (hopefully) correlates with mine. He was taken into a different room and questioned there by one of the other officers. I imagine they wanted to ask him about Andy Creighton anyway, assuming Andy spilled the beans. I wonder if he's here in the station, in a holding cell. Or if they let him go? Maybe they had him taken to a hospital; like I said, he didn't look great.

"She was sitting there and my laptop came to life and she saw what was on the screen and tried to grab my computer and delete the file." I assume that is what she was looking to do, not just have a sneak peek at my revised chapter.

"Then what happened?" He is still taking notes. What have I said differently this time from last time? Nothing. It's very worrisome. Is he going to make me take a lie detector test?

"I reached over and grabbed my computer to yank it away from her and she started to loosen her grip a little. Then suddenly with a burst of strength she tugged hard and I just let go at that point…"

"And?" He waits expectantly like this is the climactic scene in a thriller he's never seen before. But he's heard this exact tale a few times already.

"And when I let go it went flying into her face."

"The laptop."

"Yes." And there he goes again scrawling more notes. "It's just pure physics," I add this time to at least give him something legit to write down.

"Pure physics?" He is puzzled.

"Yes. Two equal and opposite forces create equilibrium, but when one force disappears, then the other force is all that's left, and boom!" Well that was more dramatic than I wanted but I need him to understand this was an accident. Not me deliberately smashing her in the face like she seems to have indicated. I am not saying she didn't deserve it, because she sure did. But I didn't do anything except let go.

"Her face looks pretty bad," he says flatly.

"I'd imagine so. Laptops are heavy and have sharp corners. Which is why we don't try to steal other people's laptops." Maybe if I stop trying to recount the events like a robot and show more emotion, he'll stop questioning me.

"We have determined that it's your laptop." Great, they are snooping around on my computer?

"As I said it was."

"We just have to be thorough." He pauses and cracks a slight smile. "You know, my last twelve hours have been exclusively occupied by cases involving you in some way."

"You're welcome?" I say. He actually laughs at that.

"Okay, I think we're done here." He stands up and opens the door. I stand, too. My butt hurts from the hard seat. "Ms. Von Slade is clearly just mad and trying to pin what happened on you."

"I should be pressing charges against her," I say. "For lying. Defamation or something."

"By the way Mr. Kopecki corroborates your story. So you're both free to go." I badly want to ask what happened to Andy Creighton but I really don't want to open that Pandora's box. Nor do I want to run into Stacy on my way out.

I need to go home and get some sleep but as close as it is, I feel like I am too tired to make it there. I may as well just crash at the cabin. Well, after I get the rest of the smashed window sealed up. Fun times. As I head toward the door, I hear commotion behind me, scuffling feet and angry voices.

"Dixon, you were supposed to wait until I said to let her out," Lenovo scolds. I turn around to see an angry Stacy Von Slade, her left eye covered in a thick bandage and a blue bruise on her forehead. Behind her is an embarrassed cop, who is reaching for her arm to prevent her from rushing at me like the crazed bitch she is.

"Ms. Von Slade, let Ms. Rylie leave first," the young policeman says gently.

"I'm warning you, Sloane!" Stacy wags a finger at me. "Don't do it, don't bring him back to life, you'll be sorry. And that's not a threat it's a promise!"

I'm so sick of threats right now I almost don't care anymore. Everyone can fuck off. I ignore her and walk out the door, leaving the two cops to deal with her sorry ass, holding her back to prevent her from assaulting me. I may need to get a restraining order against her, but that's a chore for another day. For now, I just want to get the heck out of there. Thankfully, Dylan is waiting for me in the parking lot, leaning against his Jeep. He smiles when he sees me. I can't help but notice a red stain on his front fender. A shiver flies shoots down my spine – it's Andy's blood.

"You okay, Ms…Sloane?" he asks, opening the passenger door for me and closing it gently behind me.

"Been better, and you?"

"I'm fine now, I guess." He starts the car and revs the engine a little, then backs out of the spot. "That detective didn't ask me a thing about Andy Creighton. I thought he was going to start with the blonde writer chick and then segue into grilling me about Andy, but nothing. Not so much as a suspicious look. Is it possible he didn't say anything?"

I get in the car, relieved to be done and going back to my cabin, despite it being the scene of two disturbing, violent incidents in the space of a couple of hours. I'm oddly not afraid. Instead, I'm more angry and empowered than anything else.

"If there's one thing I've learned in the last couple of days, it's that anything is possible, Dylan, anything at all."

He flashes me a smile and then drives us back to my cabin.

CHAPTER 37

SLOANE

Sunlight filters through the blinds in my bedroom and I hear the loud cheeping of baby birds in a nest that sounds like it's under the eave of my roof just above my window. My back hurts and my head is pounding. I yawn and stretch, and recoil when my left arm hits…a naked stomach? My eyes fly open. There's a man lying next to me. A man in my bed, with me. I'm in the cabin and this is not a dream. My neighbor Dylan Kopecki is fast asleep, lightly snoring as his bare chest rises and falls. I am wearing the oversized tee shirt that has been in my dresser drawer here for years, and my underwear, that's all. My sleepy mind tries to rewind to last night. What the hell happened?

Oh, right. I was in the police station with Dylan, we were both being questioned. Then I got into his Jeep after and he drove me here. Stacy's stupid bottle of wine was still sitting on the table so we foolishly decided to finish it since we were both badly shaken and needed to take the edge off. I personally would have preferred a stiffer drink, but the wine was here and that would have to do. We finished off the bottle and then I said I was tired and thanked him and told him goodnight. He put a hand on my shoulder and said he'd follow me home just to be sure I got there okay. I told him I wasn't going home, I'd just sleep in the cabin tonight. Then he got all worried about bears coming through my broken window. I laughed. I've never seen a bear around here but he said in the last few years they've been moving into these woods from further upstate. So we finished taping up the window, laughing as we went because it was sloppy and we were buzzed, me probably more than him. He warned me that a single layer of silver tape across a gaping opening would not stop a bear and I said visually it appeared to the bear the same as a wall and they'd leave it. Bears are all about the visuals and that's why the consensus is not to run from them but to play dead if in close proximity. He reluctantly agreed after considering the validity of my statement, then insisted if I was staying, he would stay over with me and keep watch. Ridiculous and unnecessary until I realized it wasn't bears I had to fear, it was Stacy Von Slade and her demand that I keep Andy Creighton dead and buried. She was free now and there was nothing preventing her from coming back here and stabbing me in the eye.

I can't remember anything after that. Dylan said he would stay up and keep watch, yet he's asleep half-naked in my bed. Did we…do anything? I leave Dylan and hurry to the bathroom. My reflection says everything. I look like I've been through it. My face is blotchy, my eyes bloodshot, and my hair wild. Wonderful. I splash some cold water on my face and pat it dry with a towel. My phone…where did I leave it? I race out of the bathroom and into the living room. There it is on the floor. Some missed calls and messages managed to come in overnight, but at this moment I have no service. I manage a slight smile when I see that the taped up window successfully held off bears, deer, foxes, or whatever wild creatures are out there. I have this nagging feeling I'm supposed to be somewhere right now, but no idea what that could be. It's just after ten in the morning. At a minimum I know I don't want to be in this cabin any longer. It's time to go home and face reality.

But first I have to get mister sleeping neighbor out of my bed and on his way. I return to the bedroom and give Dylan a gentle tap on his shoulder.

"Hey, Dylan," I say leaning over him. "Time to get up."

"Go away, Ma," he says, rolling over onto his side.

"Dylan. It's Sloane. You're in my bed." That should do it, and it does, after a five-second delay, Dylan jolts upright, eyes flying open.

"Oh shit," he says. "I was supposed to stay awake and keep watch." He seems to be skipping over the whole in my bed with me part of the scenario.

"I don't remember winding up in bed," I say, hoping he can fill in the blanks.

He rubs the sleep from his eyes and blinks a few times. "Me either." He looks me up and down and bites his lip. "Do you think we…"

"I don't know," I say honestly. Part of me desperately hopes we did, while another more sane and logical part of me would be completely mortified is we did. "Do you see any marks on me?" I ask, craning my neck and shifting my head side to side. The bathroom mirror is too small to see below my head, so I have no choice but to ask him. I step closer to the bed and Dylan narrows his eyes, searching my neck for hickies.

"Nope, nothing," he says. "What about me?" He's clean too. Not that it means we were chaste, but it's a good sign, I guess.

"Well, thanks for keeping me company," I say with a wan smile.

"Let me just use the bathroom and I'll be out of your way," he says, suddenly modest as he realizes he's only got his boxers on under the covers. His jeans are probably on the floor with his shirt.

I excuse myself and go to the living room to get myself some clothes from my overnight bag while he slips behind me into the bathroom. As soon as I unzip the bag, I hear a buzzing around my head. Out of my peripheral vision I see a bee. I duck and stand up quickly, trying to shake the insect, but it keeps buzzing around me. I think it's gone but then I feel a sharp pinch on my neck. No, not the neck, that's going to be a bad reaction. And it is, it starts to hit immediately. I begin to feel dizzy and my chest feels full. My epi pen…where did I put it?

The toilet flushes and I call Dylan's name but he doesn't hear me. I don't really know Dylan at all, other than he tried to cover up what he thought was vehicular manslaughter by hiding the body in his shed. Scared or not, that was a sketchy move. And that same man slept in my bed last night. But now I need his help. I hug myself as the bathroom door swings open. Dylan must see the concern on my face because he tilts his head, kind of like a dog, and studies me.

"You okay there?" he asks. He's dressed now, thankfully. As much as I admire his buff abs, right now I need to focus and if he's half naked and I'm about to pass out from a bee sting, I can't be objective.

"No. I was stung. Allergic. Get my epi pen, it's in my overnight bag." The words are hard to say; my mouth feels dry and rubbery.

Dylan gets on his knees and digs through my bag. Normally it's in my purse but for this occasion I am pretty sure I threw it into my bigger bag. He roots around to no avail. I steady myself against one of the wicker chairs. "Hurry," I say. No pressure. "Try pocket." The side pocket, yeah I might have tucked it in there. after what seems like hours, he comes up with the pen, lifts my shirt, and injects me in the thigh. Within seconds I can feel the epinephrine working. I can breathe again.

As he goes to zip up my bag, he sees a piece of paper that's started to unfold. His curiosity gets the better of him and he opens it.

BRING ANDY CREIGHTON BACK

The words send a shiver up my spine.

"What the hell is this, Sloane?" he asks. "Is this yours?"

"No it's not mine. I've never seen it before now," I say, taking my hand off the chair now that I feel better. Dylan is the most likely suspect to have planted it in there, so it's ironic he's the one to "find" it. Who else would have had the access? Nobody. Plus, if I passed out before he did, which is what I surmise happened, then he had ample time to do it. Why would he, though? I mean, he did ram into Andy Creighton with his Jeep. Maybe that wasn't so much an accident. Maybe he was the one who gave Andy the note to begin with. My mind is racing into bizarre and illogical and improbable directions and I can't seem to stop it. None of my thoughts make sense, and yet someone did place that note in my bag. It wasn't Stacy; she was in sight the whole time she was here.

He drops the note back into my bag and takes a step closer to me. I catch a strong whiff of his scent. Did he slap some cologne on his face just now? I look into his eyes and try to find deception and malice, but I see nothing. They're cool and devoid of emotion.

"You feeling better now?" he asks.

"Except for the note, yeah." And suddenly an idea springs into my head. If I can flesh this out then it might be a stroke of genius.

"Is this the same handwriting as the others?"

Good question and now that he asks, it's not the same at all. I have the pictures on my phone, but I don't feel like pulling them up right now. Not when Dylan is glaring at me. If it's not the same, then it's even more likely it was Dylan. I need to get my dad's rifle. After Andy and Stacy, why haven't I grabbed it yet? Maybe because I can be quite the dumbass at times. I back toward the closet and reach for the handle.

"Not the same, no."

"Then that's weird, very weird. Any idea how it got there?" He swats a fly away from his head and a memory materializes in my head, his hand caressing my hair as we lay together in bed last night. God, did that really happen?

"No idea at all. I don't feel safe anymore. I am going to get my gun out now," I tell him.

"You have a gun? That would have been good to know." If he's afraid, he's not showing it. The fly lands on his arm and he squashes it then flicks it away. Another memory returns: His hands in my hair and then his thumb brushing against my cheek. He leans in and his lips touch mine. I wonder if he remembers any of this now, too. Judging from the way he's looking at me, maybe he does.

"Here, let me see the sting," he says, leaning in. He's so close I can feel his hot breath on my neck as he studies the spot. "It's a little swollen but nothing crazy."

"Good, thank you," I tell him. When I open the closet door I almost choke; the air smells like musty old wood and stale. I can't even remember the last time I opened this door. Still hanging on the rod are a few of my dad's old jackets for those late summer and early fall nights here when it was cool out and we'd sit and roast marshmallows and talk about baseball. Dad would tell me stories, even when I was older, he'd make them up on the spot and I'd always wonder how anyone could do that. Guess I learned because that's what I do as a writer. Dad had always wanted to write a book about hunting but his dream never came true. I've had this idea for a long time, to write down all the stories I could remember him telling me and publish them in a book I'd call By the Campfire with Dad. Maybe one day after this Andy Creighton mess blows over Cabinet will feel like they owe me one and I can force them to sign it up.

The shelf above the jackets has a bunch of Macy's shirt boxes filled with old photos. Probably not the best place to keep them, but Mom didn't want them and I just couldn't deal with going through them all so I left them here. They're mostly from Dad's childhood, and I feel immensely sad all at once. He was a lonely man. I was all he had those last few years, really. The rifle is in its zippered case standing in the corner of the closet. I take it out and shut the door, relieved to be breathing in the stuffy cabin air instead of the stuffier closet time capsule oxygen.

Dylan just stands there, watching as I open the case and pull out the rifle, leaving the box of ammo in the bag. It looks fancier than I remembered. It's a 1940s Remington bolt-action rifle and the wood has a nice rich patina to it. I smile remembering Dad toting this thing around on his way to hunt in the woods back in the day. I'm so lost in memories that I don't have a chance to react when Dylan takes the gun from me.

"Hey…easy there," I start, now fully certain that he was the one who planted the note in my bag and plans to shoot me in the face.

"I asked if I could have a look at it and you said uh-huh," he says, shaking his head at me.

"Oh." I must have, yeah. He examines the gun, and tries the bolt but it's stuck. "This thing is jammed shut," he says. "It's basically useless." He uses the sight to aim just past my head toward the taped up window, and pretends to squeeze the trigger. "Kaboom," he says with a laugh. "Now if it worked, this would deter bears better than silver tape."

"Bears and Stacy Von Slade and Andy Creighton," I add. "The terrifying trio."

He smiles and hands the gun back to me. "Even though it's busted, it's still a nice looking vintage model," he continues. "My dad would love this."

I put the gun back in its case and Dylan tells me he's going to go home now. I turn to face him and a flicker of recognition burns in his eyes.

"Sloane, last night…" he says. "I think we, you know." He stops there. he must remember more than me, and that's fine because if I did I'd turn beet red and probably bury my face in my hands.

"I also think we you know," I say. I really need to get out of here. I have things to do today. And then one particularly important thing hits me. The stupid Iowa dream sequence girl is coming to New York today! Shit. I really fucked up big time. I glance at my watch, It's now 10:20. Dez Maxwell was supposed to be arriving at LaGuardia right about now. I singlehandedly may have botched the whole dream sequence contest idea before it even started. Nice work, Sloane. "Shit. I am so late, I have to run," I tell Dylan. Do I shake his hand? Hug him? Kiss him?

He solves that problem for me, taking two steps forward and giving me a gentle kiss on my cheek, followed by a light peck on my lips. "Sorry about everything," he says and I believe him. "Keep me posted on how everything goes, you know, with the book and all." In a rush of impulse that shoots through me, I lean in and kiss him on the mouth, with more conviction than just a peck, and he accepts it. A sweet little kiss that sends tingles all the way down to my core. And before I can say anything else, Dylan Kopecki is gone. He goes out the door and gets in his Jeep and drives off, leaving me alone in my cabin once again. I have this weird feeling that was the last time I'd see Dylan, that our paths will not cross again, and that makes me sad. I am about to put the rifle back in the closet when I decide to throw it into my trunk. The old Sloane would have just left it rotting in the closet. But I'm no longer that person.

On the drive back to my house, I turn on the radio, flipping through the stations trying to find a song I like but no luck. I glance at the time and switch to AM to catch the weather report that's about to come on and instead hear the announcer offer up some breaking news.

"In local news, the uproar over local author Sloane Rylie's latest book has apparently turned violent. Jenny Capstone reports from Mahopac."

I grip the steering wheel tightly as Jenny speaks. "Thanks Blake. I'm standing in front of Andy Creighton's house here on Bellview Drive. No, not the fictional character, a real life Andy Creighton. Our sources tell us that this Andy received a threatening note two days ago, and went off the deep end. We don't have details but we understand he is currently being detained after making threats to Sloane. We'll report back more on this developing story soon. Back to you in the studio."

I swallow hard. I was really hoping this story would not hit the news, but too late now. My phone is about to blow up, I'm sure. And to prove me right, it starts ringing, but it's an unexpected caller – Ellis.

"What," I say.

"Hey! Oh my god, I just heard the news report. Some lunatic made threats to you? Are you okay?"

"I'm fine," I say in a monotone, unwilling to look even more vulnerable than I already have by showing up at his place yesterday.

"I'm sorry, Sloane. I never meant to…"

"What are you sorry for? Not your fault." Ellis is on crack, apparently. I am now getting a call from Micah and another from my mom. I ignore them both.

"I didn't know this would happen. I'm sorry. I only wanted to give you a nudge in the right direction, though that maybe…oh God Sloane, I'm sorry." His voice is breaking up. Is he on the verge of tears? What the actual hell? What is he saying right now? And as I slam on the brakes almost not noticing the traffic light turning red, it dawns on me.

"You left that note for Andy Creighton? Are you fucking kidding me right now? What is wrong with you Ellis? You're a psycho, you know that?"

"Sloane, listen, I know you're upset…" My mind races forward. The second note, the one on Andy's passenger seat when his car was found abandoned in front of Dylan's property.

"And wait a minute. The second note, did you leave that for him too when you heard he was signing books in Pleasantville?"

"Sloane, I know how this looks…"

"Oh my god, I hate you so much right now." Before he can respond and confirm what I already know, I hang up. I'll deal with him later. He could have got me killed! I want to wring his neck for being a selfish prick. Did he really think he'd be able to profit from being Andy's inspiration? I slam my fist against the dash and step on the gas. I have to put a stop to this insanity right now. And it's not going to be a stupid dream sequence. I'm going to do this my way.

I ignore an incoming call from Jonah, and dial the cell number of my contact at Books and Nooks, the city's largest and best known bookstore, where I've done many book signings before. I am going to make a surprise appearance there today that will shut everyone up for good.

CHAPTER 38

MANDY

Parking in Manhattan is nearly impossible. It was always like that but it seems lately there are even more restrictions on where and when you can park. I wind up in a dirty hole of a garage on West Fifty-first Street, where I'll have to pay a fortune for however long we're here. I fully intend to show Dez St. Patrick's (despite its sharing a name with my ex-boyfriend) and Rock Center after we make the requested visit to Cabinet's offices. Meanwhile, Dez is full of questions – about the dream sequence contest. How long has that been in the works, will she get mentioned in the new edition of Sloane's book, what would they have done if nobody mentioned the dream sequence idea on socials? My head is spinning, I'm dead tired, upset over Patrick, and I just want to dump Dez into Micah's lap and let him deal with her. And where's Sloane?

As if she can read my mind, my phone buzzes just as we start the three block walk to Cabinet. It's Sloane, finally. I fumble to hit the answer button, nearly dropping my phone to the pavement.

"Oh, thank God," I say, instead of hello.

"Hi there. So it's a whole thing. But yeah I was stuck at the cabin overnight with that crappy service. Where are you?" Haha she's asking me where I am? That's rich.

"I'm with Dez Maxwell from Iowa in the city. I had to go pick her up at the airport, you know, the thing you were supposed to do?" Luckily Dez has stopped to take a few pictures so she didn't hear me. I was all worried about Sloane and now that she's on the phone my anxiety has morphed into anger. This is all her fault, all of it.

"Hey there, easy. I'm on my way back to my house and then I'll head into the city myself. I have a couple of surprises planned." I don't exactly like the sound of that. We've had enough surprises lately. And besides, I'm the damn head of publicity, there should be no surprises! I am the one who's supposed to be creating the magic.

"Surprises? What are you even talking about? You need to come here and deal with Dez," I hiss. "Micah will kill you if you don't get on this. You're the prize, Sloane. Micah's already in a panic." We turn on to Fifth Avenue and Dez gawks and gasps at its majesty. Out comes her phone again and she's snapping away. She's one of those oddballs who leaves the shutter sound on so her picture taking is audible.

"Listen, there's a lot to fill you in on," Sloane says calmly. I want to chime in "likewise" but she keeps talking. "You'll understand when I tell you. But for starters, the real life Andy Creighton went berserk and tried to kill me."

"The fuck? Are you alright?" I say, which prompts a look from Dez. Yeah now I think she is paying attention to my conversation.

"I think so. Shaken but alright."

"Listen, I can't talk now. I'm taking Dez to the Cabinet office and giving her the grand tour. Why don't you meet us there?"

I say it for Dez, though I know there's no way Sloane can get here in less than an hour and a half if she's not even home yet.

"Are you high?" Sloane says with a laugh. "Look I'll text you when I'm in the city. Keep her busy for now. And like I said, I have plans to fix everything. We will meet up soon. You'll see where and when shortly. Now I've got a call to make." And with that she hangs up.

I try to stall going to Cabinet, telling Dez that if we wait a while we can go with Sloane, but she rejects my idea. She wants to go now and refuses to wait another minute. We enter the building and right away Dez is impressed with the lobby. To me, it's just another office building entrance but she admires the immaculately clean marble floors, the colorful abstract resin sculptures on the way to the elevators, and the framed oversized vintage photos of New York that hang on the walls.

"This is so cool," she says. "We don't have buildings like this back in Des Plaines." I'm pretty sure they do have buildings just like this; Des Plaines is a good-sized modern metropolis. But I smile and agree with her. Have to keep the contest girl happy. On the ride up to thirty-three, I half expect Dez to tell me she's never ridden in an elevator before. When we get out, she gawks at the Cabinet sign above the entrance, takes pictures, asks me to take pictures of her in various poses, and asks me if they have a miniature version of the sign for her to take home. The answer is no but I tell her I'll check.

We get inside the office and she flips out at the lobby, at the framed photos of Cabinet's bestselling authors, and at the array of books on the end table between the reception chairs.

"I cannot believe I'm here," she whispers with the reverence of a library patron. I think I hear voices from the far end of the office, but seriously who would be here on a Sunday? It's probably people in the suite underneath us that's occupied by a streaming service.

"Pretty special, isn't it?" I lie. Let the girl think what she wants. The authors don't write here, the books aren't printed here, stored here, or sold here. And now half the time the books aren't even edited here thanks to Cabinet's work from home two days a week policy. It's just an office where files are kept and people make phone calls and have (mostly) boring meetings. The very idea of being here makes me yawn; that and the fact that I was just here yesterday and didn't get to sleep in today. I have to force myself to sound enthusiastic.

"Show me all the things," Dez says with her arms spread out wide, meaning I'll have to think of what I can possibly show her that would be exciting. Ah, maybe the drafts of Sloane's books in the drawer. The best thing in here is the view of the city from the conference room, and that is completely unrelated to publishing magic of any sort, but I start there. We walk in and Dez claps her hands together. "The conference room! Where all the book deals are made. This is so cool." She holds her phone up. "May I?" I am not sure that Micah would want photos of the office floating around on the internet, but too bad, he didn't prepare me for this. She takes a few shots and then asks me to snap her posing in the chair at the head of the long table. When she sees the view she practically runs up to the floor to ceiling windows and presses her face against it. "Is that Central Park?" she asks, pointing as if it's not this huge swath of green that is plainly visible.

"Sure is," I say. I need to be sitting in a rowboat on the lake there – something Patrick and I had planned to do soon – and not giving an office tour to a midwestern woman.

As we walk down the hallway and into a small sea of cubicles, the voices I thought I heard become louder. It's Jonah talking at the moment, and then a woman interrupting. I would know that voice anywhere especially since I just heard it yesterday. It's Stacy Von Slade who's in Jonah's office just beyond the cubes, with the door closed, and Jonah doesn't sound happy at all.

"Look, I understand where you're coming from. And I am really upset that he went behind my back to arrange this with you. But my hands are tied here, Stace. You shouldn't have come here."

"You literally told me to come here," Stacy says and I can picture her phony smile.

"Only after you begged to meet me. It's Sunday, honey, and I didn't exactly want to be in the office."

"I don't think you wanted me coming to your house. Audrey wouldn't have liked that much."

"Alright, calm down, Stace. Leave Audrey out of this." Audrey, his wife and mother of his stepdaughter Brooklyn. "I just…what do you want me to do?"

"Who's that in there?" Dez whispers to me as we get closer to Jonah's office, and I shush her and hold my palm up. I need to hear this.

"I want you to make sure my book gets published, that's what. It's already done and written. And you can make it happen."

"How am I supposed to do that?" Jonah asks, banging on his desk for emphasis.

"Oh, well let me give you some incentive," Stacy says, her voice dripping with sex.

"Ooh, what's going on in there, are they filming a scene from one of your books?" Dez whispers, elbowing me in the side. I've only been with her for an hour and I'm already done.

"I am about to find out," I say. "Stay here and wait." I use my stern voice, the one I used on Buster when he would misbehave. I miss old Buster. He was occasionally an asshole but as an animal, that was acceptable in exchange for his undying fealty and general chipper disposition.

I step right up to Jonah's door, turn the knob, and push it wide open. What I see might take a few years to recover from. There's Stacy in a pair of tight blue jeans and a pale pink blouse, kneeling on the floor in front of Jonah, who's sitting on his rolling chair facing her, eyes closed in indignant resignation (I'm going to go with resignation rather than anticipated pleasure). She's leaning forward as she unzips his pants when I clear my throat and say, "Excuse me!" as loud as I can, startling the crap out of both of them. Stacy quickly tries to rezip him and in the process catches her finger in the zipper and yelps, scaring Jonah, who rolls himself backwards until his chair hits the wall with a dull thud. They both look at me with a mixture of embarrassment and anger.

"What is going on here?" I ask like a mom who's caught her teenage son with a girl in his bedroom.

"Mother of pearl!" she mutters, standing up and clutching her finger. I see a spot of blood and think, *serves you* right.

"Nothing, Stacy was just leaving," Jonah says, still seated, finishing the zippering job that Stacy fumbled and then looks at me with an unwarranted level of composure. Jonah is fairly unflappable, I've noticed.

"No she's not. Sit!" I order in my best Buster command voice, and Stacy surprisingly listens. I glance back at Dez, standing in a cubicle and touching one of the junior editor's fake plants. Time to throw a further wrench into this mix. I think back to one of my favorite lines from One Night With My Brother – Your advantage is what you know and they don't. Use it wisely and use it well. Keeping everyone else off balance is the key to success. "Dez, come in here," I call and a moment later, she's standing in the doorway wide eyed. Ah, yeah she must have noticed the big old brass plate on the door and recognized the name Jonah Carlstadt from the gushing acknowledgments sections in each of Sloane's books. And a special thanks to my dear editor Jonah, for taking my mess of a manuscript and helping me knead it into something you'll all love. He's a real godsend. She laid in on thick alright. I don't think Jonah really did that much.

"Oh my Gosh," Dez says, oblivious to the scandalous scene that was on the verge of happening before I interrupted. "The editor himself," she says, extending a hand as she approaches Jonah.

"Who is this?" the editor demands, looking at me past the overenthusiastic Dez Maxwell, who's practically salivating over the sight of Jonah in the flesh.

"This is Dez Maxwell, the winner of the Cabinet Publishing Sloane Rylie Dream Sequence contest." I force a big silly smile as I come up behind Dez and put an arm on her shoulder. She's just so stupidly happy to be here. I have to remind myself this is not her fault; she's just an innocent pawn in Cabinet's stupid game. She deserves what she was promised. If she's excited to meet Jonah, then let's make the most of this. Meanwhile, Dez notices Stacy sitting there and brings a hand to her mouth.

"Oh. My. God. Stacy Von Slade is that you?" Dez starts to cry. "I cannot believe this." She lets out a little squeal and runs over to Stacy and gives her a hug. Stacy seems to forget everything else and hugs her fan back.

"I read One Night With My Brother three times that summer when it came out. I was obsessed. I should have brought it with me. I'm such a ditz. Shit. I would have loved you to sign my copy, though I'd be a little ashamed because it's kind of in rough shape – I read it seven times more after that and the cover is kind of bent." Dez pulls out her phone and calls up her Instagram account, scrolls until she finds her post from seven years ago about Stacy's book.

"Look what I said about it back then!" She hands her phone to Stacy, whose smile grows wider as she reads the post.

"Aw, honey thank you so much, this means a lot to me. And you know what? I'm sure Jonah here has an extra copy laying around the office that I'd be happy to sign for you."

At that, Jonah springs off his chair and hurries out the door. Dez and I exchange a look and Stacy just keeps on smiling. Thirty seconds later, Jonah pants back into the room, hands Dez the hardcover edition of One Night With My Brother and sits back down again.

As we stand there, my phone notification goes off. Another Sloane post! She is going to give me a freaking heart attack, that one. This must be the "plans" that she referenced on the phone. Jonah's phone dings as well. Now we're both watching the reel, with sound up, a second apart. It's text on a blue background with Sloane's voiceover reading it: "Come on down to the Books and Nooks at 3 pm today for a very special event with me, Sloane Rylie. Store capacity is only 200 and the line forms as soon as this post is live. An overflow viewing area with a screen will be set up across the street in Union Square for an additional 200 people. See you there, you don't want to miss this, all you Andy Creighton fans!"

Jonah glares at me. "Mandy, what is Sloane up to now?"

"Fuck if I know," I say. "Nobody seems to consult me about anything lately."

"A Sloane special event? Wow I am definitely in New York at the right time. Was this planned for me? Am I the guest of honor?" Dez is practically hyperventilating over Sloane's post, and Stacy is already heading for the elevators muttering to herself. Looks like we're all going down to Books and Nooks for Sloane's surprise appearance.

CHAPTER 39

SLOANE

I'm in the green room at Books and Nooks, preparing for my impromptu special appearance. When I made that phone call a few hours ago, Sasha, the bookstore manager, was so accommodating in getting things set up quickly. I knew they wouldn't be able to resist. The amount of publicity this will generate for them will be insane. They're not new to this kind of thing; they've had not just big authors here but also pretty much every celebrity who's written a cookbook or memoir. So, they were happy to oblige and will be live streaming my event on multiple platforms, and even though it was only announced a couple of hours ago, it seems like the entire greater metropolitan area is trying to get themselves down to the bookstore to be a part of history – whatever history I am about to make. I take a sip of the ice water and inhale deeply.

I was careful not to give anyone much detail – even the bookstore people don't know what I'm going to say, so nothing can leak. I'm sure Mandy, Micah, Jonah, and everyone else at Cabinet is furious with me for going rogue. I've ignored the messages and calls that came flooding in when the store made its announcement. I feel a little bad about the secrecy, but not too bad. No, after all that's happened, I need to control my own destiny.

The red light above the door flashes three times. That's my signal that I have three minutes before I need to emerge and face the crowd. I can hear them chattering nervously just beyond the door. I check the mirror and study my makeup. It's about as good as it gets, though I have to admit Brooklyn did a nice job with me yesterday. I've never thought of myself as pretty, but I look alright at the moment. Hopefully the lighting out there isn't too harsh. Two red flashes. Okay, I can do this. One red flash. I stand up and grab the doorknob. It's time.

Applause breaks out as I am introduced and walk up to the podium. Most of the seated audience members already have their phones out, ready to record and share what I say. Social media is about to blow up with posts about Andy Creighton.

"Hey everyone! Thank you so much for coming out here on such short notice. With all the excitement, anticipation, and rumors surrounding the ending of my latest book, I wanted to share with you all a bonus chapter that will be included in a forthcoming special deluxe edition, that will give you some insight and perhaps calm some anxious nerves. I place the folder on the dais and remove the sheets of paper. Adjusting the mic to my height, I begin to read:

Ciara's face blanches as she watches her lover spasm and collapse onto the table. She reaches over and felt for a pulse, but can't find one.

"Andy Creighton is dead," she says aloud. "He's really dead."

A bee lands on the table and wobbles a bit before growing still. Two deaths, Ciara thinks. Then it strikes her. The food was not poisoned. Andy was stung, and he's allergic! She lifts his unresponsive head and sees it, the stinger. It's lodged in his cheek. She reaches into his right pocket — nothing there. It's got to be in the left one, he always carries the epi pen with him. She snakes her hand in and pulls out the pen. It might be too late already, please God let it be in time, she thinks.

She stabs him in the thigh with the pen and waits, hopes, watches.

As I am reading, the audience is on the edge of their seats. I've done tons of readings before but never seen anything like this. Two hundred videos being taken, a completely rapt audience. I am so tempted to change my mind again. I am in control. This is my book, my character, my life. I can do whatever I want. Andy, Jonah, Micah, Mandy, Dez, Ellis, and everyone be damned. I can let her try to save him and fail. I can improvise and change it all. I picture the ruckus that would cause. There would be chaos and people would start crying. Some of them might try to storm the podium and attack me. It would be something. I keep going for now:

Did his eyelids move for a split second, or is she dreaming? "Andy!" she calls. "Andy, can you hear me?" But he does not respond. His eyes look swollen, and his face is blotchy and red. A severe anaphylactic reaction may require not one, but two epi shots…she'd swear she read that somewhere.

Those few in the audience who are not filming this are wringing their hands. I look toward the back rows of seats and spot Mandy sitting next to a pink-haired girl I assume is Dez Maxwell. I also see Micah, and on the other side of the aisle, Jonah and Brooklyn. This is my last chance to leave Andy dead. The next two paragraphs are it.

But if Andy didn't carry a second pen, then it wouldn't matter. She checks his pulse again. It's faint, if anything. Am I supposed to remove the stinger? No, right? She needs to find a second pen, that's what she needs. She searches her memory for any conversations they've had about his allergy. No, wait, it wasn't in person, it was through text. She whips out her phone and types "allergy" into the search bar for their chat. Nope, all that comes up is her complaining about pollen. She tries "bees" and again, nothing. It's got to be in there. She types in "Epi pen" and bingo — there are a few results. She clicks into the first one and it's him telling her "That's why I keep a spare one in my nightstand. One time I saw a bee in the bedroom and that was all it took."

She runs up the stairs, two steps at a time, bounds into his bedroom and throws open the nightstand drawer. There! She finds it. She knows time is running out.

Even the three beefy male security guards can't take their eyes off of me. I hear a helicopter hovering above the bookstore. Is this really that big of a deal? I guess so. But the moment of truth is at hand. I can leave Andy dead, the way I intended, and then escape out the back door into the alley.

She hurries down the stairs so carelessly that she slips and tumbles the last five steps. Her ankle might be busted, because when she tries to stand up, when she puts weight on it, she immediately crumbles to the floor. Luckily the pen is unharmed. She crawls instead, hands and knees as fast as she can until she's by Andy's side. She prepares the pen and jabs him with that second shot.

Come on, Andy, she thinks. Be okay. Please. I need you.

There are tears on every cheek now, not a dry eye in the house at this point. The bookstore manager herself is sobbing. They all need him. They need Andy to live. I give in. I give them what they want.

Ciara manages to pull herself up and sit on the chair next to Andy. She is bawling like a baby, mascara running down her cheeks, unable to catch her breath.

I need you, Andy.

And spontaneously the crowd chants: Andy, Andy, Andy! It's surreal, intensely touching while also deeply disturbing. I look at those faces and swear in the third row it's that woman from the grocery store. It's probably not, what are the odds of that? I read more.

What else can she do at this point? Pray? She takes Andy's hand in hers and holds it tightly. Her sobbing is loud and uncontrolled. Please, she whispers. Wait – was that a twitch? Did his finger just twitch?

I pause here for effect. I look at the paper in front of me. I still have a few more paragraphs to read. Someone in the audience whimpers – "Please be okay" and everyone applauds.

At that moment I make my decision. I deviate from my plan.

Her attention turns to his face, and through her tears, she sees his eyes flutter open just for a moment before they close again…

And then I stop reading. I look at all the faces, at all the phones capturing my words, and I say:

"What will happen to Andy? Find out for yourself. A link to pre-order the special deluxe edition will be up starting this Friday. There will be a limited supply of signed bookplates available as well. Thank you all for coming!"

The stunned silence that follows is then broken by one person clapping – I search the audience to see that it's actually Micah who's applauding. When he catches my eye he nods slowly at me. In short order, a few others join in the clapping and within seconds the entire crowd is standing and cheering. Maybe this was not what they had hoped for but it's perhaps more than they expected.

Well, that's done with. I sigh and yawn. I'm exhausted. I am about to turn and head back to the green room to wait until the store empties before leaving, but I am suddenly mobbed by audience members rushing to the podium. Security attempts to keep them back, but to no avail; one guard is knocked over while yelling "Everyone back!" My heart pounds as I watch this unfold. I know that stampedes can be deadly. At first, I think these "fans" of mine want to harm me but no, they want to hug me, touch me, shake my hand, cry happy tears at me, congratulate me, take selfies with me. I am nearly knocked over by pushing and shoving that wells up from the rear of the crowd and causes a domino effect, rippling through everyone until I am wedged up against the back wall of the store, a sea of bodies pressing against me. A few people get pushed right into me and more still are shoved around me and into the back wall, which happens to be holding a display of summer-themed books. With the impact of so many bodies against the shelves, books start to tumble – onto my head and onto the people around me. People start screaming and I actually think this might be the end. How ironic would it be for me to meet my demise in a bookstore. I want to yell, "If you crush me to death then you fuckers are never getting your bonus chapter and both Andy Creighton and I will be dead!"

Security finally starts to gain control of the crowd, with the help of several uniformed cops who were stationed at the entrance to the store. Luckily nobody seems to be hurt, well, that hardcover that landed on me might leave a lump tomorrow, but otherwise, I'm okay. I just stay where I am, letting the professionals do their thing. In a couple of minutes, they manage to get the audience out of the store. Suddenly it's quiet, and calm. It's then that I see a few familiar faces who have been allowed to stay. There's Micah and he's coming over to talk to me. I saw Mandy too, a second ago, but she's disappeared.

When Micah reaches me, he gives me a big hug. Now that man is not a hugger by nature, so it was quite an unexpected move. When I glanced at him while reading the last few paragraphs, he did seem awfully happy. But instead of just thanking me, he now wants me to come back to the Cabinet office and finish writing the chapter. He has all kinds of plans he wants to discuss with me. I protest that it's Sunday and I'm exhausted but he's not having it. He puts on his best pout-face and practically begs me, offers me a steak dinner next week if I will just go with him. Time is of the essence, he insists. I thought I'd done enough just now, but of course he's not satisfied. When this book contract is over with my next book, I am seriously thinking of leaving Cabinet. For now though, I'm stuck with Cabinet and Micah. I agree to go to the office now and he claps his hands together.

"You won't regret this," he says but there's a bit of a darkness to his voice that makes me think maybe I will.

CHAPTER 40

MANDY

I have fond memories of coming to Books and Nooks as a kid, my grandma always encouraged my love of reading and though we had a small bookstore in town where I grew up, she insisted on taking me into the city to "the biggest and best." So I'd walk the aisles all starry-eyed, and grandma had the patience of two saints. One time when I was eight she let me roam around for three hours before settling on seven books, which she happily paid for.

Back then, the store did events too, but they were all adult authors. I remember seeing a sign for Norman Mailer in here once and I asked grandma who's that and she said, "when you're older, Mandolina, when you're older." She is the only one who was allowed to call me that, even though it was my birth name. I hated it, except when she said it.

We would come mainly in July and August when everyone else was at the beach or summer camp. It was never too crowded and the cold air blasting from the vents was a relief from the hot pavement outside. Today, it's kind of warm in here, probably because of all the people gathered for Sloane Rylie's surprise event. The store arranged for six seats to be held for her publisher, and besides Dez and myself, I see Micah, Jonah, and Brooklyn talking amongst themselves just feet away from me. I don't think they've seen me yet so I call out Jonah's name. It's fifteen minutes before the event is to begin. Brooklyn lifts her head in my direction and gives me a protective stare. She nudges her stepdad and he smiles and heads over to my seat.

"Mandy! I guess you got the memo too." He laughs nervously. A second later he's joined by Micah, who is chewing furiously on a piece of gum.

"What is going on?" he says, no pretense of civility. "Whatever happens, I am holding you responsible, Mandy!" His fists are clenched. If he tries to throw a punch at least I'll have witnesses.

"I can't control Sloane, much as I'd love to. She's gone rogue," I say with a shrug. Micah glances over at the woman next to me and must recognize her from the photo that was circulated in our meeting.

"Dez? Hi there, Micah, Executive Editor over at Cabinet, lovely to meet you, thank you for flying in."

Dez flashes a broad smile, stands up and hugs Micah. He shoots me a look as she embraces him, but I shrug again. This Dream Sequence contest was not my idea.

"This is soooo exciting," Dez says. "She's going to reveal the new ending now, isn't she?"

Just then Micah's phone starts playing the theme to Cheers. He glances down and excuses himself as he answers. "I have to take this, sorry, talk to you soon Dez. Hello? Yeah I have no idea. I know. I'm trying. Okay…" and his voice trails off as he walks away from me.

Brooklyn is looking at the ceiling while Jonah introduces her to Dez. I decide it's time to get a little clarification. "Hey, Brooklyn," I say. "Mandy. Publicity Director, we met a few years back, Christmas Party."

"Oh. Okay yeah. Hi," she says.

I lean closer to her. "Listen, I was looking through the various groups on Facebook yesterday and saw a few incendiary comments from you. What was up with that? Whose side are you on anyway?"

Her face flushes and she tilts her head toward a display table twenty feet away. I stand up and walk to the table, with Brooklyn following close behind.

"I told him I should never have used my real name. Fuck." She shakes her head and bites her lip. "I was told to stir things up, to get people talking, and buying the book. That was the first day of release. Before things really got out of hand. I like to think my comments did not contribute to the insanity that followed, that it was an organic reaction that would have happened anyway." She sighs.

A tall older man takes the podium, taps on the mic and tells everyone to take their seats because the program is about to begin. Brooklyn puts a hand on my shoulder and looks me in the eye. "I needed the money, okay? I wanted to buy a new camera."

"This was Micah who put you up to it?" I ask.

"No! It was my stepdad. Micah knew nothing about this. Jonah told me he'd be furious if he found out what we were doing so I never said a word." She brushes past me and goes back to Jonah, who is sitting in the row in front of me and Dez. As soon as they sit down, Sloane takes her place at the podium and everyone in the audience gives her a standing ovation.

Dez Maxwell is not a happy camper right now. She started off ecstatic, a Cabinet Publishing contest winner sitting in the fifth row of a special Sloane Rylie event at New York City's biggest bookstore. But as Sloane began to read her revised ending, Dez grew increasingly agitated. "What the hell is going on? What about the dream sequence?" she keeps whispering to me in increasingly agitated fashion. "I know as much as you know," I reply honestly. "What about the contest?" she says. I want to answer her but I can't think of anything to say other than "I'm sure it'll be fine."

I have to admit that the bee sting plot twist isn't bad. Its far better that her saying oops the entire death was a dream, just kidding, sorry about that. She's the damn author, of course she came up with something better than some weirdo Sloane fan from Iowa.

When Sloane finishes speaking, the applause and cheering is so damn loud it actually hurts my ears. I'm happy that she came up with a solution that would not compromise her artistic integrity, but I'm also mad that she did this without consulting me. I'm also worried about Dez and how she's taking this change in plans. I decide to tell her this was part of the plan, but when I look to my left she's not in the seat next to me anymore, she's joined the throng of people pushing toward Sloane, raising her fist and yelling but her voice is mostly drowned out by the cheers and commotion. I want to go pull Dez back, and I also need to talk to Sloane but it's borderline chaos in the store and I'm thinking the safest place to be right now is sitting in my chair. The fans who are here are the most rabid ones, the ones who jumped immediately to come down and get on line, so it makes sense they are mobbing Sloane right now. It looks from where I am that we're one step away from being a stampede. Chairs in the first few rows are getting tossed aside and knocked over, people are falling down. Phones are being held up high to get selfies and everyone seems to want a piece of Sloane. This is exactly what she's been trying to avoid the last few days. Now I can hear Dez shouting frantically above the other voices, yelling "What about my ending?"

The next minutes are frightening, as bookstore security attempts to regain control, with the help of a few NYC cops, and some of the more rowdy patrons are escorted out forcefully. I have no idea where Dez wound up, but I hope she was not arrested in the commotion. I spot Brooklyn and Jonah leaving their seats and making their way toward the exit. As they go, Jonah turns toward me, puts his hand to his ear and mouths "call me" before he disappears in the crowd.

As the rest of the audience finally starts to file out, thanks to a police captain on a megaphone, ordering everyone to step away from the podium, my chance to get a moment with Sloane alone arrives – or so I think until Micah comes out of nowhere, puts a congratulatory arm around Sloane and starts talking to her. Is he telling her what he told me? My curiosity is killing me so I make my way closer and hide myself behind the sci fi bookshelf so they can't see me. From what I can make out, Micah is trying to convince her to go back to the office and finish writing the new chapter. What a nudge he is. Pushing his luck with Sloane after everything that's happened seems to be ill-advised. But in reality, he probably doesn't even know the half of it yet. I probably don't either considering she told me earlier that Andy Creighton had attacked her.

I take a few steps closer so I can hear them better now that the staff has turned on the piped in music again. Pink sings about getting the party started as I eavesdrop.

"This will be great for both of us," Micah insists. "If you finish it today, now, then we can both relax and get the whole production process going. So come on back to the office. I have a few plans and ideas I want to go over with you anyway."

"Fine. I guess. But first I want to grab an iced latte from the bookstore café," I hear Sloane say. I so badly want to talk to both of them for my nascent book, but they are off limits. It's hard to be writing a book about the death and resurrection of Andy Creighton when the two people I want to talk to most are non-starters. Which gives me a bit of a sneaky idea. What if I rush up to the Cabinet office now, and beat them there? I'd have at least a five-minute head start. Subway would be fastest and if I know Micah he will insist on an Uber, which will actually take about ten minutes longer than the train.

CHAPTER 41

SLOANE

We're silent in the cab ride to the Cabinet office. Micah is preoccupied with messaging someone on his phone the whole way there. He looks several years older than he did Friday in the board room. Or maybe it's just being this close to him I'm seeing all the wrinkles and imperfections. When we're a block away, he finally puts his phone away.

"I'm sorry, Sloane, I've been getting all kinds of messages and texts. My phone's been blowing up over your appearance."

"Messages from who?"

"A lot of people. But never mind," he says. "We're here."

I shrug and get out of the cab. I look up at the skyscraper that houses my publisher. It's a sleek-looking building but by now already fifty years old. No wonder it feels so outdated inside. We get in the elevator and now Micah is talking a mile a minute.

"Sloane, this is the best thing that could have happened. You really did a great thing. Mind you, it was a risk. I should be really fucking mad at you right now for going off script.

But I'm going to skip that part and focus on the good." The elevator dings at our floor. "I'll set you up with a laptop in the conference room so you can write with that view. And we'll get this done and into editing and production."

He sits me down at the head of the table – his usual seat – and leaves the room in search of a spare computer. I can feel air coming from the vents above but the AC is not on full blast like usual. I go to the window and unlock it, then lift with all my might until it opens. These conference room windows are the only ones in the whole office that open, and they open a good five feet high, no screen, no nothing. The first time Micah showed me I got dizzy but now it doesn't faze me at all. I look out at Central Park and long to be on a rowboat in the lake right now. Soon, I tell myself. I'll take Mandy, she'd like that.

I see some papers at the center of the table and curiosity gets the better of me so I take them. It's five typed pages and the title is "Dream Sequence by Dez Maxwell." I skim the pages quickly and yeah, it's a badly written version of how the dream sequence plays out. The last line is: Andy rubs the sleep from his eyes and smiles at Ciara. "Thank God that was just a dream," he tells her. Damn this is awful!

Micah comes back with a laptop, mouse, some USB cables, a power strip, and a can of seltzer from the vending machine.

I wave the papers in the air. "What is this crap?" I say.

He snatches the papers from me and gives them a cursory look. "Hmm, looks like this is part of our contest. Dez was here with Mandy earlier since you failed to show up at the airport." He does not replace the pages, he folds them into quarters and shoves them in his pocket.

"I'm sorry, things got out of hand last night and I was stuck at the cabin with no service," I reply. I don't feel like going into the details now. "Why did the contest include writing a chapter of my book?"

He ignores my question and fusses with the computer setup, grunting and moaning as he crawls under the table to find the outlet. He then gives me a brief pep talk (You've got this, Sloane), and just stands there looking over my shoulder. Shades of Andy Creighton last night and it makes me very uncomfortable. I ask him to leave, and he makes that pouty face again and asks if he can just watch "the magic" happen. He promises to sit across from me and not invade my space.

I open Spotify on the laptop and play some Benson Boone, partly because I love him and partly to annoy Micah, who thinks he's an "overrated throwback wannabe." The music does help me concentrate and my fingers fly across the keyboard. Now that I know what I'm doing, it's pretty easy. I am curious about Micah's plans, but I'll wait until after I finish writing to ask him. I just want to be done with this and then maybe take a real vacation to some obscure location where nobody can find me.

I take a swig of seltzer and check my word count – it's already 3,000 including the 1,200 I just read at the bookstore. The air has kicked on and there's also a gentle breeze blowing in from outside. I inhale deeply and feel refreshed. I am getting close to the ending now. I go back and reread what I've written so far. It's pretty good, considering the accelerated timeline. Honestly, under ordinary circumstances I would have taken a lot longer to write this chapter, spent a few weeks to refine and perfect it. But I don't have that luxury now. With everything that happened, I need to hurry up and be done.

Micah comes back into the conference room with a wide grin on his face.

"What are you all stupid happy about?" I ask. He stands in front of me with arms crossed and he won't wipe that smile from his face. "Well, spill it," I tell him.

"Well, I have good news and bad news," he says, his smile vanishing for a moment but then returning, and now it seems ominously phony.

"Do I get to pick what I want to hear first?"

"Nope. I will start with the good news. I just got off the phone with Pinnacle Productions. They are all in on an Andy Creighton movie! The final confirmation had to wait until after your little stunt today, but now that it's clear that Andy lives, the deal is going through." He waits for me to speak but my jaw is practically touching the floor at this point. "Sloane," he continues, "This is going to be huge!"

"Wait, what do you mean, now that Andy lives? Did I say he lives?" I want to annoy him. He deserves it. "Besides, you never mentioned that there was a deal in the works at all. That info would have been good to have." Not saying it would have changed anything, but who knows.

"Look, it's been a whole thing. But I'm sure you understand the rights business. We can't talk about deals while they are in discussion. Nothing is definite until it's definite." I hear what he's saying, but it's crap. I know for a fact that Suzanne Mexico over at Dynamo Books was involved in the negotiations to bring her book series to the big screen. Keeping it from me makes no sense.

"I do understand the rights business and you had no right to keep this from me until now." I pause. Micah is still standing there, hands on his hips.

"It's fine, Sloane, never mind that right now. Are you finished with the chapter yet?" I know I'm making great progress but it's a little presumptuous for him to expect that.

"Almost. A few more sentences."

"I'll wait," he says, sitting down.

"What about the bad news?"

"When you're done." He drums his fingers on the table while I write, which is highly annoying. But I am so close, I can finish this even if wrecking ball were to destroy half the conference room. A few minutes later, after the last word has been written and I've looked it all over, I nod and hit save.

"Done." I roll my chair away from the table. He comes over and quickly scrolls through my document. Now he's bearing a genuine smile. He pats me on the back.

"This is great, Sloane. Perfect. Upload it to the Cabinet server please and also email it to me and Jonah." He watches as I do what he asked. "Thank you. This is great. What a perfect save." He opens the email app on his phone. "Just a sec. Gotta send it to Pinnacle."

I stand up and stretch. "Well, this has been an exhausting day," I say, expecting him to offer a nice dinner as a reward for my compliance. He's possibly annoyed about me circumventing the whole dream sequence contest, but he has to admit that my solution was far better than pretending the whole thing was just a nightmare.

"Sorry about that," he says with a shrug. "Comes with the territory."

"Uh, okay." He's acting weird and I don't like it.

"Give me a moment. I need to call them." He's pacing now.

"Call who?"

"Pinnacle," he says as the call rings through. "Daniel please," he says. "Hey. Yeah, I just sent the file. I'll wait." He drums his fingers on the conference table and gives me a nervous smile. "You got it? Great. Scroll to the end." He nods his head. "Excellent. That made my day. Thank you." And with that, Micah hangs up, shoves the phone into his pocket and returns his attention to me. "Now for the bad news." He sighs deeply. My mom always does that when she's about to disappoint me so I brace myself.

"Okay, go ahead. Do your worst," I say.

"You're going to need some air," he says, rubbing my shoulder. "Let's go by the window."

I shrug and follow him. We are standing there admiring the view, and yes, there's definitely air coming in for whatever it is that will require air in my lungs.

"Pinnacle Productions is a pretty big studio," he begins. "But I'm sure you've heard a few rumors about the last two pictures they released." I search my memory. Oh, yeah. The Lieutenant Larrabee comic book adaptation and the tearjerker The Last Time I Missed You both had allegations of shady dealings. In the former, one of the minor cast members was killed on set by a falling prop and there were whispers it was intentional because he had witnessed some under the table dealings between the director and the main star of the movie. In the latter, there was a lawsuit alleging sexual harassment.

"I remember. Those are mostly rumors." Andy Creighton brought to life by Pinnacle would be a crowning achievement in my career; a couple of minor scandals would not put a dent in that. Show me a movie studio that is untouched by some scandal or another over the years.

"Mostly," he says. "Central Park looks so beautiful today, don't you think?"

"Definitely," I say, and my longing to be sitting in a rowboat returns full force.

"Well, they were very excited about this rights deal over there. Very! We were talking about incentives and bonuses to the contract. A couple that are in writing but others that are just a handshake kind of thing. A gentleman's agreement so to speak."

"Okay?" I have no idea where this is going, but I don't like it.

"If your deluxe special edition sells a million copies, then the movie rights deal increases by a million bucks. For one thing."

My eyes grow wide. A million bucks? How big is this deal if that's just a rider to the contract?

"And this is bad news?" I am confused.

"Nope. Not bad at all. But one of the riders is. Well, not for me, more for you." A hawk flies by in the distance, squawking as it passes. My vertigo is returning a little bit. I close my eyes for a moment to ground myself. Okay, that's better. I focus on Central Park. It's so green and lush. We are lucky to have that oasis in the middle of our city. And if this news is as bad as he's making it out to be then I may need to go chill there after this.

"Remember what happened with Tyrone Paisley?" he says in a low voice. Tyrone Paisley was a rival romance author at another publisher, who had a first book that got lots of critical acclaim and sold pretty well. Then after he submitted his second book, he was killed in a tragic skiing accident. The second book and the movie that followed were blockbusters.

"Sure I remember," I say. "And?"

"Pinnacle does too. So they put a clause in the contract. A handshake clause."

The acid is starting to swirl around in my stomach. "What are you talking about?"

"Andy Creighton had to live for them to do the movie deal. That was a must. That was in the written contract."

"Yeah, and he lives. How is that bad news?" Micah's hand is on my back, he's rubbing it gently. If he means it in a soothing way, it's only coming across as creepy. My arm hairs are on edge. Somewhere down below, a truck horn honks loudly, startling me.

"Well, like I said, there are some extra clauses that are not written. This one extra clause in particular, well it was very disconcerting when I first heard it. Repulsive actually, if I'm being honest with you. Made me realize that the stories about those two Pinnacle films were probably true. I almost just walked away from the entire deal based on that because at first sniff it was horrible. But when I gave it some thought, it began to have more appeal. But after the last few hours, and the bookstore just now, well that's when I knew it was the right way to go. That's when it really started to make sense."

"What are you even talking about? I don't understand," I say.

"There's an additional three million in it for us if a certain condition is met." He inhales deeply. His hand has stopped caressing and is just resting on my back. I want to reach around and move it but I don't. "But like I said it was a handshake, spoken agreement, just between me and the guy from Pinnacle, the rights director who is also one of their executive producers and a part owner in the company. I know he'll keep his word. He's a man of integrity." He chuckles. "Well, the clause itself notwithstanding, that is."

"Three million more? For us? That sounds great." What I could buy with that kind of money. My very own lake to row a boat on. "Still not getting where the bad news is in all this…"

"Oh Sloane," he says, as if I've somehow disappointed him. "Here's the thing. The us I refer to is more like me.

Not you. The clause is good news for me, but bad news for you."

"Huh?" The sun disappears behind some clouds and what was bright suddenly turns gloomy. A huge shadow now covers the entirety of Central Park. It looks very different with that gray overtone.

"The three million would be in anticipation of a gigantic increase in sales."

"Okay, so what is the clause that would cause that to happen?"

"In the event of your untimely death before the deluxe edition comes out," he says. The words don't hit me right away. No, it's not the words that I understand, it's Micah's actions. His one hand is now pushing and it's joined by the other hand on my shoulder. Instinctively, I grab onto the window ledge with my left hand, and I do a move that I learned in self-defense class a couple of years back. In one smooth move, I duck and whirl around so I'm crouched behind Micah. "What the..." he says. "Don't make this harder than it has to be. Trust me, you won't feel a thing. It's better this way..." He's grabbing for my neck, as I stand, and manages to get one hand around it. I am face to face with him; his eyes are glowing with an alien intensity that is frightening. He looks possessed. I am struggling for breath as his grip tightens. He will choke me if I don't do something to stop him. I send a knee into his groin and he yelps, but his hand is still around my throat though its grip is looser. He's off balance now, his back to the window which is a few feet behind him, and I seize that opportunity. I shove him away from me, as hard as I can and he lets go of my neck. His butt hits the window ledge and it looks like he's about to regain his momentum and composure and barrel into me, so I stomp on his foot. Another cry of pain, followed by curses.

"Sloane you ungrateful bitch, stop fighting me." Micah's body is framed against the open window. "I made you famous, it was me and me alone. I took your mediocre first Andy book and championed and pushed it until you took off, and look at you now."

"It wasn't mediocre," I yell. "You loved it."

"Listen to me, Sloane. You may be famous now, but your legacy in death will be even more amazing, you'll become a legend. Can't you just accept that?" I want to turn and run but my legs won't move. "This accidental fall will be so tragic people will flock to buy the books and watch the movie. Then there will be more movies, more money, more glory for you. Instead of being forgotten in ten years, you will be remembered for a hundred. Don't you want that?"

"Not if I have to die to make it happen, asshole!" He lunges for me now, a frightening guttural sound rising up from deep within his chest, hands poised to grab my shoulders and eyes filled with rage. I am ready for him though; I am not going to die today. I scream and headbutt his chest and he stumbles backwards. His butt hits the window ledge again but this time I need to make sure he doesn't stop. It's either me or him, and it's not going to be me. While his balance is still precarious, I shove him hard, pushing on his shoulders and he yells "Shit!" as he falls backwards out of the boardroom window and does not stop until he hits the sidewalk with a faint thud thirty-three stories below.

CHAPTER 42

MANDY

I fly out the bookstore doors and sprint all the way to the Union Square station, flying down the steps so fast I almost trip. Luckily, a train is just pulling into the station, and I hop on it breathlessly. Insanely, this will be the fourth time in the office this weekend.

I do beat them to the office, but I have to figure out where to hide myself. I check her location on my phone; she's a few blocks south. I don't have much time. I didn't really think this through. I need to be able to spy on them but in order to do that, I have to know where they plan to be? Will they go into Micah's office? Will he set her up in the guest office, or an empty cubicle? I must have been standing in the office lobby longer than I thought, because the elevator ding startles me. Shit. I have to hide, and quickly. I scurry down the hall and duck into the boardroom. Great, a wide-open space. If they come in here, I'm caught. Then I remember – there's a walk-in closet in here, the kind with wooden slat folding doors. When they have big meetings with vendors or industry execs, everyone hangs their coats in there but most of the time it's empty.

I'll just hide in here until I figure out where they are, then I can move closer. I can hear their voices now, they sound friendly and pleasant, thank God. I was afraid they'd walk in here arguing over the details of the chapter.

I am expecting them to keep walking but instead, they walk right into the boardroom. It's all I can do to force myself not to gasp. Sloane sits down at the head of the table and Micah leaves the room, telling her he'll bring her a drink and a computer. I'm suddenly wanting to chicken out of my plan and make a run for the elevators. If I am super quiet, I can probably sneak out because Sloane's back is to me. But then again, Micah could walk back in at any moment, and them catching me in the closet looks a lot worse than just me in the office generally. I could get fired. I debate the merits of sneaking out for too long, because in walks Micah carrying a laptop and a can of ginger ale. He sets them both down and I watch him futz with the wires until it's connected.

"Hey, can we open a window, it's stuffy in here," she says. You want stuffy? Try standing in a closet.

I watch Micah go to the nearest window and give it a yank until it opens. He lifts it about four feet and even from in here I can feel a breeze wafting in.

"Ahh that's better," she says. "Okay, I guess I'll get to it then."

"Happy writing," he says, plopping himself into a chair diagonally across from her.

"Do you have to literally sit there and watch me?" she scoffs, glaring at him.

"Have to, no. Want to, yes." Oh Micah, ever witty and often annoying. The more I think about it, the more I want to quit. But not yet. Not until I can do my book research.

Micah puts his feet up on a neighboring chair and plays on his phone. It might actually be the same candy matching game I play. I'll have to look him up and invite him to my team since we have an open slot. For a while, nobody speaks. Sloane puts on some Sabrina Carpenter, and after five songs, Micah asks how it's going. Sloane tells him she's almost done, and Micah claps his hands.

"That's my girl," he says.

"I'm not your girl," she says, tapping away on the keyboard.

"Yeah, okay. I need to tell you something, Sloane," he says, rolling his chair closer to her, a broad smile on his face.

"What are you all stupid happy about?" she asks. Micah stands up, nodding slowly.

"You ready for this? It's big."

"Can you just tell me instead of dancing around?" She types another sentence and then hits save.

"Pinnacle Productions has bought the rights to your Andy Creighton series to turn it into a movie," he says.

"Really? When did this happen?"

"It's been in the works for weeks, but the details were ironed out yesterday, well today actually. The moment you made your decision to keep Andy alive. It all hinged on that."

"Hmm," Sloane says. Her face betrays no emotion, which is odd, for her.

"I thought you'd be happy," Micah sounds confused.

"Pinnacle Productions is one of the top studios in Hollywood," she says thoughtfully.

"I mean yeah that's why this is so exciting." Something about Pinnacle sticks in my head though. I search my memory. Oh, yeah. There was talk of sexual abuse and financial shenanigans on their last two pictures, and even an untimely death of one of the stars. I didn't watch either Lieutenant Larrabee or The Last Time I Missed You, but I read all the rumors and innuendoes.

"Hmm," she says again. Andy Creighton brought to life by Pinnacle would be a crowning achievement in her career; even a couple of minor scandals would not put a dent in that. Most movie studios have been hit by one scandal or another over the years. "Central Park looks so beautiful today, don't you think?" she adds. I wish I was in Central Park right now instead of the boardroom closet.

"Definitely," Micah says with conviction. He turns to her again. "Sloane, they were very excited about this rights deal over there at Pinnacle. Very! We were talking about incentives and bonuses to the contract. A couple that are in writing but others that are just a handshake kind of thing."

"Well, I have good news and bad news for you, Micah."

"Do you now? Well, good news first," he says.

"Obviously."

"So, spill it, what's the good news?"

"This movie deal would make us a fortune."

Micah looks confused. "Okay, well yeah. We knew this. So, what's the bad news then?"

"I'm not handing over the chapter until we renegotiate my contract and make movie rights sixty percent for me and forty for Cabinet." I don't think I've seen Sloane this mad before.

"Sloane, we can't do that no, at this point it's too late." Micah is practically stuttering.

"It's never too late. There's no rule. You can change it now. So why don't you go grab it and we can revise it now and I'll initial the change?"

"I can't do that."

"How about now?" Sloane picks up her laptop and unleashes a primal scream as she swings it wildly at Micah's head, making solid contact that sends him reeling sideways.

"Sloane, what the hell," he manages, holding his head as he steadies himself. I can see blood start to coat his hair. What the hell?

"You had a movie deal brewing all along and didn't bother to tell me? Concocted this idiotic dream sequence contest and tried to cajole me into changing the ending? Do you know how much I've always wanted the rights to my books picked up? How many times have I told you this!" she screams, swinging the laptop again. This time he ducks, and she almost loses her balance. "I would have just changed the ending right away if I knew. Now go get the contract!"

"Calm down. Let's talk this through," he says. "I should press charges for what you just did but I'll chalk it up to everything you've been through lately." He touches the side of his head gingerly and looks at the red stain on his palm. "Shit, I'm bleeding." His voice is shaking.

"I'm sorry. Okay. Jesus. I'm so sorry, Micah," Sloane says, fighting back tears. She puts down the laptop and brings her hands to her face in horror.

"Alright. It's alright. Let's talk this through," Micah tells her. "Breathe, Sloane, breathe." Knowing Micah, he will press charges but he's not going to announce that. He wants to calm her down before he calls the cops. For a second I think it would be a good time for me to come out of the closet and interrupt this confrontation, to automatically de-escalate the situation. But then again, with Sloane in rage mode, I don't want to be the next recipient of a laptop beating.

"Okay, fine. We can talk. After we change my contract."

"Sloane, I told you I can't do that for this book." He is studying the blood on his palm. "But for the next one definitely, whatever you want," Micah says, his lips curving into a forced smile.

"No deal," Sloane says and charges Micah, barreling into him and ramming him in the stomach with the side of her arm. I watch in horror as Micah reels backwards, calling out her name as he falls straight out the window. And just like that, he's gone.

This can't be happening. She didn't just do that. I pinch myself in the face and it hurts. This is not a dream. She really did this. She pushed Micah out the window of the thirty-third floor of the Compton Building on Fifth Avenue.

The bile is rising from my stomach. I am trying not to be sick, trying not to make a sound. Claustrophobia is also setting in real fast now. I need to get out of here but I am trapped. Sloane leans her head out the window for a second and then backs away from the opening, shaking her head slowly.

"If I can kill Andy Creighton, I can kill anyone," she says. She turns toward the closet, and I'd swear she sees me, but a second later she leaves the room with her laptop. My guess is to the bathroom to wipe the blood off. Which gives me a chance to make a run for it. I quietly open the closet door and make sure I close it fully. Then I sneak toward the boardroom door, and poke my head out. The coast is clear so I run for the lobby, and out the door. I press the elevator button hoping it comes fast and also that Sloane does not try to leave. She'll call 911, won't she? If she tries to flee that will look bad.

When I get to the building lobby, I hear sirens. If I don't hurry the police might lock down this building and I'll be trapped and forced to answer questions. Sloane will find out I was in the office.

I go through the revolving doors and breathe a sigh of relief when I am on the sidewalk. That is, until I look to my right and see the gathering crowd of people gasping and crying and standing around what must be Micah's broken body.

EPILOGUE 1

THREE MONTHS LATER - SLOANE

Life is good.

For a while there I didn't think the storm would ever blow over. But it did within a week or two, and now things are so much better.

I just received the advance copies of my deluxe special edition sprayed edges hardcover of All Things Must, with the new bonus chapter included. It's a stunningly gorgeous book, I have to admit. Micah's last idea was a good one. I will miss him.

The movie deal that he had going fell through after all due to the slightly crazy situation at Cabinet, but that's okay because a few weeks ago, Netflix bought the rights and wants to turn the books into a series. Three-season guarantee! I much prefer that to a single movie anyway.

Best of all, I came to an agreement with Stacy Von Slade with the blessing of the Cabinet editorial board, what's left of it after Micah's death and the two senior editors who quit. Stacy will take over my Andy Creighton book series now that he is alive and well once again. I forgave her for nearly attacking me at my cabin after she apologized profusely. Authors can get a little feisty when pushed to their limit, believe me, I know that all too well. But things are great between us now and she is thrilled that the book she had already written will be published with a few tweaks to fit into my new ending. Jonah read it and loved it. So, Andy will find new life again and while I'm sure some readers will turn up their noses, I think her book will do spectacularly well. I can't even tell you how many containers of banana pudding she's given me in the last month!

I am now busy working on my final Cabinet Publishing book. I haven't told them yet that I plan to ditch them. Mandy has been talking about starting her own publishing company and signing me up as her first author. How sweet that will be. We are getting along well now. I feel like she and I are closer than ever before. She comes over a few nights a week and we chat or play cards, usually over a shared pint of ice cream. It's like the old days again.

Detective Lenovo checked in on me often those first few days after Micah's fall. Well, let me be more accurate here – questioned me. Yes, at first, he questioned me more than checked in on me. But after that, he was calling me just to see how I was doing. It was so sweet. And though back then I was still slightly obsessed with Dylan Kopecki, I finally came to the realization that he and I would never work. And no, it's not the age difference. That does not bother me anymore. It's more that I am just not sure I could ever fully trust him after he hit Andy Creighton with his car.

But Lenny, as the detective likes to be called by his friends, well, he and I started dating. I finally let go of Ellis – don't know and don't care who he's dating now. But Lenny and I are a thing. Very low key hush hush though. I have not told anyone, not even Mandy, and I know he hasn't either. We want to see if this can become serious before we start telling people, because we both know how easily people gossip and don't want it to be a distraction in either of our lives. It's fine; I just put my hair up and wear a baseball cap when we go out. And of course nobody recognizes him, he's just a guy.

What he doesn't know – and I don't plan on telling him based on how it went to Ellis' head when he found out his connection to Andy Creighton – is that he is the inspiration for my new book's lead character, who happens to be a detective. I had already intended to have Ciara fall for the detective who investigates Andy's death, and now I can write that novel just as I had planned minus the investigates a death part. In Stacy's book, Ciara has broken up with Andy and it goes a whole new direction. So I am free to continue with my favorite FMC. And now I conveniently have a perfect model for Detective Crenshaw. I didn't plan it this way but he kind of fell into my lap so I would be foolish not to seize the moment.

To be honest, I am not thrilled with how we hooked up, but it's whatever.

Lenny – back then he was still Lenovo to me – had just asked me a rather difficult question about Micah's death. I mean the question itself was not difficult, but the answer was going to be. Even though the death did not take place in his jurisdiction, he still wanted me to come down to the station to "tie up some loose ends" as he put it. Instead of answering his question, I got up and walked over to his chair and kissed him full on the lips.

Our relationship was born from that moment. Maybe the kiss came out of necessity rather than desire, but I am being honest when I say that what happened after was organic. So we'll see where it goes. For now, I just know Lenny's too busy thinking about me to think about Micah or Andy Creighton or anyone else. I keep him distracted and happy and he kind of makes me happy too in his own way. I'll keep this up as long as is necessary because now that I think about it, maybe Stacy Von Slade was right about me when she said in that article – "She's a devious one, that Sloane Rylie."

I've let people walk over me for too long, use me as they wish for their own purposes, because I didn't realize what I was capable of doing to protect myself, to watch out for me.

Now I know. And once you know, there's no going back.

EPILOGUE 2

THREE MONTHS LATER - MANDY

I am still working on my book. It's almost finished now. When Jonah was promoted to Executive Editor and Publisher, he reviewed all the existing book contracts and of course, was surprised to find mine because Micah had kept it secret from everyone. At first, he was wholeheartedly against it and wanted to use one of the "disaster" clauses in my contract to negate the whole thing, but the next day he reconsidered and felt that it would make for good publicity to air the entire thing out. We agreed that for now, it was best to continue to keep my project a secret from Sloane, the way Micah had originally intended it.

It's very exciting to be nearly done with the book. Back when everything was going down, I had not even started writing. Once I did, I really got into it, spending countless hours going through social media posts and Cabinet files. Ellis was a great help since he was around the author herself for so much of the time while Sloane was writing the book. Now that he and I are actually dating, he's quite willing to share his observations and memories. I didn't start things up again with him just to get access to his thoughts, but it's definitely a perk. In return, I might have promised him that he'd get a lot of credit for being the inspiration for Andy

Creighton. I already know that stuff is ninety percent his inflated ego talking based on a couple of off the cuff remarks by Sloane a while back. But it's fine, I'll let him have his moment of glory in the book.

I do spend a lot of time with Sloane, and it's nice. Like old times. Until I remind myself what she's capable of. You know what they say: keep your friends close…

There are times when I question my own sanity, when I search my memories and try to determine what is true. It's not easy because at times it seems…unreal. Yet I know what happened. I was there.

As I sit here at my computer, I am certain that my tell-all book will be a bestseller, I can already feel it.

The ending will be devastatingly sad, but also shocking. It will be the kind of ending that kicks a review up to five stars, though in this case it's not some creative piece of fiction, it's just me recording events as they happen. In this case, the event I'm referring to has not happened yet, but it will, I have this deep-down, tragic feeling that it will.

Unfortunately, Sloane Rylie will commit suicide.

Why would she do that?

My guess is that a secretly recorded and highly incriminating partial audio tape of her conversation with Micah just before his untimely demise will be anonymously released to the media, and it will differ greatly from whatever story she told the police. And faced with the looming consequences, she will be driven to the desperate act of killing herself.

At least that is what everyone will believe, because I will be the one to find her body, and they will believe me, her best friend.

Now that's a great ending to my book, isn't it?

Pinnacle Productions seems to think so or they would not have offered me three million for the movie rights.

THE END

ACKNOWLEDGMENTS

This book was born from an amazing reading adventure last year that saw me broaden my horizons and devour a wide variety of books, including *Fourth Wing*, *Iron Flame*, and *Onyx Storm*, the *MindF*ck* series, and an assortment of thrillers and romance titles. A special thanks goes to Amanda for introducing me to new genres and authors, and engaging with me in conversations that got me thinking about writers, readers, and publishing in general, inspiring me to create this book. *Andy Creighton is Dead* reflects a year in which I was immersed in books and intense discussions about beloved (and not so beloved) characters that fueled the fire and drove me to finish my novel (with ongoing encouragement from Amanda). And special thanks also goes out to Ever After Cover Design for the stunning cover

ABOUT THE AUTHOR

Richard Panchyk has been writing since the age of seven. He sold his first "book" – trivia questions on a folded sheet of looseleaf paper – to a third grade classmate for a nickel. Richard is the author of *Escape '56* (Triangle Square Books), a young adult novel based on a true story of his family's escape from Hungary after the failed 1956 revolution. He is also the translator of three of Austrian writer Joseph Roth's 1930s novels into English, including *The Hundred Days*, the story of Napoleon's final days in power from the viewpoint of one of his servants. *Andy Creighton is Dead* is his second thriller. His first, *Fletcher's Plan*, was released in 2025. The first chapter was released as a short story in early 2025 and, reached #3 among 30-minute Literature and Fiction Reads on Amazon.